MENUCHA PUBLISHERS

a novel

dancing
IN THE DARK

SHOSHANA MAEL

Menucha Publishers, Inc.
© 2013 by Menucha Publishers
Typeset and designed by Gittel Kaplan
All rights reserved

ISBN: 978-1-61465-094-2

No part of this publication may be translated, reproduced, stored in a retrieval system, or transmitted in any form or by any means, electronic, mechanical, photocopying, recording, or otherwise, without prior permission in writing from both the copyright holder and the publisher.

Published and distributed by:
Menucha Publishers, Inc.
250 44th Street
Brooklyn, NY 11232
Tel/Fax: 718-232-0856
www.menuchapublishers.com
sales@menuchapublishers.com

Printed in Israel by Chish

Dedicated

to those who have walked beside me.

Acknowledgments

Each of my sisters played a pivotal role in the evolution of this book. Deena, Nechama, and Devora, your critique and enthusiasm to read more made the writing process so rewarding.

Bobi, it was an honor to watch you enjoy reading my book and your encouragement meant so much to me.

Abba and Mommy, you are both natural editors and I was blessed to have your input while writing this book. More importantly, I have extreme *hakaras hatov* for everything you've done for me. You've always believed that I can do anything I put my mind to, and that faith has helped me go far.

It is with utmost sincerity that I thank *HaKadosh Baruch Hu* for giving me my individual *kochos* and abilities. It is with His help that I've been able to accomplish all that I have.

1

I always thought the day my mother was committed to the hospital should've been more dramatic. I wouldn't have minded an ambulance, a couple of police cars, plenty of flashing lights, and maybe even my mother in handcuffs, pressed up against the side of a police car. There should've been more people. The cops, of course, and maybe a few psychiatrists, and then in the same way that criminals have their rights read to them, someone should've stood next to my mother and said in a solemn voice, "Aviva Coleman, you have the right to remain silent. On grounds of you being a danger to yourself and your family, you are being committed to the state psychiatric hospital for an unidentified amount of time. Do not pass go. Do not collect two hundred dollars."

None of that happened. It was a completely silent affair with none of the attention it deserved. As soon as my father made Havdallah, he led my mother into the living room and spoke to her in a gentle voice.

"There are some people who've heard about your powers, Aviva. They want to talk to you more about the lights and the messages. Why don't we go see them tonight?"

My mother was completely unhinged. She hissed at my father to keep his voice down. "How do you know they can be trusted? Secrets of this magnitude can only be communicated over secure connections. Do you want me to be kidnapped for my powers?"

The indignation in her voice was so real, for a moment I wasn't sure my father's tactic would work. He'd always been the one who could control her, working with her delusions to keep some semblance of normalcy in our lives.

It was a joke. Nothing about our lives was normal.

My father was speaking again, talking to her paranoia, explaining that because the secret of her power was so classified, it was imperative that they meet with the experts in person. "Quick Aviva, we need to hurry. If they know where we're going, they might try to follow us. Let's leave now. The girls will take care of things."

I wondered why he bothered to mention us when she so clearly didn't care. Several moments later, I heard my mother slip out the back door and my father walked into the kitchen, exhaustion evident in his eyes.

He studied me for a minute and then asked, "You heard that?" I nodded. He looked away for a minute, attempting to maintain his composure. "She's in a bad place, Rikki. She hasn't been taking her medication regularly and I'm really scared she'll hurt herself."

He was never this honest with me. At that point, I started to realize this wasn't like the other times. Ima was more far-gone than we'd ever seen and one week on a psychiatric unit wasn't going to be enough to fix her. The idea of a longer hospitalization was oddly appealing.

"Abba...tell them that she—" His eyes narrowed in concern

and I stopped midsentence. Now was not the time to add salt to his wounds. "Forget it," I said, moving toward the sink to start washing dishes. "Just call us when you have information."

Daniella breezed into the house just as I was putting the candlesticks back into the breakfront. I glanced at the clock, startled to see it was just past midnight. My older sister stood in the doorway of the dining room, texting quickly. Just seventeen months older than I was, Daniella was my closest friend in the world. I watched her text, wanting her to stop so I could tell her what was happening, but also wanting her to continue forever, so she could never know the tragedy that had become our family life. Too quickly, she finished her text, tossed her phone on the table, and came over to me, giving me a quick hug.

"Hey, Cinderella, where's everyone else?"

Anger flared in me, so fast that I almost missed it. She had this irritating ability to deal with situations by escaping. I probably could have escaped too, but someone had to stay around to witness the madness. Even though her nonchalance was a thorn in my side, I could never stay mad at Daniella. I needed her more than I needed oxygen, and for as much as she escaped the chaos in our home, she was always there when I really needed her.

"Uri is still at Donny's," I told her without looking up. As soon as we made eye contact, there was no more hiding anything. "He called asking to be picked up but I asked Mrs. Elias if he could sleep over tonight. I said we'll get him tomorrow afternoon."

Daniella stopped in the middle of taking off her scarf. Strands of her long hair clung to it as it hung midair, giving her a slightly electrocuted look. "And why didn't you want Uri at the house tonight?"

"Because it was just me here, and Donny Elias is a lot more fun than I am."

Daniella put her hands on her hips. "Are you going to tell me where Ima and Abba are or do I have to play Twenty Questions?"

I mimicked her stance and glared at her. "Would it really take you twenty questions to figure it out?"

She dropped her hands and walked back over to me. Taking my hand, she pulled me into the kitchen and made me sit at the table. "I'm making coffee," she said calmly. "Talk."

I took a deep breath, willing myself to stay calm. "They're at the hospital. Abba's trying to get her hospitalized."

Once I started talking, it was hard to stop.

Shabbos had seemed to start okay. We knew Ima was manic, but we were trying to ignore it, since in many ways, the mania was a lot more enjoyable than the depression. Ima had cooked straight from Thursday morning through Friday afternoon — literally. I'd heard the food processor going at three thirty in the morning, and by five, the smell of potato kugel had made its way to my room. When she lit candles on Friday night, she stared so hard at the flames that she seemed to have gone into a trance.

"Ima," I said quietly. "Did you make the *berachah*?"

She turned to me, with fire blazing in her eyes, and said, "Rikki, the fire makes a *berachah* on me. We're so connected, it speaks to the flame of my *neshamah*." Then she grasped my hands, closed her eyes, and davened quietly for so long that eventually I just pulled away.

During the Friday night meal, we almost enjoyed ourselves. She insisted that we all sing together, and we sounded good. Uri looked almost happy, as if we were a normal family that always sang at the Shabbos table. My mother served us five courses as if we were at a state dinner. At some points, I'm not even sure she knew who we were. Throughout it all — the singing, the serving, the eating, and the senseless conversation — she didn't take her eyes off the candles.

I don't think she slept Friday night. I heard her pacing in the living room and dining room, her frantic, pressured speech and my father's low, calm voice. My father came into my room before he left for shul with Uri. I was awake, but Daniella was still sleeping.

"Rikki, can you keep an eye on Ima until I get back?"

I nodded. As soon as he walked out, Daniella opened her eyes. "He needs to hire a babysitter."

Despite Daniella's knowledge that Ima was close to the edge, she went to her friend's house after lunch, taking Uri along too to drop him off at Donny's. To her credit, she asked before she left.

"I'll stay if you want." I knew she meant it; Daniella always meant what she said. But Daniella was the only reason I had gotten any sleep at all that Friday night. When my mother was manic, I became an insomniac. Daniella had her own room, just down the hall from mine, but the only way I could sleep was if she was in my bed with me. I stayed close to the wall, and she had the rest of the bed. My human shield, protecting me from the insanity that lurked outside the door. I told her to go, that I'd keep an eye on things at the house.

My father was downstairs learning and I was sitting on the couch reading a book when my mother came out of her room. At first I just stared. She was wearing her sheitel, four-inch heels, and nearly all of her jewelry. She sauntered smoothly into the kitchen and I heard her rummaging around. When she wasn't manic, my mother couldn't walk ten feet in heels without stumbling. I waited to see what would happen next. She entered the dining room carrying a box of Shabbos candles. I watched with morbid fascination. She began setting up rows and rows of candles in front of the *lichter*, speaking to herself as she arranged and rearranged the candles in intricate patterns.

I didn't want to talk to her. I didn't want anything to do with her unmedicated mind. If she wanted to be *mechallel Shabbos*, nothing I said was going to stop her. I just hoped Hashem understood she was completely out of control, and that I was a helpless bystander in this situation. She lit a match and began lighting the candles, one after the other, until the table was ablaze and the lights from the fire were reflected back in her wide eyes. I'd moved off the couch and was standing on the opposite side of the table.

She bent forward so she was eye level with the flames and stared, without blinking. I alternated between watching her and glancing down at the flames to try and see what she was seeing. Without warning, her head snapped up and her gaze locked on mine.

"I can hear the fire, Rivka."

I backed away. "Ima, come on, it's Shabbos." I figured I should at least try.

Moving into the kitchen, I stood at the top of the stairs and called down to my father. "Abba, I think you should come up."

It was as I stepped back into the dining room that it happened. Ima was waving her arms around the flames, almost as if she were doing *hadlakas neiros* on a community of candles. As she leaned forward to encircle the entire blaze, the edge of her sheitel caught fire.

"Abba!" The word stuck in my throat as I stumbled back. Ima hadn't noticed. The flames crept up toward her face but she was completely oblivious, her eyes locked intently on the flickering lights.

My father exploded into the room, "Rikki, what happened?" Seeing my mother's sheitel on fire, he grabbed her by her arm and pulled her into the kitchen. In one fluid motion, he grabbed a dishtowel and smothered the flames.

The conversation that ensued between my parents was so tragic that I locked myself in my room for the rest of Shabbos. My mother was beyond delusional. I knew she was bipolar, but her mental state had deteriorated past anything we'd ever seen.

"Daniella, she could have killed herself," I said, noticing for the first time that I was gripping my coffee mug so hard my fingers were white.

Daniella's laughter was so unexpected that I jerked out of my chair. I stared at her in disbelief. "What's wrong with you?"

At the look on my face, she tried to control herself. "I'm sorry, Rik, it's really not funny, but seriously? You can't die from your sheitel catching on fire. It comes off, you know."

Frustration knotted my stomach and all of a sudden there were tears in the back of my eyes. Daniella stopped laughing. "Listen, it's better this way. We don't need her here, she's just getting worse." Her tone was so cavalier, so effortlessly unaffected, that I wished, for the thousandth time, that I was more like my sister.

"Yeah, it's better. But it's harder too. Every time it gets harder, because now Abba's going to be a wreck, and Uri won't know what to do with himself, and we never know what to say when people ask about her."

Daniella snorted. "Trust me. We'll figure out what to tell people. That's the least of our problems." Daniella didn't seem to have a conscience when it came to lying about our mother's condition. I'd lost track of how many different ailments she'd created to avoid revealing where Ima really was.

Four months ago, at my cousin Shevy's wedding, a bunch of my aunts had cornered Daniella and me and had asked with genuine concern, "Where's Aviva?" At that time, my mother was on a psychiatric unit after swallowing an entire bottle of her mood-stabilizing medication. I'd hoped that if it didn't kill her, it might stabilize her mood for a while, but I was out of luck.

Without missing a beat, Daniella had said, "She's dealing with postpartum depression." I was so stunned all I could do was stare at her. My aunts were apparently as shocked as I was.

"Did…she just have a baby?" Aunt Liora asked hesitantly.

Daniella looked down at the floor as if the answer was difficult to share. Clearing her throat, she said, "There's…no baby…anymore."

When they walked away, I turned to her. "You're such a liar. And you're so good at it, it scares me."

She flashed me a big smile. "Thanks."

Daniella refilled my coffee cup and sat down across from me. Under the bright kitchen lights, I studied my sister. Everyone said we looked alike, and we were often mistaken for twins. We had the same tall, lean frame and long, thick, light-brown hair. Beyond that, I was unsure how we resembled each other. Daniella's eyes were green, tinged with blue at the edges, while mine were solidly brown. She was known for her infectious smile. It wasn't that she smiled so often, but when she did, it counted. It usually started off as a smirk, then it would spread slowly across her whole face, and by the time she was done smiling, everyone else usually was too. I had to remind myself to smile. Lately, I was aware that I'd been walking around with a serious expression, which, according to my friend and next-door-neighbor Kayla, made me look like a snob. I wasn't a snob. Far from it. Sometimes it was just hard to smile.

"Why are you giving me coffee at one o'clock in the morning?" I pushed the mug away from me, even though I felt the irrational urge to gulp it all down.

"I don't know. You looked like you needed it. Coffee fixes things."

"Tell that to Ima's doctors," I muttered. "Maybe that's all she needs."

This time, Daniella's laughter made me smile. My cell phone beeped, signaling a text message. I stared at my phone momentarily, frozen, until I remembered that my father never texted. It was from Kayla. *Can I have a ride 2morrow morn?*

"Oh my gosh." I dropped my head to the table, harder than I'd intended. "Ow."

Daniella reached for my phone, reading the text out loud. "I totally forgot about that," she said. "Dance tryouts are at nine."

She stood up, stretched, and collected our mugs, bringing them over to the sink.

"Go to sleep, Rikki."

"Are you coming?"

She cocked her head and stared at me. I usually slept alone when my mother was in the hospital. I kept quiet, silently begging her not to question me. Not now.

"Yeah. I'll be there in a minute."

2

When I'd signed up to be a dance head for the school production at the end of tenth grade, my mother had been relatively stable. Production was what I liked best about school, and I'd naively assumed that there was no reason I shouldn't sign up to be a dance head. I was popular enough that the GO committee had chosen me, and well-behaved enough that the staff advisors hadn't rejected their choice. On top of that, I was a good dancer, and they knew I could choreograph well because I'd made up the color war dances since I was in ninth grade. Daniella was a dancer too, but she didn't have the patience to create the dances. She wanted to be taught the steps, and then just dance.

My co-dance heads were all seniors. Zehava, Atara, and Laya were easy to get along with and didn't seem to care that I was only in eleventh grade. The truth was that they were so preoccupied with seminary decisions and college courses, that my lack of knowledge on both subjects was refreshing and kept them from discussing it ad nauseam when we got together. Zehava and I would be heading two dances, and Atara and Laya had two of their own. With twelve girls in each dance, counting the heads, that left forty slots for over one hundred hopeful dancers.

"I'm so glad I'm not trying out for dance," Kayla said, looking wide-eyed at the crowds of girls milling around the auditorium. She was a singer, with a rich, low voice and an ear for harmony.

"Me too," I agreed. "I hate going into this knowing that so many girls are going to end up disappointed. No one tries out for dance as a second choice."

In our school, being in dance was a status symbol. Preproduction, you may have been shy, socially awkward, or downright nerdy, but making it into dance got you halfway to cool. It couldn't do it all — there were definitely some dancers lacking social skills or a fashion sense — but it was impossible to be in dance and be a total loser.

"You're too nice," Daniella said from behind us. "The production isn't a *chesed* project. You can't accept girls just because you feel bad for them."

"I know," I shot back. "That's why I'm not so sure you'll get accepted, and I'm trying to figure out the best way to tell you."

Kayla laughed. She was used to our conversations and knew there was little we could say to each other that would actually sting. Daniella slung an arm around each of our shoulders right before we parted ways at the corner of the hall.

"All right kids, it's time to get serious. I have to pick Uri up at one, so be at the car at twelve forty-five. If you're not, I'm leaving anyway."

Daniella twirled away from us and was immediately swallowed up by a crowd of girls calling her name and greeting her as though they hadn't seen her in years. She flitted from girl to girl, sporadically giving out hugs, examining hairstyles and jewelry, and seamlessly becoming the center of attention.

"She's such a drama queen," I said, shaking my head, as she moved with the pack into the auditorium.

"I know, but she's hilarious." Kayla started walking down the hall toward choir tryouts but then stopped. She stood in place for a moment and then walked back until she was standing in front of me.

"Is everything okay with your mother?" she asked, her eyes searching my face, not probing, just concerned.

I broke her gaze, my eyes travelling down to my green-and-black sneakers. I'd taken time picking out my outfit this morning. It was rare that we were allowed to be at school out of uniform and I'd wanted to make the most of it. I hadn't dressed up, since this was dance tryouts, not a *chagigah*. Still, I was wearing a short, black skirt over black leggings, a black T-shirt, and a green zip-up that coordinated with my shoes. Since I'd walked in the school building less than ten minutes before, I'd had at least three compliments on my sneakers.

I forced myself to look Kayla in the eye. Out of all my friends, she was the only one who had even the smallest clue as to how sick my mother really was. And that was just by default, with her being my neighbor. Kayla had witnessed more than one of my mother's breakdowns, and not only had she kept our secret safe, she'd given me her friendship despite knowing the truth about us.

I was well aware that having a mentally ill mother wasn't exactly a way to win friends. Mental illness freaked teenagers out. I heard my classmates make comments about people they knew who "weren't one hundred percent" or who were "a little off." The tones of their voices made it clear just how little they thought of these people.

I didn't blame them. If I hadn't grown up in my house, I probably would've been one of them. They possessed a superiority that was borne out of blessed ignorance. And because of how much I wished I too possessed that ignorance, I couldn't bring myself to blame them.

Luckily, there was Kayla. She was literally the only friend who was allowed in my house. My mother adored her, which bothered me more than I let on, since she didn't seem to care much for her own children.

"How did you know?" I asked Kayla, truly curious.

Kayla hesitated, then said, "She knocked on our door yesterday afternoon. She wanted to know if we had any extra candles. And she looked sort of…dressed up."

I knew Daniella would've laughed at her passé description of my mother's getup. But I wasn't Daniella. I inhaled deeply, willing the stress that was creeping up my throat to disappear. I couldn't deal with this now. It was my fault for having locked myself in my room until Havdallah. Clearly my father wasn't capable of keeping her craziness contained to our house.

"She's completely lost it. My father took her to the hospital last night. I think they're still waiting for a bed at St. Lucas." Saying the name of the local psychiatric hospital hurt. I saw a slight grimace pass over Kayla's face, and then it was gone.

"Rikki…" Kayla didn't have to say anything more. Her eyes said it all. Compassion. Uncertainty. Concern. "Are you okay?"

I couldn't look her in the eye anymore. Glancing around the rapidly emptying hallway, I opted for honesty. "Me and Daniella will be fine, but my father's a wreck. He knows he can't control her anymore and he thinks that this time she'll be in there for longer than usual. And Uri doesn't even know yet. We're telling him when we pick him up later. He's going to freak out. My father already has no time for him, and if he's visiting my mother at the hospital every night, it's just going to be the three of us at home." Speaking my concerns out loud made my stomach hurt. The anxiety was like a fist, clenching harder and harder as the realizations set in. "Like, we can cook for him and take care of him, but we can't help him with Gemara or play sports with him. He suffers the most from all of this."

Kayla raised an eyebrow.

"Well, we all suffer," I amended. "Still, he's young. He doesn't get it."

"You should see about getting him a mentor." Kayla was a problem solver. That was one of the reasons why I was even partially okay with opening up to her about my problems. Rather than psychoanalyze me, she always offered solutions. "My brother Shlomo had a boy he mentored a few years ago. It was a ten-year-old kid whose parents were divorced and the father wasn't *frum* anymore. Shlomo took him out once a week, played sports with him, learned with him — basically they just had fun together. Uri would love it. He'd get out of the house with a cool older kid."

"It's a good idea," I said, grateful for something concrete to think about. "I'll ask my father when I see him."

Kayla smiled, and although I knew she didn't mean for it to be patronizing, the pity in her eyes was clear.

"I'm fine."

"I know." Just like that, she was looking at me normally again. "I have to run to tryouts, and you better get in there before anyone has a nervous breakdown. Let's hang out later." She started walking backward down the hall toward the choir room. "See you at twelve forty-five, don't be late, or Daniella's leaving without you!"

I grinned and walked into the auditorium.

3

It was like walking onto another planet. The energy level in the room was intoxicating.

"Rikki!" Zehava called my name out before the door had even closed behind me. Suddenly, over one hundred pairs of eyes had turned to look at me. Seeing Laya and Atara standing next to Zehava in the front of the room, I realized they'd all been waiting for me.

"Hey, Zehava!" I called out, threading my way through hopeful dancers watching my every move. This was what being a celebrity had to feel like.

"When I reached the three girls, we formed a quick huddle.

"How does this usually work?" I asked.

"Let's break them down into two groups," Atara said. "We'll teach half, and you two will teach half. Then they'll try out, three at a time, first for us, then for you."

We nodded. Breaking up the huddle, we stood still for a moment, waiting for someone to make the first move. I shrugged and hopped up on a chair. The room fell totally quiet.

"Hi, everyone. Welcome to dance tryouts." The girls looked at me eagerly, and I realized, with a start, that they all had pinned their hopes on me. "I know you're all anxious to try out already, so let me explain how this is going to work and then we'll get started."

A few feet in front of me, two freshmen girls shuddered in anticipation and I had to laugh. "Listen, try not to be nervous. I know this can be intimidating. I remember trying out for dance when I was in ninth grade. I was so worried, I didn't eat for two days beforehand."

Tense laughter rippled through the room.

"It's true," Daniella called out. I hadn't seen her sitting over on the radiator with a group of her friends. She was learning against the window with her feet propped up on the back of a chair, a picture of nonchalance. "She made me so nervous that I didn't *stop* eating for two days beforehand."

The mood in the room lightened considerably and I heard people whisper, "That's her sister."

I quickly outlined the tryout process. "You only have ten minutes to learn the steps, so don't focus too much on each move. Just try to get the sequence down. We know it's quick so we're not looking for perfection. And don't forget to smile!"

Zehava and I crossed to the other side of the room and the girls on that side converged on us. Someone hooked up the CD player and the Yeshiva Boys Choir filled the room. For the next hour, I lost myself in the dance. The tryout sequence was perfect. We'd spent over two hours putting together a concise combination of steps that were alternately graceful, sharp, coordinated, and energetic. If someone wasn't a natural dancer, it would be obvious fairly quickly.

The girls' faces blurred together as group after group stepped up before us and watched as we danced the steps over and over again. "Like this?" they asked. "Am I doing this right?" To be honest, I didn't really look. This was tryouts, and they either could pick it up, or they couldn't.

When the last girls had been taught the steps and the room was a writhing mass of dancing girls, I got back up on the chair. My hair was in a messy ponytail, my sneakers had been tossed off long ago, as had my sweatshirt, and I had the sleeves of my T-shirt pushed up to my elbows. My face was flushed and suddenly the room seemed overwhelmingly hot.

"Congrats — you're ready for the real tryouts now!"

Excitement swelled in the room and I had to wait a moment for them to quiet down before I could explain the procedure. When I jumped off the chair, Daniella appeared at my side, a bottle of Powerade in her hand.

"Drink, Rikki."

"I'm fine. I'll have later."

She grabbed my wrist, tightening her grip when I started to pull back. "You haven't eaten anything all day." She held the bottle out again. When I hesitated, she pressed the back of her hand against my cheek. "You're really hot."

Daniella's cool skin against my flaming cheeks accentuated the fact that I was dehydrated. I took the bottle and started to drink. The first sip ignited the thirst in me and I didn't stop drinking until I was halfway through the bottle.

"Thanks," I said, grinning sheepishly. "I guess I got a little distracted."

"You're on fire, Rik. The freshies can't stop talking about you. You're their new hero."

I rolled my eyes. "They just want to get into dance."

"Maybe, but I'm *shepping nachas* while it lasts!" She grew serious suddenly and took a step closer. "Are you going to be done by twelve forty-five? I'm not getting Uri without you and I don't want to wait any later to tell him."

I glanced at the clock. "We should be, but I'll tell Zehava I need to be out by then. She'll be cool with that."

"With what?" Zehava asked, handing me a clipboard with sheets of paper. I glanced down and saw that as the girls had come into the auditorium, they'd written their names on score sheets so we could keep track of their performance. There was a ten-point rating scale and a small space for comments.

"I need to leave by twelve forty-five."

"Then let's get started." She stood on the radiator and I smiled as the room quieted down again. The power of being a dance head was ridiculous.

"The sooner we get done with tryouts, the sooner we can start working on the dance lists," Zehava announced. "So start getting into groups of three and line up against the wall here."

Laya caught my eye from across the room and we both laughed. The speed of tryouts had absolutely no bearing on the selection process, which was a joint effort between the four dance heads and the teacher advisor. Zehava just wanted to get out of here on time as much as the rest of us did.

Once again, time faded away as girls danced their hearts out. After a while, the hopeful looks on their faces started to get to me and I stopped paying attention, focusing solely on their moves. The worst were my friends, who assumed they were automatically in, just because they had "connections."

"If there's a jumpy dance, I want to be in that one," Riva Winters whispered to me conspiratorially before she headed out of the auditorium. I stared after her in disbelief, wondering where she got the nerve to make such a request after she'd just performed a dance that looked nothing like the sequence we'd taught her.

It was also hard to watch the younger girls who were so

intimidated by the whole process that they forgot the steps as soon as the music began. A thin, blonde girl and two of her friends stepped up in front of us.

"What are your names?" I asked.

"Ayelet Klein," the blonde girl said.

A GO representative handed three papers to Zehava and me. I took Ayelet's sheet and gave the other two to Zehava. There was something about Ayelet that intrigued me. I didn't pay much attention to ninth graders. Not because I looked down on them; I was usually too preoccupied with my own life to notice what went on in school outside my circle of friends. Ayelet looked young, even for a ninth grader. I watched her pull her sleek hair into a ponytail. Her fingers were long and delicate and her chin was pointed, giving her an elfin look. When she saw me watching her, she offered me a shy smile and I smiled back.

"Ready?"

Zehava hit the Play button and the music started. She counted off until the first beat and the girls started dancing. The other two girls danced the routine decently, but Ayelet completely froze. She stepped back as her friends finished, and crossed her arms self-consciously across her chest.

"What happened?" I asked her when the music stopped. She shrugged, color rising in her cheeks as her friends looked at her in confusion. I rewound the music thirty seconds. "Go ahead, I'll play it again."

She scrambled forward, positioning herself in the starting pose. The music started and she blew us away. She wasn't just graceful, the girl was fluid. She danced the steps better than I did. When the music stopped, there was a moment of silence and then Zehava turned slowly to look at me.

"I'm glad you gave her another chance."

By twelve thirty, every girl in the room had tried out. Daniella had us on the floor laughing when she danced an original composition that included every incorrect dance step we'd seen that day. She then danced the tryout routine exactly as I would have; her imitation was perfect.

"That's freaky," Atara said, looking back and forth between us.

After that, Daniella performed our tryout routine in the styles of hip-hop, Sephardi, ballet, and tap. Just when I thought I'd stop breathing if Daniella danced it again, she glanced at the clock and raised her eyebrows.

"We're heading out," she announced, balancing on one foot at a time as she pulled her sneakers on and laced them up. Still balancing on one foot, she turned toward the other dance heads, cocked her head to the side, and in a perfect imitation of one desperate tenth grader from earlier that morning, begged, "Please, please, please, I really want to be in dance!"

With their laughter ringing in our ears, we headed out toward the parking lot.

"How were tryouts?" Kayla asked, pushing herself off the car, where she'd been waiting for us.

Daniella ruffled my hair as she unlocked the car. "Rikki was a total rock star. She could've started doing the chicken dance and everyone would've followed along."

Smoothing my hair back down, I slid into the front seat and kicked my sneakers off. My feet were alive with fatigue, throbbing as they adjusted to their new, relaxed state. Propping them up on the dashboard, I tilted my seat all the way back and lay down, closing my eyes. I was exhausted. I still hadn't consumed anything besides the Powerade, and suddenly, I was ravenous. I thought about our fridge at home, packed full with the results of my mother's frantic cooking frenzy, and just as suddenly, my appetite was gone. I pushed my seat back into a sitting position, irritated that the reality of the situation had ruined my mood.

"What's your problem?" Daniella asked, noticing my face.

"*I* don't have a problem."

Daniella glanced at Kayla in the backseat. Kayla looked out the window.

"Ima tried to borrow candles from the Kaddens."

Daniella's face was completely neutral. I'd watched her do this a thousand times, but every time she did it, I was fascinated all over again. She had the ability to wipe every trace of emotion off her face. Although I could read her better than most people, at times like this, her feelings were a mystery.

"So…" She drew the word out and I realized it was an invitation to continue.

"So Kayla knows."

"She knows what?"

Kayla was uncomfortably quiet. In was no secret that Daniella disapproved of my trust in her. Daniella was a firm believer in keeping our business at home. She was perfectly fine with full-blown lies, told with a straight face to family members, friends, and strangers alike, yet she continuously questioned my reasons for confiding in Kayla. I rarely did something that Daniella didn't like, but this was one of those few things.

"Chill out, Danz. She's not telling anyone."

"She knows what?"

The controlled calm of her voice irritated me more than I expected.

"She knows whatever I told her, okay? It doesn't matter."

Daniella continued driving, her face a perfect mask. She started whistling, the same song that we'd been playing all morning for tryouts. I wanted to grab the wheel and force her to pull over to the side of the road. I wanted to stare at her until her face cracked and she became human again. Her neutrality was infuriating, especially when my insides felt like a tornado.

"I told her Ima's in the hospital and Uri doesn't know yet." The words were out before I could stop them. I couldn't not answer Daniella's question.

Her whistling stopped abruptly. We drove through two lights in silence. One block away from our house, Daniella flipped down her visor and tilted the mirror so she was looking at Kayla in the backseat.

"Kayla."

I turned around in my seat just in time to see Kayla give me a panicked look.

"Yeah?"

"Did you lend my mother any candles? Because if you did, we'll totally give them back. Just because she's crazy doesn't give her the right to borrow without returning, you know."

The smile she flashed us both was so disarming that all we could do was stare at each other.

4

"How are we telling him?"

We sat in the car down the street from the Eliases'. Daniella was braiding thin sections of her hair, knotting the ends of each braid when it was done.

"You do realize those aren't going to come out."

She rolled her eyes at me. "Yes. I know knots don't come out. Thanks, darling."

"You're welcome. Now how are we telling him?"

"How about, 'Uri, Ima tried to light herself on fire so she's locked up in a hospital for safekeeping until someone can figure out how to shut the voices off'?"

"Yeah, that's perfect if you want him to have nightmares until he's thirty."

She reached for my hair, twirling a small section on her finger. "Can I braid this?"

I pulled back. "You're not tying knots in my hair."

She pouted. "You are so boring sometimes."

"Can you please focus?"

Daniella started the car up and started cruising down the street, one arm hanging out the window. A few houses down from the Eliases', she grasped my hand gently. She spoke, keeping her eyes locked on the road ahead of us.

"You know I'll figure out how to tell him. We both will. Because it's what we do. We figure out how to protect Uri, because Abba is useless right now. And you don't have to worry because while we're taking care of Uri, I'll be taking care of you. So please, stop stressing out, and trust me that things will be okay. And if it makes you feel better to talk to Kayla, that's fine, but please, try to keep things quiet. We don't need everyone looking at us because of this. If you need something, I'll take care of it."

Her grip tightened and so did my chest. We sat in front of the house for a few minutes, hand in hand, until finally she turned off the car and drew in a deep breath.

"Let's do this."

Uri was waiting for us on the front-porch swing. His light-brown hair was spiky in front and needed to be brushed, and he was wearing Donny's clothes, which were too big on him. When he saw us both walking up the front steps, he slumped back in the swing, squeezing his eyes shut momentarily before opening them again and looking at us dully.

"Wow. What a welcome. Nice to see you too," Daniella said gently.

She sat down on the swing next to him and I sat on the other side. For a while, we sat there, swinging gently. Uri was motionless, even when Daniella reached over and smoothed down his hair.

"You okay, Uri?" One of his sleeves was rolled up to his elbow; the other had become undone. As I reached over to refold it, he caught my eye.

"Ima doesn't have a peanut allergy."

I swallowed hard, refusing to look at Daniella, even though I was sure she was staring at me.

"You're right, Uri. I just needed to give Mrs. Elias a reason for why I wanted you to stay here."

"Can we leave?" He stood angrily, crossing his thin arms across his chest. He reached under the swing and pulled out a small shopping bag of his clothes.

Mrs. Elias appeared in the doorway, Donny right behind her.

"Hi, girls, how's your mother?"

"She's fine," Daniella answered carefully. "Thanks for keeping Uri here for the night. It was kind of scary at home."

Mrs. Elias nodded. "I'm sure it was. Please let me know if you need anything."

Uri threw his bag into the car and sat down in the back. The sound of his seat belt clicking furiously spoke volumes.

"Uri, what's your—"

He lashed out with his feet, kicking the back of my seat. "Every time, *I* get sent out of the house. Why do *I* always get sent out if she's doing something wrong?"

His words dissolved into sobs and he curled over on himself, burying his face in his knees. Daniella hadn't made it off the Eliases' street, but she pulled over and we both climbed into the back.

"Uri, we're not trying to punish you. It's scary at home when Ima's sick. We don't want you to have to see it."

My words meant nothing to him. His thin shoulders shuddered as he cried. I felt tears building in my eyes, but I refused to let them out.

At eleven, Uri was no longer a baby, but he missed Ima more than any of us. Daniella and I doted on him and gave him as much attention as we could, but that didn't stop him from feeling the pain of an absent mother. His relationship with my father was painful to watch. The more my father tried to show him affection, the more Uri wanted my mother's attention. My mother couldn't have cared less about what Uri wanted, and my father became resentful at Uri's lack of reciprocity toward him. Daniella and I had watched helplessly as my father stopped trying to reach Uri. Their interactions were short and stiff. Uri was hyperalert when Abba was around, his eyes tracking Abba's every move.

Uri sat up shakily, swiping tears from him eyes. He let us hug him, unashamed to be given so much affection from his big sisters. Looking into his eyes, I saw raw fear, and finally understood.

"Uri, we're never going to leave you. If we want you to leave the house because Ima's not safe, it's only so you'll be safe."

"That's true. We don't want Ima to hurt you by accident. She doesn't know what she's doing sometimes," Daniella added.

"I wish you didn't ever have to leave," I said honestly. "I wish you could always stay home with us."

"And if I had to choose who would leave the house, it would be Ima. Not you."

I caught Daniella's eye as she said this, uncertain that this was the message we wanted Uri to be hearing. She looked back defiantly.

Moving right along, I made my final point. "We'll always come back to get you. Always."

Uri gave us a halfhearted smile. "Donny's mother kept asking me about peanut allergies. She wanted to know what happens to Ima when she eats peanuts, so I said she sneezes a lot and she can't stop."

Daniella stifled a laugh. "That's perfect, Uri. You got the right answer."

5

*I*n my dreams, she always caught me. Before my mother got really sick, if I ever dreamed about being chased, I always woke up right before I got caught. Not anymore. My dreams continued past the point of horror, filled with torture and unadulterated fear.

I jerked forward in bed, my hands clawing at my throat, half crying and screaming and half unable to breathe. Terror threaded its way through my body, leaving me trapped in its grip. Images, emotions, and memories flooded through my brain so rapidly that I had no idea what was real and what wasn't. Someone touched me and I reacted in panic. Screams choked their way past my throat and I struck out with my arms, trying desperately to get away.

"Rikki, stop!"

Her hands were pushing me down on the bed, restraining me, trying to hurt me. I fought back, hard, my fist connecting with someone, not knowing or caring who it was. The fear was a gaping hole in my chest and to stop fighting would've been to succumb to it, to lose my mind forever in the endless waves of terror.

"Rikki, you're okay. It's me. Look at me."

Her voice was rhythmic. Endless. I struggled to rise above the panic, to focus on her voice. Daniella? She wasn't going to hurt me. Breathe.

She was holding me by my arms, pinning me down on the bed. Her face hovered above mine, her eyes black in the dim light. The fear was fading. Ima wasn't here. She couldn't reach me.

I was breathing hard, my heart hammering in my chest. I'd seen her. She'd been right here, with me, hurting me. My mind told me it wasn't true, that it had been just a dream, but my body refused to calm down.

Daniella slowly relaxed her grip on me, waiting, to make sure I wouldn't strike out again. With one hand she slowly stroked my cheek, and the tenderness of the gesture brought tears to my eyes. Her calm voice was my lifeline out of the hopelessness that yawned beneath me.

As the fear faded, the shaking set in. This is how it always was after a nightmare. My body trembled relentlessly as my mind processed what had just occurred. I was soaked with sweat and my sheets were a tangled mess. Daniella helped me to the bathroom, where I stumbled into the shower and turned the water on so hot that it nearly scalded my skin.

When I came out, she was sitting on the floor holding fresh pajamas, her head leaning against the bathroom cabinet, her eyes half-closed. Her right eye looked swollen and I wondered if that's what I'd hit when I lashed out. She'd remade the bed with fresh sheets and even though she'd added an extra blanket, once we were under the covers, the shaking started all over again. Tears leaked out of my eyes as I curled in on myself, trying to control the tremors.

"Don't fight it," Daniella said quietly.

She knew how it went just as well as I did. Some nights I'd tremble for hours, tears seeping out of my eyes even though I didn't feel like I was crying. I turned my head, burying my face in her sweatshirt, hearing her heartbeat.

"I can't do this," I whispered, the words coming out in shaky gasps. "How do you do it?"

She was silent for a while, rubbing slow circles on my back. When she spoke, I knew she was being honest, and her words had an almost hypnotic effect on me.

"You have nightmares when you sleep, but I get them during the day. I'll be driving or sitting in class, and then these memories come into my head…and they're so real. I see it happening, Rikki. She's right in front of me. And it's always the worst stuff, the things we never talk about. They replay over and over in my head. The worst part is that I never know when it'll happen. The weirdest things will bring the memories back, certain music, certain smells…it's awful. But since I'm awake, and there are people around, I can't freak out. So I look like I'm fine on the outside, but inside, I'm totally falling apart."

Her hand stilled and just as I was wondering if she'd fallen asleep, she spoke again, her voice so low, I had to listen hard to hear her. My body stopped trembling, as if it too, were waiting to hear what my sister would say next.

"I'm not nearly as strong as I look. I know you think I'm a lot tougher than you but it's not true. You wouldn't want to be more like me."

"Do you ever feel like you're going to completely lose it? That one day everything will just blow up in your face and everyone'll know you've been faking the whole time?"

Her laugh was low and mirthless. "All the time, Rikki. All the time."

6

When the alarm rang the next morning, there was a split second, right before I moved, before I breathed, before I opened my eyes, that everything felt fine. Then I swallowed, and my throat responded with such sharp pain that for a moment, I was positive I'd swallowed a knife. Opening my eyes, I saw Daniella sitting up sleepily, her hair curtaining half of her face as she struggled to open her eyes completely. She turned and gave me a half smile and every trace of fatigue vanished as I shot up in bed.

"What?" she exclaimed, leaning backward as I stared at her wide-eyed.

I pressed my hand against my mouth, shame rising in my stomach as I realized what I'd done. Her right eye was bruised and swollen. Even in the bleak morning light, I could see the dark colors that reached up to her brow and down to the top of her cheekbone.

"I gave you a black eye."

I lay back down on the bed, burying my head into my pillow. Out of the corner of my eye, I watched her slowly finger the edge of the swollen skin. Rising, she walked over to the mirror and examined her face from every angle.

"It could be worse," she said nonchalantly.

"Really? Tell me how it could be worse, because I'm not so sure it could be."

"You could've broken my nose."

"Oh, you're right. *Baruch Hashem* I only hit you in the eye."

She flopped back on the bed and looked down at me, tilting her head to one side. After studying me for a minute, she said, "You gave yourself laryngitis."

It was true. My throat was raw, and burned every time I spoke. My choked screams from the night before had taken their toll.

"I can say it's from dance tryouts. I was yelling a lot."

"And I can say this is from…dance tryouts too. Maybe I tripped over my feet."

The mischievous look dropped from her face, and her eyes narrowed as she leaned closer to me.

"Oh, Rikki…" With one hand, she tugged down gently on the front of my sweatshirt. "You scratched your whole neck up."

Now it was my turn to stand in from of the mirror and survey the damage. She was right. In my panic the night before, I'd clawed at my neck, trying to release myself from invisible hands. Dark-red scratches ran from beneath my chin down to right under my collarbone. It looked brutal, like someone had tried to choke me.

I looked at Daniella in desperation. "I'm not going to school like this."

"Yes you are. I'll do your makeup for you."

"Makeup is not going to cover this up. People are going to think that I…"

I trailed off, realizing that I had no idea what people would make of the angry-looking marks.

"What am I supposed to say? I can't make up random things the way you do."

"Tell them your cat scratched you."

"We don't—"

"That's the point."

The conversation was over.

Daniella started getting dressed, pulling out my uniform as well and tossing it at me. Our Bais Yaakov uniforms were pretty standard — long, pleated black skirts and solid-colored button-down shirts. The one unique policy of our school was that every grade was assigned a different colored shirt. Freshmen wore pink, sophomores wore yellow, juniors wore green, and seniors wore blue. Since Daniella and I were the same size, that meant we only needed to argue over which uniform skirt belonged to whom, since the shirt situation was blessedly obvious.

We were silent as we finished putting our clothes on and ironed our hair. We were obsessive about our hair. We had two Chi irons, since we used them so often we couldn't afford to share. Every morning, we spent at least twenty minutes ironing our hair into sleek, straight sheets. Daniella's process that morning was somewhat complicated by the knotted braids she'd added to her hair the day before. She tied them together loosely at the top of her head and ironed the rest of her hair, releasing the braids from on top once she was finished. On other people, it would've looked juvenile. On her, it looked exotic.

When we'd both decided that our hair was satisfactorily straight, Daniella sat me at my desk chair and examined my neck.

"There's no way I'm putting makeup on this," she said slowly, holding my chin gently and tiling my head up. "It's too fresh."

I stood up and faced the mirror.

"Fine, just put a lot of makeup on my face then. Maybe people won't notice as much."

Ten minutes later, my eyes were smoldering with shimmery shadow and looked twice their normal size thanks to eyeliner and mascara. Daniella had attempted to cover up her bruised eye, but the swelling made it look so disturbing that she removed all of her makeup and decided to go completely natural, with only neutral-colored lip gloss.

We stood next to each other facing the mirror. Daniella cracked a smile first, and I couldn't help it, I smiled too.

"We look crazy," I said helplessly, grinning wider at myself in the mirror.

"Today's going to be interesting."

Daniella insisted I eat breakfast, even though it was the last thing I wanted to do. I attempted to drink a cup of orange juice, but nearly choked from the pain as it hit my raw throat. While I forced down a bowl of Cheerios, Daniella woke Uri and got him ready for school.

"What happened to your eye?" I heard him ask.

"I walked into a doorknob."

"Doorknobs aren't that high."

"I know. But I was on my knees."

"So if you were on your knees, how were you walking?"

As they walked into the kitchen, Daniella shot me a mock-serious look. "Take note, the doorknob is a bad cover story. Uri blew through it in two seconds."

I rolled my eyes at her and turned to Uri, who was looking frustrated at the lack of explanation. "Uri, it was an accident. I banged into her last night when it was dark in my room."

He looked satisfied with that answer and went to pour himself a bowl of cereal.

Daniella looked at me with an awestruck expression. "Rikki, you're so much smarter than me."

I rolled my eyes at her again, smiling despite the seriousness of the situation. She really didn't take herself seriously, and if I wanted to make it through the day okay, I was going to have to adopt some of that detachment. Pushing away my half-eaten bowl of cereal, I started making our lunches. Uri was picky about his sandwiches so I cut his crusts off and sliced the bread twice, creating four equal triangles. After I packed his lunch into a paper bag, I grabbed a Post-it note and scrawled, *We love you Uri, <3 Danz and Rik.*

Five minutes before we had to leave, Kayla knocked on the front door. She rode with Daniella and me to school every morning, and in exchange, Mrs. Kadden drove Uri to school with her sons.

As soon as Uri left the house, after a hug from me, and excessive hugs and kisses from Daniella, Kayla asked, "Your father isn't back yet?"

I glanced at Daniella, gauging her mood to see how much I could say in front of her. She glanced at me and gave me a small nod, letting me know it was okay to talk.

"He came back late last night for about twenty minutes, just to shower and get some more clothes. There's no bed at St. Lucas yet so she's still waiting in the emergency room."

Kayla looked confused. "How can they just keep her in the emergency room? Can't she leave if she wants? What's she doing there?"

"Kicking back and taking a break from her stressful life with three demanding children and an unhelpful husband," Daniella said coolly. "It's not easy being a mother these days."

Ignoring Daniella, I answered Kayla's question.

"They can keep her there as long as they want because the emergency room psychiatrist assessed her and said she's a danger to herself and to other people. They're committing her, so she's got no choice in the matter. If she tries to leave, security will bring her back. My father said she's very medicated right now so she's calm."

Daniella cleared her throat, giving me the impression that she thought I'd said too much. "Are you guys ready to go?"

We followed her out to the car. Before we made it to the street, Daniella stopped and spun around to face us. Kayla stepped back in surprise, but I just waited patiently.

"Kayla." Daniella pulled me up next to her so that we were both facing Kayla. "What do you think?" she said, gesturing to her eye and my neck.

I felt bad for Kayla, who looked like she had no idea what the right answer might be, but I was curious to hear her response.

"I think…that you got punched in the face and someone tried to choke you?"

"Perfect answer. Thanks." Daniella twirled back around and headed for the car again.

"Why does she have so much energy in the morning?" Kayla whispered to me.

I didn't have a clue. Although Daniella had spent several hours the night before talking me down from a state of panic, she looked wide awake, whereas I wanted to lie down on the driveway and take a nap. I always felt sick the day after I had a nightmare. Although the anxiety was gone, my whole body felt uncertain, not trusting that danger wasn't going to strike at any moment. Besides for my aching throat and neck, my head throbbed steadily and my stomach clenched involuntarily, making me wish I'd refused to eat those Cheerios.

"Sorry I never called you yesterday," I said quietly to Kayla. "We took Uri downtown to the sports park and played catch with him. He was really upset about the whole…situation."

"It's fine," she said sincerely. Reaching into her pocket for her cell phone, she said, "I'll text you the number for Adina Begin. She runs the Jewish Big Brother program."

"Thanks."

Daniella turned on music once we started driving, and I was grateful for the chance to close my eyes and rest. Her phone started ringing as she turned into the school driveway.

"Can you get it, Rik?"

It was her best friend, Tali Hassan.

"Hey Tali, it's Rikki."

"Rikki! How's it going, cutie?"

Tali, like Daniella, was generous with her affection. She called me "sweetie" and "honey," and although she was only one year older than me, I always got a warm, big-sister vibe from her. Although she was Daniella's best friend and Daniella spent more than half her life at the Hassans', Daniella had made it clear to me on multiple occasions that Tali knew nothing about our mother's condition.

"I'm good. How are you?"

"Great. Hey, I heard you were a total celebrity at tryouts yesterday."

I smiled, remembering the scene. Had it really just been yesterday? "It wasn't that big of a deal. Daniella likes to make everything sound more dramatic than it is."

Next to me, Daniella pretended to be mortally offended by my assessment of her character.

"I didn't hear it from Daniella. I heard it from my sister, who tried out, and half a dozen of her friends. It was all 'Rikki this' and 'Rikki that.' All afternoon. Seriously, if I didn't love you, I'd be sick of you right now."

I laughed, immediately regretting it when my throat protested.

"You okay, sweetie? You sound sick."

"Yeah, I'm fine, thanks."

"Good. Listen, tell your dramatic sister that I'm getting her off first period to help with scenery."

"Why? She can't paint."

Daniella, who could apparently hear Tali through the cell phone, laughed.

"So? They need some creative geniuses to help them come up with good ideas. I can't paint either."

"Okay. I'll try to convince her to take off. But she might want to go to class. I'll do my best."

"Yeah, right. Bye darling, go drink some tea. See you later!"

I hung up the phone, exhausted by the combined energy of my sister and her friend. My phone beeped and I looked down, seeing that I had a new text. It was from Kayla. *You sound horrible. U okay?*

I closed my eyes briefly, wishing desperately that the honest answer was yes. But it didn't pay to lie to Kayla. If I started lying to her, she'd know.

Not so good. Tell u soon.

She reached around the side of my seat and squeezed my shoulder gently. To my irritation, tears sprang to my eyes. Lately, that happened every time someone showed me any physical affection. When Uri had hugged me the night before, hanging on to me a beat longer than usual, I had to lock myself in the bathroom for five minutes afterward before I was sure I wouldn't dissolve in a puddle of tears. I didn't know if it was because I was starved for meaningful contact, or if I was just overly sensitive in general, but whatever the reason, it bothered me. Daniella parked the car and I forced myself to get in control of my emotions.

Daniella turned to face me, and I nearly started crying all over again once I saw her eye. In the light of the sun, it looked awful. Noticing my expression, she winced.

"Is it that bad?"

I nodded. Sighing, she got out of the car and tucked her uniform shirt in. Leaning down to look in the rearview mirror, she experimented with sweeping her bangs across her swollen eye. After a few failed attempts, she flung her hair back off her face and straightened up.

"Whatever. Let's do this."

As soon as Daniella left to go find Tali, Kayla seemed to relax. "I'm sorry, Rikki, but she drives me crazy."

"I know she does, but she's not trying to be that way."

We had this conversation a lot. Kayla was always on edge when Daniella was around. My sister wasn't mean to her, she just had a way of making Kayla feel insecure and uncertain of her place. My sister had that effect on a lot of people; if she hadn't been my sister, I probably would've felt the same way.

"So what happened to you?" Kayla looked pointedly at my neck. "Is that related to her eye?"

I didn't want to tell her. I was okay with talking about my mother's craziness. That allowed me a certain level of superiority because it was all her problem. When it came to me, I wasn't so forthcoming. My nightmares weren't normal. I didn't know exactly how abnormal they were, but they definitely didn't happen to the average teenager and I wasn't sure I wanted Kayla knowing just how much damage they caused. I opted for half the truth.

"I really don't want to talk about this. Let's just say neither of us slept well last night. And things are weird at home. It honestly feels like we don't have parents anymore."

"Do you guys need…help?" Her tone was uncertain, as if she didn't really know what she was asking.

I laughed quietly. "Of course we do. But I don't think that type of help exists." Sobering, I said, "I actually really need help making it through today. I just want to sleep. I really don't feel good."

"Rikki, take it easy today. And listen, Daniella doesn't always have the answers. So if you guys need help with something, anything, big or small, just tell me. My family'll help you." She offered me a half smile, and I wanted to hug her out of gratitude, but instead I smiled in return and turned to go to my class.

Almost immediately, I realized I needed a plausible excuse for the scratches on my neck, and I needed it fast.

Riva Winters stopped short in front of me, squinting as she peered at me. "Oh my gosh, what happened to you?"

Luckily, before I had to time to formulate an answer, she followed up with, "Did you decide which dance I'm in? I won't tell anyone."

I wanted to shove her out of my way. Controlling my voice and avoiding her eye, I simply said no, and continued on my way to class.

The first lie I told was to Shira Jaffee. She asked the standard "What happened?" question and I paused for a moment to channel Daniella's imagination before telling her that I'd had a mishap with an old sweatshirt and a broken zipper. No one doubted the story, and after I'd repeated it to Tehilla, Rina, and Sora Leah, it started to feel true.

Mrs. Zilber, my first period Chumash teacher, glanced at my neck when I came into her room, but thankfully she didn't say anything. I sat down at my desk, wanting nothing more than to put my head down and rest for five minutes, but my friends flocked over to me to chat until the bell rang. Their voices swirled around my head, talking about tryouts, the production, random Sunday activities, and other inane topics, and I tried my hardest to at least look present. It was odd how my friends didn't seem to care if I participated in the conversation or not. It was as if talking near me was more important than talking to me.

I pulled out my cell phone, keeping it concealed under my desk, and texted Daniella. If Mrs. Zilber saw me with a cell phone, I'd be in big trouble. *Is this day ever going 2 end?*

My sister's reply was instantaneous. *I feel u. hang in there xoxo*

When the bell rang and Mrs. Zilber started teaching, anger flared in me. I didn't want to be here. No offense to what we were learning, but I had more important things to take care of. My mother was in the hospital, my father was unavailable, my brother was feeling neglected, and I was having nightmares so bad that I'd assaulted both my sister and myself in my sleep. Chumash didn't really make it on my list of priorities. I watched Mrs. Zilber without hearing a word she said. She was a good teacher, animated and down-to-earth, yet I felt resentment toward her, toward the subject, and toward the whole school. Didn't anybody realize this was unimportant? Was I the only person in the whole room who didn't care about what she was saying?

Twenty minutes into class, I hadn't taken a single note and I had the distinct feeling that I'd been glaring at Mrs. Zilber without even realizing it. I thought about what Daniella had told me about having nightmares in the middle of the day. I would never have guessed. She was so ridiculously composed all the time. Her flamboyant personality, her cocky attitude and witty remarks made it impossible to detect the turmoil that I didn't doubt she was experiencing. She was a master of disguise when it came to her true feelings. It took a heart-stopping nightmare to evoke real openness from her. And when she was honest, it tore me apart. The thought of her reexperiencing our worst moments during class was awful. I wondered if her silences in our conversations were as meaningful as I'd imagined, or if she was just off in her head, stuck in some nightmarish memory.

Frustration seeped into my muscles and I stretched out my hands in front of me, flexing and clenching my fingers. I glanced up at the clock and saw there were three minutes left to class. I closed my blank notebook, closed my Chumash that had been opened to a random page for the duration of the class, and twirled my pen between my fingers under my desk. When the bell rang, although I'd been expecting it, the noise made me jerk out of my seat in fright. Trying to look nonchalant, I went over to the cabinet to take a siddur.

"I'll give you notes later," Kayla whispered as she passed me on her way to the cabinet.

Still jittery from the clanging of the bell, I nodded distractedly and returned to my seat. My seat in Chumash was front and center. Three weeks ago I'd gotten a seventy-two on my Chumash test. I didn't think that was so terrible, but on the test before I'd gotten a ninety-eight, so Mrs. Zilber thought maybe I needed help staying focused.

Hearing the girls around me start davening quietly to themselves triggered another wave of frustration. I spent the davening period in a daze, obsessing about Uri, Daniella, my mother, and our future. Daniella's friends spent all their time discussing which seminaries they wanted to apply to. Daniella refused to discuss seminary, and if I ever brought up the issue, she got agitated and changed the topic so fast that I didn't have the heart to push it.

I thought about my father, his haggard face as he pushed through the door at eleven thirty the night before. He was still wearing his clothes from Shabbos. He spoke to us briefly, updating us on Ima's status, not before making sure that Uri was safely in his room.

"I really don't know how long this wait will be. Thankfully, they realize she needs to be watched around the clock now, so they aren't trying to send her home."

We'd all breathed a sigh of relief at that. The year before, they'd sent her home to wait while a bed at St. Lucas opened up, and that had been disastrous. My father left for the hospital again before we had a chance to ask him why my mother was so much worse than usual, or how we were going to manage without any parents in the house. Uri hadn't come out of his room until he heard my father's car pull away.

"Maybe they'll lock him up at the hospital too," he said hopefully, watching my father's car turn off our street.

Lost in thought, I stared down at my siddur until the words swam in front of my eyes. Feeling suddenly self-conscious, I looked up to see Mrs. Zilber looking directly at me. My right hand had unconsciously been tracing the scratches on my neck and she was watching my every move. I lowered my hand and dropped it to my lap, holding it steady with my left hand to keep them both from trembling. It felt as though she'd caught me doing something very wrong.

She looked down, and I felt heat rise in my face. I glanced at the clock. Nine thirty-seven. It was too early in the morning to be feeling this horrible.

I was the first one out the door when the bell rang, scared that Mrs. Zilber would pull me aside to ask how I'd managed to cut my neck in that manner. Luckily, she didn't try to stop me.

Kayla caught up with me outside of the classroom. Usually, we didn't talk much in school. It wasn't that we weren't friends there, but our relationship was mostly contained to outside of school. We had entirely separate groups of friends with very little overlap. We spoke to each other throughout the day, but I think she sensed that I needed the space to protect my image of a "Coleman sister." Today, however, apparently I didn't look like I needed space.

"Why don't you go to the nurse's office?" she suggested as we walked toward Ivrit. "You look like you're going to faint."

She was right about that. Not only did I look I was going to pass out, I felt like it too. The last thing I needed was to draw attention to myself. A scratched face was one thing. Fainting in front of a roomful of girls was another.

"I don't want to. I'll just go to the library and lie down for a bit."

The seats in the library were notoriously comfortable for sleeping and I fully intended to take advantage of that. Using my jacket as a pillow, I arranged myself in two of the chairs, pushed as far back in the corner as they'd go. Since it was still early morning, the librarian wasn't there yet and the lights in the library were off. I wondered, briefly, if I'd have a nightmare there, but exhaustion won out and I drifted off into a desperately needed nap.

7

When I woke up, the lights were on in the library and I could hear voices. I pulled out my cell phone and did a double take when I realized I'd slept straight through second and third period, and lunch was halfway over. Remembering that I was supposed to meet with the other dance heads to start the selection process, I dragged myself off the chairs and stretched, my cramped limbs protesting at the movement. I had five unread texts on my phone and was unsurprised to see that three of them were from Zehava, asking where I was.

I texted her back, *Sorry, where r u, I'm on my way.* She texted back with a room number and I headed there, reading the other two texts as I walked. Both were from Daniella. The first said *take note, stopping-a-carjacking story didn't go over too well either.* The second one lacked any trace of humor. *I'm sort of in trouble. Rabbi S wants 2 c me after school.* I texted back a quick *what happened?* but my phone stayed silent.

It wasn't unusual for Daniella to be called to the principal's office. She was regularly sanctioned for inappropriate attire, including untucked shirts, colored nail polish, and hair accessories that could only be considered a distraction. While she wasn't outright disrespectful to teachers, she deliberately flaunted a "don't care" attitude that irked them to no end. She'd become an expert at toeing the line, often making school staff wish she'd crossed it, just so that they could punish her. Despite the fact that our principal's request to see her was not out of the ordinary, it made me nervous. Today was not a day that either of us wanted any more scrutiny than necessary.

I reached room 203 and took a deep breath before stepping inside. Despite the long nap, I still felt shaky from fatigue. I wondered what my voice sounded like, because my throat hurt worse than ever. "Hi," I whispered to myself, one hand on the door handle. My voice was ravaged. I wished I had a drink.

Stepping inside, I plastered a smile on my face and greeted them as normally as I could.

"What happened to you?" Atara asked.

"That seems to be the question of the day," I joked. "It's a long story, I'll tell you after. Sorry I'm late."

We were narrowing down the list of potential dancers from one hundred and eighteen to forty. Ms. Palmer, the teacher advisor for dance, sat in a circle with us four dance heads, overseeing the process. It quickly became clear that her purpose was not to help us with the selection, but rather to make sure our discussion stayed on track and didn't dissolve into a *lashon hara* fest regarding the weaknesses of the dancers we didn't want.

"Remember," she said for the third time since I'd walked in, "you don't need to explain why are you aren't choosing someone. You only need to pick out the girls you want."

Ms. Palmer was young, and I remembered that she'd been dance head four years ago. Her pirate dance and circus dance had been innovative and legendary. She'd revolutionized the image of Bais Yaakov dances, demonstrating that although our dances were tamer than what most of society would've deemed entertaining, it was possible to inject spirit and talent into a dance so that it could be classified as both *tznius* and incredible. She only taught ninth grade and had never been my teacher, but I liked her.

On the desk in the middle of our little circle were one hundred and eighteen pieces of paper with the names of all the girls who tried out. In one circle off to the side was a group of about twelve papers. Those were the girls whose skills were so obvious that there was no discussion about them being accepted. I was relieved to see Daniella's name in that pile, and was also pleasantly surprised to see that Ayelet Klein had made that cut, despite her rocky start. Ms. Palmer was trying to discourage us from creating a pile of automatic rejects, but eventually she realized that it would be immensely difficult to sort through the rest of the names without doing so.

The end-of-lunch bell rang, once again startling me so much that I jumped. The four of them looked at me in surprise and I smiled sheepishly.

"I guess I just really got caught up in the process!"

We were up to thirty-one names in the "yes" pile.

"Can you get us off first period?" Zehava asked Ms. Palmer. "I think we can finish this up."

She agreed, and left to go get us passes from the office. As soon as she stepped out of the room, the atmosphere changed. Laya reached and slid two names from the "yes" pile over to Zehava.

"Shaindy and Devora can't dance that well. You can't put them in dance just because they're your friends."

Zehava rolled her eyes. "I knew you'd say that. You can't not put them in dance just because they're not your friends, either."

Laya shook her head. "It's not about that. I'm just saying, there were a lot of girls who were better than them."

Atara pulled another name out of the "yes" pile. "What about Aleeza? I feel like Ms. Palmer said yes to her just because she wants her to be in dance, so she'll stay out of trouble. Not because she's that good."

I'd actually been the one to suggest Aleeza. And not because I thought she needed to stay out of trouble, whatever trouble they might be referring to. Her moves were slick and I'd seen her doing cartwheels in the back of the auditorium. Adding gymnastics to dance routines always spiced things up.

The three of them went back and forth, pulling names from all three piles, accusing each other of favoritism and prejudices. They kept referencing drama I was completely oblivious to, and I finally started watching the door, waiting for Ms. Palmer to return so they'd all go back to pretending they agreed with each other.

"Rikki, you decide."

"What?" I asked in alarm, as they slid six slips of paper over to me.

"You don't know these girls, so you'll just judge them by their dance skills."

I read the names off the papers. There were four seniors and two freshmen. Glancing up at my three coheads, I saw them looking at me expectantly. Realizing they were planning on listening to what I said, I decided to be totally straight.

Rearranging the papers as I spoke, I said, "Hadassah is definitely in. She has a ton of natural skill, and she'll be able to pick up whatever style we want her to. I'm not sure about Shaindy. She got the moves, but she wasn't doing them in any special way; it was too automatic. She'll be able to pick up the steps, but she won't necessarily make it look great. Let's put her back in the 'maybe' pile because she's definitely a lot better than some other people. She'd probably do well in a sharp dance because she'll do the moves exactly like we teach her. Devora's in. She's been in dance since ninth grade for a reason. Chaya, I'm not sure about. She does the moves really well, but she can't seem to remember a sequence. But after a hundred hours of practice, I'm assuming she'll get it all. So put her back in 'maybe,' but as a 'probably.' Put Shira back in the 'maybe' pile. She'd probably do well in a graceful dance, but she might also be too loose with the moves. And leave Aleeza in the 'yes' pile. I want her in my dance."

I pushed the scrap with Aleeza's name into the "yes" pile and sat back. "That's all I've got."

The three girls looked at me in awe.

"I'm fine with that. Are you guys good?" Zehava asked.

They nodded just as Ms. Palmer came back into the room. She handed out our passes and sat back down at the circle. Studying the piles, she noted the changes we'd made and nodded her approval.

"You're doing good, girls. Keep it up. If we can get the lists up by the end of this week, a lot of people will be happy."

"And a lot of people won't," I added.

My cynical comment seemed to spur everyone on and by the end of the period, we had thirty-nine names in the "yes" pile and were debating between Dina Jacoby in the tenth grade and Perry Lieberman in the eleventh. Perry was one of Kayla's friends and we spoke to each other whenever we happened to be in the same place. But I couldn't put a face to Dina's name, even though I'd rated her dancing skills as a eight and a half and had scrawled *Graceful, smiles, perfect beat*, on her score sheet. When the girls looked to me to make the final decision, I desperately wanted to pass.

For the first time since we'd started with the selections, I realized how much of an impact I had in the next several months of these girls' lives. If they were in dance, they were bound to have fun, being part of the elite group that garnered the most attention and the most applause at every concert. If they didn't get in, they might end up in ensemble, which had the reputation of being the group for "dance rejects." I didn't want to do that to Perry. Yet Dina Jacoby, whose smile, grace, and impeccable timing had captured my attention, didn't deserve that either.

The pressure of the decision made me want to bolt from the room. It was easy to move girls in between the "yes" and "maybe" piles. Those decisions weren't definite. But here, we were down to the wire. As my anxiety built, I realized that out of the all the stressors in my life, dance cuts were probably the least of my worries, but for whatever reason, this decision seemed overwhelming.

"Can you please decide?" I said weakly, turning to Ms. Palmer. "I've made too many decisions today. My head hurts."

Ms. Palmer finished writing the list down in her notebook and then gathered the scraps of paper together. "Sure. I'll figure it out tonight. Ladies, thank you for your hard work, you've done a great job. Let's meet again tomorrow and start breaking the groups down."

Laya and Atara left the room quickly, their heads bent together, talking quietly about who they hoped to have in their dances. Zehava turned to me as she slung her knapsack over her shoulder. "So what happened to your neck?"

I tiredly recited my fake story, tripping over the details that were starting to blur together in my mind.

"And what happened to Daniella's eye?" she asked innocently.

That was a problem. I didn't know what story Daniella had decided to go with and the last thing either of us needed was for there to be two false stories going around.

"That's something you'll have to ask her about," I said lamely.

When we hit the hallway, Zehava asked when I wanted to get together to start choreographing.

"We can start tomorrow," I said, "but can we do it at your house? There's no good space in mine."

"I have ten siblings; we don't exactly have space either."

I wished my stomach would stop clenching every time something went wrong. "So why don't we just stay late here? The teachers don't leave until five thirty. We'll get permission from Ms. Palmer. Nobody will mind."

She nodded thoughtfully. "That'll work."

Turning toward her classroom, she tossed back over her shoulder, "You were great today, Rikki. I'm really glad we're working together."

Her sincere words burned as they hit my skin and I felt the too-familiar prickle of tears in my throat. What was wrong with me?

"Thanks, Zehava," I said hoarsely. "You too."

8

By the end of the school day I'd attended a total of three and a half out of eight classes, having slept through two, gotten off for one, and cut the last one and a half classes of the day. I hadn't intend to walk out of English class, but Mrs. Sidransky, who was doing a unit on creative writing, said, "Today's writing assignment is called 'Family Portrait,'" and I walked out of the room without waiting to hear what it actually entailed.

Once I'd already cut half of my English period, I figured things couldn't get worse by skipping gym. It was usually my favorite subject, but my whole body hurt and the last thing I wanted to do was play another game of *machanayim* with a bunch of girls who prattled on about such trivial things that I wanted to slap them. Their naïveté about the real world and real issues made me nauseous.

Daniella had never responded to my text and I couldn't keep myself from worrying about her. After texting her no less than six more times, she finally responded, *They want u in Rabbi S's office. Tell Kayla to find a ride home.*

I texted Kayla and made my way to the office. I wondered if they'd already been told about the sleeping and cutting class. Passing by a wall mural inlaid with mosaic tiles and small pieces of mirrored glass, I caught a glance of my reflection.

I looked ridiculous. With my overly made-up eyes, which I now saw drew more attention to my neck than detracted from it, it looked like I was trying too hard to hide something. In fact, Ms. Palmer had told me as much. In between second and third periods, she passed me in the hall and pulled me aside for a moment.

"You look a little fancy for school today. Are you going somewhere later?" Her eyes flickered from my neck back up to my eyes.

"No," I said self-consciously. "I just felt like looking nice."

"Well, you don't have to try so hard to look nice, Rikki. You're naturally very pretty. Remember that, okay?"

I knew she meant well, but her tone felt so patronizing that I wanted to tell her that she didn't know anything, and the next time she tries to boost someone's self-esteem, she shouldn't bother with me. Instead, I thanked her awkwardly, and walked off as quickly as I could.

It wasn't just my throat that looked hurt. My eyes were bloodshot and the makeup hadn't concealed the bags under my eyes. Swallowing hard, I continued down the hall to the office.

I was grateful there were no students in there. The secretary sat behind the desk on her computer and Mrs. Zilber was filling out some papers next to her. Mrs. Zilber smiled when she saw me.

"Hi, Rikki."

I tried to smile back, cringing to myself as I turned to the secretary and said, "I think Rabbi Sacks wants to see me."

She nodded and said, "You're Rikki Coleman? Your sister is already back there speaking to him. I'm not sure if they're finished yet." Turning to Mrs. Zilber, she asked in an undertone, "Did they want you in on this?"

My body was suddenly on high alert. What would they need Mrs. Zilber in on? She hardly even knew me. Sure, she was my *mechaneches*, but that didn't mean I actually talked to her.

"I said I'd be here if they needed me, but I won't go in there unless it's necessary."

I looked back and forth between the two of them. "What's going on? Am I in trouble?"

Mrs. Zilber shook her head quickly. "No, Rikki, you're fine. Rabbi Sacks just had some concerns he wanted to discuss with you." Turning to the secretary, she said, "I'll go see if he's ready."

I followed her down the back hallways toward the principal's office. The only time I'd been in there was the year before, the day I was chosen as dance head. Rabbi Sacks had sat the four dance heads in his office and gave us a quick talk about our responsibility to pick dancers who were refined, *tzniusdik*, and would comply with the school guidelines regarding approved and unapproved dance steps. I didn't have much of an opinion of him, as he kept a respectful distance from the girls, mostly staying in his role of public speaker, disciplinarian, and parent diplomat. Mrs. Landau, the assistant principal, was the one who dealt directly with the students on a day-to-day basis.

When Mrs. Zilber knocked gently on the door and it opened from within, I was taken aback to see not only Rabbi Sacks and Daniella, but also Mrs. Landau, and Mrs. Moskowitz, the school social worker. It was more serious than I'd anticipated. Daniella's eye looked worse than I remembered. Throughout the day, the bruising had deepened, and her eye had swollen halfway shut. She looked at me when I came in, but didn't smile, which concerned me even more than the crowd in the office. Under ordinary circumstances, Daniella would've done something — a wink, a raised eyebrow — to put me at ease. Her lack of expression meant even she was scared.

"I'll be in the main office, if you need me," Mrs. Zilber said, pulling the door closed behind her.

Rabbi Sacks motioned for me to sit in the empty chair next to Daniella.

"Rivka," he began.

"It's Rikki," Daniella said, grasping one of the small braids from within her hair and examining the knot at the end, effectively avoiding eye contact with anyone in the room.

Rabbi Sacks glared at her, momentarily silenced, before continuing.

"Rikki, in our school, the safety of our students is the most important thing, even more than their education. Our staff is trained to notice signs of unsafe situations, or red flags that something is going on outside of school, maybe at home or somewhere else." He leaned forward slightly and went on. "This morning Daniella's teacher asked her what happened to her eye, and the answer she gave wasn't exactly believable."

I glanced over at her, remembering her "carjacking" text. She was attempting to unknot the end of her braid, and didn't look back.

Rabbi Sacks continued. "I had three separate teachers approach me today, concerned about her black eye, which, as I'm sure you know, isn't something that we see in this school very often. Then one of your teachers approached me about some marks on your neck."

I involuntarily tilted my chin down, as if that would undo the damage that had already been done. My hands started twitching and I knotted them together in my lap to still them.

"We need to know if there's something going on at home, if you girls are being hurt. Daniella seems very much against us calling your parents."

Daniella jerked forward in her seat, looking about to say

something, but then slumped back, her hands dangling off the edges of her chair in defeat.

Rabbi Sacks delivered the final blow. "If you're not able to explain how you were injured, I'm really sorry, but we're going to have to contact child protective services and make a report of suspected abuse."

My heart slammed in my chest and I could hear my blood pounding in my ears. Of course they'd made the connection between our injuries. How could I've been so stupid? Three sets of eyes rested on me.

Mrs. Moskowitz spoke calmly. "Rikki, can you tell us how you got injured?"

I needed to say something, but my throat seemed to be stuck. *Daniella, help me*, I thought as hard as I could. But she remained completely still, her arms now folded across her chest.

The first words that came out sounded harsh and defensive to my ears. "Daniella doesn't want you to tell our parents because they don't know anything about it."

"Okay," Mrs. Moskowitz said slowly, "but you do."

Frustrated, I turned to Daniella. "Why didn't you just tell them the truth?"

She finally turned to me, her eyes blazing. "Because it's not my truth to tell." Her words were bitter, but I understood the meaning behind them. She'd been trying to protect my privacy, in the same way she carefully guarded her own. She was willing to spend hours under the scrutiny of our principal, vice principal, and school social worker, all so she wouldn't reveal anything negative about me.

Relaxing slightly, Daniella said, "You can tell them." Seeing the uncertainty in my face, her voice softened even more and she said, "Really. You can."

The three of them watched us intently, waiting for the scene to play itself out. I resented that they expected me to talk openly in front of a crowd. Didn't they already assume the situation involved physical abuse? Did that warrant a full-blown interrogation? This didn't seem the best way to elicit the truth from an abused teenager, but hey, I wasn't the expert.

Shifting uncomfortably in my chair, I looked at Rabbi Sacks and said, "I did it."

No one moved.

"What?" I said, irritated at the lack of response, and the look of disbelief in his eyes. "I did. I get really bad nightmares sometimes and I did this to myself. Then Daniella tried to wake me up and I hit her in the face. It was an accident."

Mrs. Landau spoke first. "Daniella, is that true?"

Daniella nodded.

"Why were you so concerned about me calling your parents?" Rabbi Sacks asked.

Daniella shot him a bitter look. "I told you already — they don't know." Her voice dripped with anger and even I was surprised at her level of disrespect toward our principal. "And they don't need to know. It has nothing to do with them."

"I disagree," he said simply. "If Rikki is having nightmares that bad, your parents need to know. You're her sister, Daniella, not her mother."

He couldn't have said anything worse. Daniella was out of her chair before I could even react. "You kept me in here for three hours, trying to get me to admit that I'm being abused, threatening the whole time that you're going to call my parents or CPS. Then she comes in here and *tells* you what you want to know — and now you're going to call them anyway?"

Rabbi Sacks stood slowly from his seat. "I'm going to step out for a minute and let you ladies finish talking." Eyeing Daniella warily, he slipped out of his office.

"Daniella, please sit down." Mrs. Moskowitz's voice was

admirably neutral. Daniella stared at her for a moment too long and I started wondering if she was having a flashback. I let myself breathe when she finally sat down and then shifted my chair slightly closer to hers.

"I won't call your parents," Mrs. Moskowitz promised, and I felt Daniella relax. "However, I'm extremely concerned about both of you." She let her words hang in the air.

"We're fine," Daniella said tiredly, as her voice had lost its fight.

"I'm not jumping to conclusions, but I do know that nightmares of such intensity are usually a sign that something bigger is going on."

I felt Mrs. Moskowitz's eyes on me but I refused to meet her gaze.

"I can't help but wonder what's causing them, and what they're about. I'm guessing they're not fun to deal with, if your neck and Daniella's eye are any indication." Her voice was so gentle that tears started up in my eyes again.

Daniella's next words made them evaporate. "She does need help. They're really bad. But my parents have a lot going on, so I don't want them to have to deal with it. Can you see her about them?"

I turned to her, shocked and feeling betrayed by her sudden change.

She met my gaze, unflinching. "You do need help. It's okay."

I felt sick, cold, and furious. Daniella was infuriating. She thought she ran my whole life. "I'm not seeing anyone about them," I said hotly. "This was a one-time thing. I'm fine."

Daniella didn't respond. Mostly because she knew it was a lie, but also because she knew, that in this situation, she was unequivocally right. I needed help.

Mrs. Moskowitz said she would be happy to see me, but if I wanted to see her more than twice, I was going to need parental consent. I didn't even plan on seeing her more than once, so I wasn't concerned. But Daniella assured her that if I needed parental consent, she'd make sure I got it. Mrs. Moskowitz gave me an appointment for Wednesday at nine thirty in the morning. I didn't bother protesting, since I knew Daniella would drag me from my classroom if I tried.

When Daniella noticed what time it was, she flew out of her chair and grabbed her knapsack from the floor. "We need to get Uri. Now."

She turned to Mrs. Landau and Mrs. Moskowitz, and in her most polite voice, explained. "I told my parents I'd pick up my little brother from school, and we'll be late if we don't leave now. Can we please go?"

The teachers exchanged glances and Mrs. Landau said, "Rabbi Sacks—"

"I'll talk to Rabbi Sacks tomorrow," Daniella said. "And I'll apologize for being *chutzpadik*. I'll write a letter, or whatever he wants, but we really need to leave. And please tell him not to call anyone either. I promise…we're okay."

She inched toward the door as she spoke. Realizing she wasn't going to stay even if they told her to, Mrs. Landau nodded that we could go.

Daniella ran to the car and I followed after her, realizing that even if she sped, we were still going to be late for Uri. That meant that he'd have another hard night, feeling angry at us for forgetting about him, and being sad that Ima wasn't there. I didn't have time for his emotions when I could barely handle my own.

Luckily, Daniella resigned herself to being late and drove safely.

"I can't believe you did that," I said bitterly.

"Did what?" I had a feeling she wasn't being facetious, since she'd done a lot of things that day that could've warranted my comment — and that only irritated me more.

"What am I supposed to say to Mrs. Moskowitz if she wants to know what I'm dreaming about?"

"I don't know what you dream about. Tell her whatever you want."

I jerked sideways in my seat, so I could glare at my sister directly. The truth was, she didn't know. I spoke about my nightmares in the vaguest of terms, mostly because they were blurry amalgamations of horror that imitated real events, with a raw, inhumane twist.

"If I don't tell *you* about them, why do you think I'd tell her?"

"Because she's not me."

"What does *that* mean?"

Daniella sighed. "Why *don't* you tell me what they're about?"

I considered the question. "There's a hundred reasons. I don't want to talk about them. I don't know how to talk about them, it makes me feel worse to even think about them, there's no point in repeating them, you don't need to deal with my nightmares—"

"That one," she said, cutting me off. "The last one. Even if you wanted to tell me about them, you wouldn't, because you think I can't handle it. Or you'd feel guilty telling me."

"That's not true."

"No?"

She let her question hang in the air, just a beat too long, in typical Daniella fashion, so that it answered itself. Indignation sizzled in my stomach.

"I'm so sick of you acting like you know me better than I know myself," I said, turning to face forward. I didn't want to watch her as she psychoanalyzed me. I didn't care if she was right or not — I just wanted her to stop.

"I'm sorry. Rikki, seriously. Just ignore me, okay?" Keeping her eyes focused on the road, she ran her hand through her hair, pausing halfway to let it rest on her head.

When I didn't say anything, she pulled over to the side of the road and put the car in park. She held both hands up in front of her face, and we watched her fingers tremble for a moment. Turning toward me, she held my gaze for a short moment before looking out her window down the darkening street.

In a hollow voice, she said, "It's just easier to act like I know what's going on with you, than it is to admit I have no idea what's going on with myself."

9

Uri was so angry with us for being late that he refused to talk during the entire ride home. He slammed his car door and stalked into the house, throwing his knapsack across the front hallway and tossing his jacket on top of it. His thin shoulders heaved with anger and I was almost impressed by the scowl that he kept plastered on his face.

"Uri," I tried. "We got sent to the principal's office. We left as soon as we could."

He turned away from me, indifferent to my excuse. "Leave me alone."

I was surprised by how much his dismissal hurt.

"Fine," I said, flinging my knapsack on the floor as well.

"Uri, what do you want for dinner?" Daniella asked from the kitchen.

"Nothing."

He made his way toward his room and I watched him go, too exhausted to try and comfort him. I tried to remember what Ima had been like when I was eleven, curious if I'd been able to comprehend that her illness wasn't something I could control. But I could hardly remember what I'd eaten for lunch that day, much less my emotional capacity five years earlier.

"I don't know what to say to him," I told Daniella as she stared blankly into the pantry.

"There's nothing to say. We screwed up and we were late. That was my fault for being rude to Rabbi Sacks."

"It's not your fault. He was threatening you."

"I know, but I was being a jerk. That's why he called in Mrs. Landau. I really want to know which teachers told him about my eye." She pulled a can of vegetable soup out of the closet and set it on the counter. "You want? It'll be good for your throat."

I nodded, and handed her the can opener.

Once the soup was heating up on the stove, Daniella turned to look at me, resting her back against the countertop. "How was your day?"

The scene stunned me momentarily; it was how I imagined a mother should look after a long day — preparing dinner, asking genuinely interested questions. This was the best I'd get.

"It was horrible."

Daniella was a good listener, and I could feel my chest loosening as I told her about sleeping through my classes, the inane banter of my classmates, and the irritating dance selections during lunch.

"So who do you think Ms. Palmer will choose?" she asked, once I told her about the final two candidates for dance.

I shrugged. "I don't even care. I just couldn't deal with making any more decisions."

"So…did I make it into dance?"

I raised an eyebrow at her. "Are you kidding? Of course."

"Well, there's your answer. Both girls can get in because one of them can have my spot."

I scanned my sister's face, looking for signs of humor or playfulness, but she was solemn.

"Why…"

"Uri," she said simply.

The unfairness of the situation struck deep and I felt the familiar icy burn of anger.

"That's ridiculous. You shouldn't have to miss out on dance just to pick him up. We can get him another ride home from school."

"It's not just about that, Rikki. You know that. I need to be here for him when he gets home. He needs me."

There was nothing to argue about. "I don't know what to tell Ms. Palmer."

Daniella smiled at me. "You're always so worried about what to tell people."

"Yeah, well, not everyone can lie like Daniella Coleman."

10

At eight thirty, Daniella, Uri, and I were sitting at the kitchen table, where we'd been since Uri had come out of his room an hour earlier, his face tear-stained and sad. Daniella hugged him tight and let him have waffles for dinner.

Uri was doing his homework, and Daniella and I were pretending to do ours. In reality, I was sketching choreography patterns, trying to create new setups and arrangements that hadn't been used before, and Daniella was doodling her name on a piece of paper, tracing and retracing the edges of her block letters until her name seemed to rise from the paper. None of us spoke, and although the atmosphere wasn't unpleasant, a distinct heaviness permeated the room.

The sound of the front door unlocking startled all three of us. Uri sat stiffly in his seat, clenching the pencil so tightly that his fingers were turning white. Daniella stretched a hand out toward the edge of my paper, pencil poised, and scrawled, *I can't deal with this*, before quickly scratching it out.

Abba looked surprised to see us all in the kitchen, which made no sense because that's exactly where we always were at that time of night.

"Hi. How's everyone doing?"

Uri got up and left of the room.

"What's wrong with Uri?"

Daniella started to respond but then seemed to think better of it.

"He'll be fine," I said. Noticing my father's fresh shirt and tie, I asked, "Are you coming from work?"

He nodded, loosening his tie as he sat in Uri's vacated seat. "Ima got a bed around noon. After they admitted her, I went into the office."

"Thanks for letting us know," Daniella said icily.

"Daniella…"

"What?"

"I didn't want to bother you girls at school. I figured we'd get a chance to talk tonight when I got home."

"Well, that was very considerate of you." Her voice dripped with sarcasm and I was grateful I wasn't on the receiving end of her barbs.

"How's Ima?" I asked, after the silence had stretched on uncomfortably long.

It took Abba a minute to tear his gaze away from Daniella, who had now outlined her name so many times that the pencil was cutting straight through the paper. When he finally focused on me, I found myself wanting him to look away again, uncomfortable with the vulnerability in his eyes.

"She's not doing very well."

My father hated talking to us about our mother. He was fiercely protective of her and forever seemed to be striving for the perfect balance between adequate disclosure and maintaining her dignity. He always erred on the side of caution, leaving us with unanswered questions.

"Can you just tell us what the deal is?" The exasperation in Daniella's voice mirrored my feelings exactly.

"She's doing worse. Before, her bipolar mostly manifested itself in episodes of mania and depression. You know, the highs and lows—"

"Yes. We know what bipolar is," Daniella cut in.

Abba acted like he hadn't heard, but I noticed that he directed his next words toward me. "She now has…psychotic features." He waited. I wanted to urge him to go on and explain, but I knew Daniella would take care of that. And I wasn't sure I wanted to hear what else he had to say.

Daniella pushed back her chair from the table abruptly and stood. "Are you going to tell us what this means or not?"

"Sit, Daniella," my father said quietly. "This isn't easy for me."

She sat, and after a moment, he continued. "Bipolar isn't a curable disease. It can only be treated with medication and therapy, but it's an ongoing process. Even after the patient finds the right combination of medications, various factors can knock them off balance again. That's why Ima's been hospitalized more than once…because her medications needed to be readjusted."

"Or because she stopped taking them," Daniella said.

"Or took all of them at once," I added.

My father nodded. "That's true. Medication noncompliance complicates things a lot. And people with bipolar don't always want to give up the manias, since they can be very pleasurable. So they often stop taking their medication, even though it helps stabilize their moods. That's what's happened in the past with Ima, and every time she's gone back into the hospital, they've been able to restabilize her. The thing is…" He paused, stretching his neck and shoulders uncomfortably before continuing. "The more times someone plays around with their medication, the harder it is to restabilize. More complications can come up and it's not so easy to get back to the previous level of functioning."

"What does that mean?" I asked.

"It means that when Ima stopped taking her medication this past time, she didn't just slip back into the old pattern of mood swings. Things got worse, and she started seeing things that weren't there and hearing voices in her head. Basically…she's become psychotic."

The word hung in the air, threatening and ugly. My mind didn't want to accept that that label now applied to my mother. "Bipolar with psychotic features" was a lot different than saying my mother had become psychotic. Was it really a clinical word? My friends used it jokingly whenever someone did or said something strange. But what my mother had been doing was on a whole new level. My brain rejected the word, sending it spiraling back at my father. The question I asked next was so out of character, I almost thought I heard Daniella asking it.

"Why did you let her stop taking her medications?"

Daniella raised an eyebrow at me, smirking slightly. She was impressed with my question, which made me feel horrible.

"She's a grown woman, Rikki. She's not a child. It's her responsibility to take care of her health."

"That's not true. You just committed her to a psychiatric hospital."

"Yes, because she was a danger to herself."

"So you didn't realize that would happen if she went off her meds? You knew she'd get like this. Why would you put her in charge of her medication?"

Daniella chimed in, "Aren't there blood tests that show if she's taking her meds? How come no one caught that?"

My father looked confused by our questions. "Girls, I don't control Ima. I don't try to take her rights away unless someone will get hurt."

"Well, maybe you should've thought of that before things got this bad," Daniella said. "Or maybe you should've asked us, because we both could've told you how dangerous she could get."

In the silence that followed, I felt my respect for my father slipping away. How couldn't he see that it was his responsibility to make sure she took her medication? If he didn't do it, who would?

He cleared his throat. "Girls, I'm sorry you feel this way. I wish I could've kept her safe, but bipolar is a complicated disease."

I didn't want to hear his excuses. "What are they going to do for her at the hospital?"

Abba seemed grateful for the question. "They're going to put her on an antipsychotic medication to try and stop the hallucinations and delusions. It may take a while for it to take effect, but they aren't in any rush. I need you to realize this won't be a quick hospitalization. Ima may not be home for several weeks, maybe more, and I'll need your help with Uri." He hesitated. "There's something else. Ima isn't ready to have visitors at this point."

"Isn't ready, or just doesn't care enough about her own kids to let them visit?" Daniella's voice was tight and I could see she was clenching and unclenching her jaw.

"Daniella, you know it's not like that. I know you and Rikki will understand, but Uri will be really upset that he can't see her." He first gave Daniella, then me, a pleading look.

"We need money," Daniella said suddenly.

My father look startled. "What? Why?"

"Because we're running this house," she snapped. "We need money for groceries, and laundry detergent, and gas, and new shoes for Uri, and everything else that needs to get done around here."

My father sighed, defeated. "I'll go to the bank tomorrow and take out some cash. Girls, I'm really sorry you have to deal with this. I may have to work some overtime but I'll try to make it home by six. Thank you…for everything."

He left the room, leaving the two of us looking at each other. Daniella spoke first. "He didn't even notice our faces."

11

"Do you want me to sleep in here tonight?" Daniella asked, lingering in my doorway. It was early, just past ten o'clock, but I was bone-tired and my brain was racing so fast I was sure that if I didn't lie down soon, it would split through my skull. She seemed exhausted too, leaning against the doorframe as if she couldn't have supported her body weight without it.

"Not a good idea. We don't need a repeat of last night."

She crossed the room and lay down on my bed. "True, but will you sleep okay?"

"Probably not." There was no way I was going to make it through the night without dreaming. My mind was fragile, just barely holding itself together. My only hope was that the exhaustion would prevent me from reacting to my dreams with the same violence as the night before.

"So let me stay." She crossed her arms over her chest and stared at the ceiling.

"Daniella, no. I can't deal with that again."

"It's fine, I won't try to grab you if it happens. I'll just wait until you calm down."

"It's not like that. I don't know if I'm in control of what I'm doing." I sounded crazy. I thought about Mrs. Moskowitz; the idea of telling her about the dreams made my stomach clench. I crawled into my bed and lay against the wall.

I let my eyes rest on the mural painted on the wall directly in front of my bed. It was a scene depicting a sunset on the beach. Faint footsteps traversed the length of sandy landscape, and blue-green waves seem to move gently between the golden sand and the purple-hued sky. It was my mother's handiwork, painted at the height of her mania, in a stunning fourteen-hour painting marathon. She'd painted straight through the night, while I'd slept fitfully, alternately excited about the scene unfolding on my wall, and nervous about the limitless energy that seemed to be radiating from her as she worked.

It represented the best of my mother and reminded me that although she was incredibly sick, she also possessed unbelievable talent. It was heartbreaking that her illness brought out the best of her creativity. It wasn't surprising that she wouldn't have wanted to give up the periods of mania.

Daniella had propped herself up on one elbow and was gazing at me. "I won't be able to sleep. I'm going to Tali's for a bit, okay?"

"Now?"

She shrugged. "It's better than tossing and turning. I'll just keep you up."

"I already said you're not sleeping here. I'll be fine, I don't need you."

When she looked at me, I could've sworn I saw tears glistening in her eyes.

"But what if I need you?"

Neither of my parents knew about Daniella's habit of going to Tali's late at night. It didn't usually bother me, and she was good about keeping me updated via text so I knew when to expect her back. I did wonder what they were doing at that hour, but whenever I asked, Daniella promised they were just hanging out. I had no choice but to believe her. I knew that one of these days my father would catch Daniella driving off at midnight, but I also knew he had very little control over her.

As soon as she left, my exhaustion vanished and was replaced with hot, angry energy. Rabbi Sacks's threats, Ms. Palmer's patronizing comments, Daniella's request to be removed from dance, my father's explanation of my mother's psychosis. It all swirled in my head, leaving me vibrating with rage-laced restlessness.

I prowled around my darkened room, running my hands against the smooth walls, stopping to trace the waves of the ocean, which were slightly textured from layers of paint. The sensation against my skin further irritated me and I found myself wanting — no, needing — to feel something more. I skimmed my hands across the fresh cuts on my neck, pressing slightly, just enough so that I could feel the pain. It hurt, but it wasn't strong enough.

I continued moving in impatient circles, my eyes and hands roving over the items in my room, seeking something that would give me relief from the pent-up swarm of emotion. I stopped in front of my desk, opening and closing the drawers recklessly, deliberately avoiding the top drawer on the right. I desperately looked for something — anything — other than what lurked in that drawer, but right now, it was the only thing I could think of. Cold fury shrieked across my brain, obliterating all other thoughts.

Without having any say in the matter, my hand opened the top drawer and cradled a book of matches. Self-hatred mixed with relief, and within seconds the latter feeling had totally wiped out the former. Caressing the small object, I walked toward my bed, feeling lightheaded with anticipation. I lay back on the sheets, not bothering to slide close to the wall as I always did. For now, I was safe to relax.

As I struck the first match, I felt some of the knots of tension in my body ignite, and then slowly begin to burn away. The flame was intoxicating. It seemed to suck the unhappy energy from my body into its blue-white flame and fling it into the air with tiny, happy sparks. I waited until the heat from the flames touched my fingertips before blowing it out.

With each subsequent match, the stress ebbed from my body. As the flame consumed the thin match, I watched, fascinated, as the fire inched closer and closer to my hand. It became a game, daring myself to let it burn longer and longer before blowing it out. The tips of my fingers tingled and then burned, but it felt so good.

On the fifth match, I got too cocky. The fire seared my finger and I dropped the match in shock. The flame drifted to my shirt in a heartbeat, lighting on the thin fabric of my pajamas. Before it could go further, I flipped onto my stomach, extinguishing it. Heart pounding, I sat up shakily and examined my shirt. A tiny, singed hole was all that remained of the match. That, and the undeniable, exhilarating feeling of being completely alive.

A knock at my door nearly made my heart beat right out of my chest. Uri stuck his head in and I relaxed slightly, struggling to wipe the drunk look off my face.

He wrinkled his nose as he stepped inside. "Why does it smell like smoke in here?"

I casually crossed my arms over my shirt. "I burned my hair."

"I thought you iron your hair in the morning." He was suspicious, but at least he was talking to me.

"Yeah, well, I thought it would save time to do it tonight."

He glanced at me skeptically, but didn't push it. "Where's Danz?"

"She…had to get something from Tali's. She's coming right back." It was so hard to know how much to tell him.

He inched more into the room, and I motioned for him to sit on the bed. He tucked his knees to his chest and rested his chin on top. "What did Abba say about Ima?"

"She's not doing so good. She'll probably be there for a while."

Uri dropped his head further down, resting his forehead on his knees so I couldn't see his face. In a muffled voice, he asked, "Can we visit her?"

"Do you want to?"

He looked up quickly, startled. "Do you?"

How could I tell him I didn't want to see our mother? Uri retained an unfailing love for Ima and no amount of psychosis could change that. Of course he wanted to see her.

"I don't think she wants to see us," I said finally, sticking to the truth of what our father had said. "She's pretty sick right now. But I'll tell you what — when she does want visitors, I bet she'll want to see you."

"I really want to see her," he said plaintively.

I pulled him into my arms and he relaxed against me, his anger from earlier in the day completely gone. "I know you do." I stroked his soft hair, and noticed he desperately needed a haircut. I suddenly felt ashamed of how inadequately I was caring for my little brother.

"We'll take care of you. We're not going to be late to get you anymore and you won't have to be here alone with Abba if you don't want." The gratitude in his eyes hurt. "But, Uri…why won't you talk to Abba? He wants to help you with stuff."

Uri shook his head, twisting to look at me. "I can't trust him. He put Ima in the hospital."

His simple logic rendered me speechless for a moment. "Uri, Ima was sick. That's why she went to the hospital."

"Yeah, but Abba let her get sick. I heard what you said about the medication. It's Abba's job to make sure she takes it."

Guilt slithered through my veins. That's what acting like Daniella had accomplished. I'd cemented Uri's view of my father as the cause of our mother's insanity.

I walked Uri back to bed and tucked him in, after several futile attempts at convincing him that our father was not the enemy. I realized he wasn't interested in my logic; he just wanted to see his mother.

When I finally got back into my bed, it was just past midnight and I had a text from Daniella. *b back in 5. hope u r sleeping, luv u.*

When she slid into the bed next to me, I pretended to be asleep. Maybe if I faked my way through the night, I'd manage not to cause any physical damage. Just when I thought she'd fallen asleep, my phone vibrated.

ur a bad faker. if u need me, wake me up no matter what. i am here.

12

The days dragged on, a blur of sleepless, dream-interrupted nights. I woke during the night often, tears streaming down my face, cobwebs of nightmares slowly lifting as I regained full consciousness. Daniella stayed in my bed every night and it was her calm, gentle voice that talked me down from the height of panic.

In the mornings, we dragged ourselves out of bed, straightened our hair, did each other's makeup, tucked in our uniform shirts, and got Uri ready for school. Abba was gone before we awoke, off to shul and then straight to work. I stayed late for dance practice most days, and had dinner with Daniella and Uri when I got home. Abba would visit Ima in the hospital during visiting hours, seven to eight thirty, so he wasn't home until after nine.

Life became depressingly routine, and I started hoping Ima wouldn't stabilize any time soon. School, however, remained intolerable. My frustration increased daily as I was forced to sit through classes that not only didn't speak to me, but infuriated me. I didn't want to hear about *bitachon* and *emunah*. I wasn't interested in Chumash and Navi, because it didn't matter. This wasn't what I needed to know in order to make it through life. I needed to be learning how to deal with my ever-increasing night terrors. I needed to know how to keep my family together, when all we seemed to be doing was drifting apart. I needed to figure out where I was headed in life, because if I didn't, it was going to drive me crazy.

After being called to Rabbi Sacks's office twice for cutting class and having my grades threatened, I forced myself to stay in the classroom, fidgeting in my seat as I counted down the minutes until the end of class. I was ashamed at the anger I felt toward my teachers, but I was undeniably mad. I took bathroom breaks as often as I dared and blew my co-dance heads away with intricate ideas for dance formations, born out of extreme levels of boredom.

My first meeting with Mrs. Moskowitz was a disaster. Rattled from a particularly disturbing dream the night before and jacked up on too much coffee, I was barely able to make myself sit down in her office. Her tone was kind and nonjudgmental, but I was so paranoid she'd call my parents that I promised her the dreams had stopped. When she pointed out that I was fidgeting intensely on her couch and stated calmly that she didn't believe me, I channeled the tears that rose in my eyes into an uncharacteristic outburst.

"I don't have any anything to talk about. I don't need to be here. You can't force me to talk to you."

I would've loved for her to throw me out of her office. But instead she only asked me to come back the following week. Her final words, "I know it's scary to talk about, but sometimes the only way out is through," had me crying in the bathroom for ten minutes before I could compose myself enough to return to class.

Dance seemed to be the only thing going right in my life. In practice, I was floating. My moves were unique, powerful, and tasteful, earning the respect of both students and staff. I was hard on my dancers, pushing them to perfect the moves and the timing. They responded with enthusiasm, and I almost started to feel bad for Atara and Laya when our dances started to overshadow theirs.

When I was dancing, I was free. The music pulsed through my veins, and emotion coursed through my body like electric shocks — there was nothing between me and the movement. When I danced, I forgot about my nightmares, my mother, my family, my heartache, and my fears. When I stopped dancing, everything came crashing back down on me.

When Zehava drove me home after practice, I felt my body weaken as her car approached our house. I wanted to see Daniella and Uri, but the thought of going home to the cold sadness made me want to cry.

It had been difficult pulling Daniella from the dance selection. Ms. Palmer had asked way too many questions, as did the other dance heads. Unable to come up with any good excuses on my own, I ultimately stonewalled and told them they needed to ask her themselves. Rumor was that she'd given every excuse from arthritis in her ankles to a school punishment for having her shirt untucked too many times.

Daniella's transformation after my mother's hospitalization was subtle, yet significant. Her attitude seemed to increase incrementally by the day and she texted me from the principal's office more and more often. I knew she wasn't paying attention in class or doing her homework, mostly because she spent the evenings helping Uri with his, making dinner, or keeping the house clean. She slept fitfully at night too, and although I told her numerous times she could stop babysitting me, she wouldn't leave my bed.

When I passed her in the halls at school, she grinned and hugged me, and she was surrounded by her posse of friends, always. Yet I couldn't help but notice the sadness in her eyes and defeated aura that clung to her — so artfully shed when around others, yet always creeping back when we were alone. We didn't speak about our pain. It was too big to put into words, and to do so would have risked cracks in our carefully created facade.

So we forged on, cracking jokes at the dinner table, trying to make Uri laugh, greeting Abba with forced happiness each night, smiling at our friends and teachers at school, and waiting until the early hours of the morning to fall apart. It was unsustainable, but we had no other choice.

13

"Can you show me the last eight beats again? I think I have it mixed up." Ayelet Klein's face was flushed, but she was smiling. Dance practice was over and we'd just finished the first minute of our jail dance, which had resulted in celebrations all around.

"Rikki, I'm going to get the copies of CDs from Ms. Palmer. I'll be right back," Zehava called over her shoulder as she left the room.

I repeated the dance steps for Ayelet. She caught on quickly, performing them so well that I was once again reminded of why I'd chosen her for my dance.

"Thanks, Rikki." She flashed me another smile and started putting her shoes back on.

"Hey, can I ask you something?" I noticed the room had cleared out and it was just the two of us. Ayelet looked nervous, and I wondered if this was a question I wanted to hear.

"Yeah, sure."

"Why did you give me another chance, during tryouts?"

I smiled inwardly. So it was that type of question. The sort of non-question that didn't require an answer at all, it just served as a segue into conversation. She didn't want to know why I gave her a second chance, she wanted to talk to me.

Not for the first time, I wondered about Ayelet. She was quiet, but not shy. While she got along with the other dancers and wasn't a loner, there was something solitary about her that suggested a depth atypical of many of the freshmen in our school.

"I had my eye on you," I said truthfully. "You looked like you'd be a dancer. I wanted you to do well, so when you messed up, I wanted to give you another chance." Smiling, I added, "And I was totally right."

She bit her lip. "You're sweet." She pulled her long blonde ponytail over her shoulder and started playing with the ends of it. "I don't know what I would've done if I didn't get into dance. I hate school, so this makes me able to tolerate it. Sort of."

There was so much she wasn't saying. I wanted to ask more, but I recognized where this was going. A lot of my classmates had friends in younger grades who looked up to them as "big sisters." Ayelet wasn't the first underclassman to strike up this sort of conversation with me. Even though she intrigued me, I wasn't exactly a role model at the moment. The last thing she needed was a mentor who was mental.

I couldn't help myself. I looked into her hopeful eyes and saw that whatever I had to give, she needed. "So you're not a fan of school."

She made a face. "No. Definitely not. I never have been. That's why I've always done extracurricular stuff. At my old school, I was in dance and on the basketball team. This school really only has concert, so it was like, I needed to get into dance or that was it."

"Where was your old school?"

"Los Angeles. We moved in the summer."

She wanted to talk. That much was evident. Surprisingly, I wanted to listen. But just then, Zehava returned.

"Here, Ayelet, you can have the first copy," she said, tossing her a CD. "Rikki, you ready?"

When I turned back to Ayelet, she was bent over, putting the CD in her knapsack.

"Yeah," I said, slowly. "I'm ready." Kneeling down next to Ayelet, I said, "Hey, listen, I'm really glad you're in dance. You're an awesome dancer, and I know all about not liking school, so I totally get why this means so much to you. We'll talk again, okay?"

When she nodded, I straightened and followed after Zehava.

"Thanks, Rikki." Ayelet's words followed me as I made my way out to Zehava's car. For once, I didn't start feeling sick on the way home.

I hadn't even closed the front door when Uri appeared in the hallway. "Daniella's crying," he said solemnly.

The door to her room was locked. Although it was silent inside, I sensed her presence. "Danz, let me in," I said quietly as I sank to the floor.

Uri sat cross-legged on the floor opposite me. "I don't know what happened," he said, leaning his head back against the wall. "I was doing my homework, and she finished making dinner, and then she was just crying. She said, 'I'm fine,' but then went and locked herself in her room."

Danz open the door, I texted her.

Her response was slow in coming. *I'm sorry I just need space. I'm fine. Really.*

It was hard to argue with that, but I needed to see her. And I was so used to saying I was fine when I really wasn't, that I couldn't believe her.

plz. I need to see u.

r u ok?

Great. Now I'd made it all about me. Her concern was touching but I felt queasy at the thought of Daniella breaking down. Daniella showing weakness was so rare that I had no idea how to respond. I chose the cowardly option.

I'm fine but ur scaring us. Plz…

The door opened, startling me more than it should have. Uri stood up. "I'll go to the kitchen, but don't lock the door, okay? I don't like it out here alone."

Nodding, I slipped inside her room. I rarely spent time in there. We spent our nights in my room, and somehow Daniella's clothing had made its way over to my closet, so we essentially shared a bedroom. Daniella's walls were bare, save for one that held a mural — another testament to my mother's creative brilliance. Daniella had taken forever deciding which scene she wanted. In the end, she'd decided on a skyline reflected in a glistening river. The mural was stunning, a complicated creation of glassy lights, realistic reflections, and shimmering waves.

Daniella stood with her back against the painting, her arms folded tightly over her chest. Her hair was pulled into a haphazard ponytail and although her expression was stoic, her swollen, bloodshot eyes and red nose indicated that Uri's report was accurate.

"What happened?" I crossed the room quickly and placed my hands on either side of her face, looking worriedly into her red-rimmed eyes. Immediately, tears sprang to her eyes and her lips quivered. I knew this feeling. She slid down the wall to a sitting position and cried. I sat down too and wrapped my arms around her, letting her cry against my shoulder. I fought down strains of panic at my sister's uncharacteristic display of emotion and held her tightly, trying to let her feel I was strong for her, that it was okay to cry.

When her sobs faded, we sat there quietly, paying respects to her grief. She spoke first. "I'm so sorry for being like this—"

I couldn't let her finish. "Danz, you don't have to apologize. It's fine."

"No, it's pathetic. I shouldn't be crying over this."

I waited for her to continue.

"Tali…she's really mad at me. She knows I've been lying about Ima and all…it just…it all blew up today. She's going on and on about how she can't trust me anymore, and she doesn't even care about what's wrong with Ima, she just thought I was her best friend and now she knows I've been lying."

My mind was having a hard time keeping up. "Wait, how does Tali know?"

"She was using my phone and she saw what I'd been searching for in Google."

"What were you searching for?"

Daniella's shoulders sagged and I could feel the sadness move through her again.

"First I was looking up the contact information for St. Lucas. Then I was looking up statistics on bipolar, the recovery rates and all that…"

She pulled her ponytail out and ran her fingers through her hair. She was calmer, but her eyes still leaked tears. I went to get some tissues and returned to my spot on the floor.

"So what happened?"

"She saw the stuff on my phone last night. Then today at lunch, she was like 'Okay, I don't usually pry into your life, but I feel like you're lying to me, and I'm your best friend so why can't you just tell me the truth?' But I was an idiot. Instead of apologizing, I got mad at her for going through my phone, which is stupid because we do that with each other's phones all the time."

Best friends. Daniella was hiding half her life from her best friend. No wonder that had blown up in her face. "So you didn't tell her the truth?"

"No."

"Daniella!" I turned to her, exasperated. "Why can't you be honest with her? She's your best friend. She's not going to care. She obviously would rather you be honest with her than pretend that everything's okay."

"I can't be honest. It doesn't work that way for me. I seriously don't how to tell people the truth."

"Why?"

"I don't know. I feel like it'll kill me if I do that."

"Daniella…" I pulled her close to me, feeling her start to cry all over again.

"I can't deal with this now…"

"I know," I said, holding her tighter, because I did know. We were in full survival mode, functioning beyond our capacity, and any additional stress was a threat to our equilibrium. Tali had no idea how much Daniella needed her, and unfortunately the recent incident was only going to push Tali further away.

"Just talk to her…"

"I can't."

"So text her."

Daniella stared at her phone for a full three minutes before pushing it toward me. "You write something." Her hands were shaking.

I took the phone and started typing. When I was finished, I held it out to her. She scanned the text quickly: *I'm sorry I lied. It's hard 2 talk about this, but plz give me a chance. Can we talk 2morrow?* Wincing, she nodded, and I hit the Send button.

She buried her face in her knees while we waited for Tali to respond. When the phone beeped less than twenty seconds later,

I thanked God that Tali was as addicted to her phone as Daniella was. I let Daniella read the text first and started to relax when a ghost of a smile flitted across her tear-streaked face.

meet b4 first period? xoxo

14

"I'm glad you came to see me again."

It'd been two weeks since I'd last sat in Mrs. Moskowitz's office. After my first anxiety-producing session, I'd fabricated a dance practice to avoid seeing her the following week. When she passed me in the hallway later that day, her knowing yet pleasant look told me she was on to my game. I hadn't dared try that again.

Mrs. Moskowitz sat comfortably in her chair looking at ease, while I sat on the edge of her couch, ready to bolt at the slightest sign of trouble.

"I didn't know I had a choice." Daniella had given me a pep talk the night before, about the importance of talking to someone about the nightmares. I'd promised her that I'd give Mrs. Moskowitz a second chance.

"You seem anxious about being here," she said conversationally. "Yet you came back. Is there some part of you that does want help?"

I shifted uneasily, wondering why the couch had seemed so comfortable last week when we used the room for a dance heads meeting. Now, it was hard as nails. "I do want help. I just don't think talking is going to help me."

"So what do you think might work?"

"I…don't know."

"Can I take a minute to explain to you what I'm here for? I think it might help you understand my role. Then you can decide if you'd like to give this a chance."

If she wanted to talk, I was fine with that.

"As a social worker, it's my job to help the girls when they have a problem that's affecting them at school. It might be an issue with friends or teachers, or something going on at home that's causing them to have difficulties. Whatever the case, I work with students by exploring the problem, coming up with solutions, and sometimes, if the problem's bigger than what I can deal with, referring them for additional help. Does that make sense?"

Once I nodded, she launched into a speech about confidentiality, and what she legally could and couldn't repeat from our conversations. This is where I started to pay attention.

"So…what if I told you about something that happened in the past, and even though it was never reported, there's no chance it would happen again? Would you still have to report it?" I tried to make my tone nonchalant, but it was hard to keep my voice steady.

Luckily, she was calm enough for both of us. "It depends. It's not only about keeping you safe. Even if someone no longer has access to you, they may still be able to hurt someone else. That's why it's important to report all incidents of abuse."

"No, but let's say they can't hurt anyone. Like…let's say they got locked up."

"In prison?"

"Sure."

Mrs. Moskowitz looked thoughtful. "It sounds like you have something specific in mind."

I was silent.

"Rikki, I won't push you to say anything you're not comfortable saying. And the reason I'm so clear about confidentiality from the start is because I don't want you to regret telling me something when you realize that I have to report it. This way, you know what the guidelines are. As for this specific situation, it sounds like whatever it is, it's really bothering you. And while I can't guarantee it's not reportable, if there's a way for you to talk about it comfortably, I'd really encourage you to do so."

I couldn't say anything. I looked at her, wishing she could get inside my head and fix things without me having to say a word.

"Is this related to your nightmares?"

I nodded.

She picked up a pen from her desk and turned it slowly in her hands, watching me. "Do you remember what I told you last time we met?"

"The only way out is through."

"Exactly. If you continue to keep the nightmares to yourself, they're only going to get worse. The more you refuse to face the memories head-on, the more they'll literally haunt you in your dreams. It probably seems like you can't deal with them, that they're too big and too scary and too unspeakable. Every time you convince yourself of that, you're reinforcing that you're not strong enough to deal with them. But Rikki, it's not true. You are strong enough. You can face this, whatever it is, and I can help you, if you'll let me. It's not going to be easy, and facing this is going to hurt so much you'll probably be sure this was a big mistake. But if you can make it through, it'll all be worth it."

She had no idea how much her words cut me. If I'd opened my

mouth, I would've started howling in pain. To turn around and face the nightmares, instead of running from them, was tantamount to suicide. The only way to survive was to fight them, to bury them, to deny they even existed.

"I don't know how to do this." Squeezing the words past the bricks in my chest took every bit of my strength.

She reached into a desk drawer and pulled out a spiral-bound journal. "A lot of people find that writing is easier than talking. Next time you wake up from a nightmare, try to write at least a few sentences about what you experienced. It doesn't need to be detailed, I just want you to acknowledge what it is. Can you try that?"

I took the journal and stuffed it into my knapsack, avoiding her gaze.

"One more thing. I'd like to meet with you again, but I'll need one of your parents to sign a consent form. Will that be okay?"

"Yeah, I'll get it signed."

I started toward her door, and then turned to face her. "Look… I'm really okay. Like, I'm not crazy or anything. Everything else is fine, besides the nightmares. I just don't want you to think that I'm—"

She waved her hand dismissively, flashing me a warm smile. "I know, Rikki. You're okay."

15

My father came home early from work that night, which meant that dinner was mostly a silent affair. Uri's avoidance of him had reached epic proportions and as soon as Uri finished his vegetables, at Daniella's insistence, he went to do his homework in his room, closing the door loudly behind him.

"Does he talk to you?" my father asked helplessly.

"Yeah, he's not mad at us," Daniella said calmly.

"So he's mad at me?"

Before Daniella could give a snarky reply, I interrupted. "Abba, you should call Adina Begin. She runs the Big Brother program. It would be good for Uri to have someone to take him out."

Abba looked relieved. "Do you have a number?"

I wrote it on a piece of paper, and then remembered my own form that I needed signed.

"Can you sign something else from school?" I slid Mrs. Moskowitz's form across the table, giving no explanation, and watched his face.

"Do you want to talk about this?" he asked slowly.

"No."

He signed the paper and slid it back to me. "I hope this helps." Hesitating, he turned to Daniella. "Do you want to see her too?"

"Why?" Daniella narrowed her eyes at him. "Do you think I have a problem?"

"Actually, yes, I do." My father stood, staring her down. "Your attitude is a big problem. You seem to have no respect for me, and based on the calls I've been getting from your school, you're not much better there."

Daniella had been waiting for this moment. I could see it in the way she pulled her shoulders back and tightened her jaw. She wanted to hurt him.

"I have no reason to respect you. Or them."

"Since when do you need to have a reason to respect your parents? Or people in authority? You're not a child, Daniella. You know this."

"Clearly I don't. And you know what? I don't need you to give me a reason to respect you. I just need you to stop giving me reasons to hate you."

There was venom in her voice and there was no turning back now. My father's jaw clenched repeatedly as he struggled to stay calm, but she was nowhere near through.

"Uri's brave enough to show it, you know that? He hates you and he ignores you because he's not a faker like the rest of us. You keep choosing your crazy wife over us. You let her get sick and then you just check out of our lives to go baby her while she's in the hospital. And you let her choose to ignore us, you let her make decisions about whether we should get to see her. But she's crazy. So you pick and choose when she should get to decide things. She wants to skip her meds? Fine. She wants to shut us all out? Fine. She wants to burn our house down? Whatever. But then all of a sudden you want to come in and save the day and sign her into the hospital and work extra hours so we have enough money, and we're supposed to love you? Get real. You're crazier than she is."

My father turned stiffly to face me. "Is that how you feel too?" His pain-filled eyes pinned me to the spot and I felt an ache spreading in my chest.

"I don't know how I feel anymore. But nothing makes sense, and if you don't do something, none of us are going to be okay."

My father cleared his throat and sniffed, blinking rapidly. "Daniella," he turned toward her and I willed her to be silent. "I'm only human. I don't always know the best decisions to make, especially when it comes to Ima. But please believe me when I say that I'm doing my best. I don't want any of you to get hurt, but Ima is my wife. I have obligations to all of you and I'm trying my hardest to do the right—"

"Then you should divorce her."

Mission accomplished. Anger flashed across my father's face and when he spoke, his voice was barely controlled. "Daniella, you are completely out of line. That's an extremely inappropriate thing to say."

"Well, it needs to be said. She's not going to get better, is she? So it's either her or us. As long as you're still married to her, you'll keep living at the hospital, and playing games with her medication, and we'll be on our own. So why don't you choose?"

Her defiance was frightening.

My father's voice was deadly quiet. "Who do you think you are?"

And just like that, all the fight went out of her. Her shoulders slumped, she took a step backward, and barely looked at him as she said, "I don't know. Just a kid with a crazy mother and an attitude problem."

16

"I couldn't believe she said that," I told Kayla later that night. We sat on two lawn chairs on her back porch, looking up at the stars sprinkled across the sky. "I thought he might snap and hit her or something."

"She's too reckless," Kayla said carefully. "Honestly, I think she's getting too…" she floundered, searching for the right word.

"What?"

"Too *chutzpadik*." She grimaced. "I know, that sounds really lame, but it's true. It's like she doesn't care about anyone or anything anymore. Like, Daniella never cared what people thought of her. She was always confident and would do her own thing. But now she's pushing the limits. She knows people like her, so she's seeing how much she can get away with."

"Rabbi Sacks doesn't like her that much anymore."

"Yeah, well, there's a rumor going around that she owes him one hundred eighty dollars in fines for having her shirt untucked, but she's refusing to pay it."

"Really?"

"Yeah. And that's so typical Daniella. She picks something that he can't argue with. Since it's not legal or anything, and he can't punish her for not paying. He's probably mad at her for making a statement."

"I don't get it. What's her statement?"

"That he can't control her. That no one can."

"That's true," I said quietly.

We sat quietly for a while, the peaceful air settling my nerves. Daniella was at Tali's — apparently they had made up that morning, I was still waiting for details — and I knew I wasn't going to be able to sleep until I could talk to her.

"How's everything else going?"

Kayla's voice startled me.

"What?"

"I hardly ever see you anymore. You're always in practice or off with Zehava."

"I know. It's intense. But it's keeping me sane."

"Really?" Kayla looked skeptical.

"What?" I asked in mock indignation. "Do I look like I'm losing it?"

She smiled halfheartedly. "No, but you look stressed-out all the time."

I couldn't argue with that.

"Are you eating?"

I raised an eyebrow at that question. "Why? Do you think I'm losing weight?"

"I don't know." Kayla sighed. "I don't know what's up with you. But I worry about you a lot. You trust Daniella too much and I don't think she's the greatest role model."

"I've been talking to Mrs. Moskowitz," I confessed. I was grateful for the dim light so Kayla couldn't my cheeks flushing at that admission. "About these nightmares I've been having. She wants to help me with them."

"Yeah? How's that going?"

I slid off the lawn chair and pulled the hood of my sweatshirt over my head. Then I lay back on the soft grass and stared straight up at a sheet of stars. It was easier to talk that way.

"She gave me a journal and told me to write about them."

"And?"

"I haven't written anything."

"But you're still having them?" She joined me on the grass, her arm up against mine.

"Every night."

"Rikki, can I ask—"

"No," I said quietly. "Please, don't."

When Daniella came home twenty minutes later, she joined us on the grass, lying on the other side of me. She seemed calm, but didn't say much. When Kayla went inside, I started to get up, but Daniella took my arm, pulling me down.

"Stay out here for a bit. It's so peaceful."

That was undeniable. Not knowing where to begin, I lay quietly.

"So…" she said, drawing the word out, giving me the feeling that she didn't know where to begin either.

"How'd it work out with Tali?"

Daniella seemed grateful for the direction. "I think we'll be okay. I apologized for lying. But then she started asking questions and I got freaked out. So she got a little mad all over again when I wouldn't tell her anything, but I told her I hate talking about it, and I pretended to get all sad, so she felt bad and dropped it."

"You pretended to get sad?"

"Well, yeah. Or I really was. I don't know."

I rolled my eyes in the dark. "You were too harsh on Abba tonight."

I felt her turn sideways to look at me. "You really think so?"

"You're kidding, right?" I sat up so I could look at her directly. She sat up too.

"No, I'm not. You really think I was too harsh? You didn't think what I said was true?"

"I didn't say it wasn't true, but you can't just talk to him like that."

She threw her hands up. "Why? Why do I have to fake-respect everyone all the time? Why can't I just say the truth?"

She had a point, but it didn't jive with the culture we were raised in. She knew as well as I did that respect was something to be given to anyone in a position of authority, regardless of whether or not they earned it. "Don't you think it's ironic that you're upset that you can't say the truth?"

"Why's that ironic?"

I laughed. "Because you hate telling the truth."

Daniella cracked a small smile. Leaning in suddenly, she hugged me fiercely. "I don't know what I'd do without you."

I pulled back slightly. "Why does your hair smell like…nail polish?"

"Oh, right." Her grin stretched across her face slowly. In the moonlight, she looked so beautiful, I couldn't help but stare. Gathering her hair into a ponytail, she rose from the ground and held out a hand toward me. "You've got to see this. You'll love it."

Brushing grass off my skirt, I followed her across the lawn back toward our house. Once we hit the lights of our back porch, my eyes widened, and I caught sight of the blue streaks in her hair.

17

The attention Daniella's black eye garnered was nothing compared to what happened when she arrived at school with blue-streaked hair. I was relieved to see Tali with matching streaks, but that did little to staunch the steady stream of comments that came my way.

Girls kept asking me why she'd done it. Was I supposed to know? I thought it looked cool. And the more I repeated that to them — "She likes how it looks. I like it too, I think it looks cool" — the more I started to believe it. And the more I believed it, the more frustrated I became that everyone seemed confident that blue hair was enough to diagnose underlying *hashkafic* issues. Because, really, that's what everyone was asking indirectly. Beneath every "why," was an unspoken "What's her problem? What statement is she trying to make with blue hair? What'll she do next? Will she pierce her nose and start wearing jeans?"

I would've been lying if I'd said that those same thoughts weren't crossing my mind, but nothing else about Daniella indicated an internal struggle with her faith. Just the blue streaks. And apparently, that was enough.

"You guys need to get over it," I said irritably to the group of girls gathered around my desk before third period. "It's just blue hair."

"Yeah, for now," Riva Winters said, looking at me significantly.

"What's that supposed to mean?"

"Nothing! I'm just saying…it could be a cry for help."

"Riva." I glared at her and felt the girls around me quiet down. "Just stop talking, okay? Especially if you don't have anything important to say."

The look on her face made me want to be sick. I got up abruptly from my seat and walked out of the classroom just as my Ivrit teacher was stepping inside.

"Rikki, where are you going?"

I ignored her and proceeded down the hall. I didn't stop until I was in the stairwell furthest from the main office. I sank down to the bottom step and rested my head against the railing.

I pulled out my phone and texted, *what were u thinking?????* and waited for a response.

we got called to Rabbi S's office. lol but we did nothing wrong!!!

Yeah, except ruin my day.

stop doing stupid things. its annoying, all the questions

ya sorry abt that. 4got ppl r so closeminded

no u didn't. u just don't care.

r u ok???

fine. bhave w/ rabbi s

I always do :)

I tossed my phone onto my knapsack. It slid off, skittered several feet across the floor, and hit the wall. I kicked the bottom of the railing as I stood to retrieve it.

"Rikki?"

I froze. Mrs. Zilber stood at the top of the stairs looking down at me. I'd forgotten the offices of the *mechanchos* were on this side of the building.

"Hi."

I searched her face, wanting to know if she'd seen me texting, but she showed no particular emotion and came down the stairs. "I won't ask what you're doing here, even though I know you're supposed to be in Ivrit right now, but that's only because I need to speak to you."

"Oh. Okay."

"Don't worry, you're not in trouble. Normally I would've pulled you aside after class, but you have a habit of mysteriously disappearing as soon as the bell rings."

That was true. And that was precisely because I tried to avoid meetings like this.

I followed her to her office, thankful that she hadn't commented on my disregard for school rules as I retrieved the phone and stuck it in my knapsack.

Once inside, she wasted no time. "Rikki, I have a question. But before I ask, I want you to know I'm not judging you, or thinking negatively about you. I'm just concerned about something I've noticed and wanted to ask you directly, because I care."

"That was a long introduction for one question."

She laughed, and I started to relax slightly. Then she got serious and asked, "Why don't you daven?"

Now the disclaimer made sense. My initial reaction was to deny it. How would she know if I davened? Then I remembered my seat was front and center. Mrs. Zilber watched me not daven five days a week. Lying wouldn't accomplish anything. But what was it to her? It wasn't a school requirement that I say the *tefillos*, and it wasn't like I was disrupting class or anything. Was she even allowed to ask me a question like that? Didn't that, like, violate my right to freedom of speech? These myriad of thoughts must've been playing out across my face because she was watching me intently.

When I answered, I hadn't made a conscious decision to be honest. It was more like I was so worn down from questions about Daniella that morning that when I was finally asked one I had an answer to, I couldn't hold back.

"It's not worth it." Cringing at how that sounded, I added, "For me. It's not worth it for me."

She waited for me to continue. If she'd started talking, even just one thing, I probably would've stopped there and bluffed my way through the rest of our conversation. But her silence made me feel like she wanted to know.

"It doesn't even work. Every time I've davened for things to get better, they just got worse. And when I don't daven, things get worse too. So I just stopped davening because it doesn't make a difference."

I told myself to stop talking. Really, I said it one hundred times in my head, but I was angry and frustrated, and I had nothing better to do.

"I'm so sick of hearing stories about people who daven and daven for the things they want or need and then they get it. Yeah, that's wonderful, but that's not real life. In real life, prayer doesn't do anything except waste time. I swear, Hashem doesn't care about my prayers."

Too late, I realized my choice of words could be construed as offensive, but Mrs. Zilber didn't react.

"And I don't want to be a hypocrite. So I'm not going to sit there and pretend to say the words in davening when I don't feel it. I'm not fake-praying. I hate fakers. And Hashem probably does too. So it's better off this way. I don't pray and Hashem doesn't help me out."

In the silence that followed, the reality of what I'd just confessed set in. I stood shakily, horrified by what I'd just revealed. Mrs. Zilber stood too.

"Rikki, it's okay. If that's what you feel, then you can say it."

"No, I can't," I said quietly, inching my way toward the door. "I don't need to make Hashem any madder at me."

She moved quickly for a teacher wearing high heels. She stood next to the door, not quite blocking it, just letting me know she didn't want me to leave. "Why do you think Hashem is mad at you?" Her voice was fearless and unassuming, and in her eyes I saw genuine curiosity and concern.

"Because I'm mad at Him."

Saying those words out loud was the last straw. I broke down, sinking into a chair and pressing my face into my hands. This wasn't me. This couldn't be a conversation I was having. What happened to keeping it together on the outside? Mrs. Zilber put an arm on my shoulder and I flinched so strongly that she jumped too. When I'd finally gotten in control of myself enough to stop the tears from streaming, I stood and tried to leave.

"Rikki, no. You're not leaving like this. Just take a minute and let yourself breathe." She pushed a box of tissues toward me and I took them gratefully.

When my breathing had slowed to normal, she asked simply, "What's going on?"

I went for the easiest answer. "Have you seen my sister today?"

"Blue hair?"

"Yeah. Everyone's saying all these things about how she's doing it for attention and it's a sign she's going off the *derech*, and that's not true at all. Daniella's much more spiritual than me. She davens every day and does the things she's supposed to. But more than that, she talks to Hashem. It's almost like she's friends with Him and she feels her life is run by Him. And then there's me.

Everyone looks at me and thinks I'm fine, that I'm all *frum* because I don't put braids in my hair and I don't get in trouble in school and I'm dance head, but I'm really the one who's doing stuff wrong. I'm just faking it. She's being real about who she is and everyone has it all backward. It's just making me really mad at everyone."

I stopped to breathe, and glanced at Mrs. Zilber to gauge her reaction. Waiting until she was sure I'd finished speaking, she reached into her desk drawer, pulled out a water bottle, and held it out. I took it gratefully and drank.

"Rikki." Her tone was careful. "You can't compare yourself to Daniella that way. You're right, it is wonderful that Daniella has that connection with Hashem and I hope that one day you'll have that as well. But you need to realize that the way you treat other people, the halachos of *bein adam lachaveiro* — those count too. And you seem to really shine in that area." The unspoken words that followed were, *and Daniella does not*.

"I understand that today's been very stressful because of her hair, but this seems like an ongoing issue for you. Do you want to talk about it?"

No. I didn't want to tell her anything. I didn't want to tell anyone. But there I was, talking, hearing myself as though I were outside my own body.

"My mother has bipolar. She's in the hospital now, she's been there for three weeks already, and she's not getting better. She's been sick for years, but this is the worst she's ever been."

There was no going back now. The damage had already been done, so I might as well finish digging my own grave.

"She's not just bipolar. She's psychotic too, like, totally out of her mind. So Daniella runs our house. I mean, my father's there, but he's always working or visiting her. And she won't see us. Like, Daniella and me, we don't want to see her. But my little brother, all he wants is to see her. He's miserable all the time because he misses her and she won't let him visit."

I took a drink of water, hoping it would staunch the flow of words, but I kept going.

"And every night, every single night, I get these horrible nightmares, remembering stuff that happened with my mother, and I wake up all crazy, screaming and crying, and it takes Daniella forever to calm me down. So then we get to school and we're tired and I don't feel well and I'm still scared, and then we're supposed to sit in class and just listen to stuff. And I don't care about it. I'm sorry, I just don't."

I checked her face to see if I was offending her, but it didn't look like it.

"And Daniella doesn't care anymore, so she just gets in trouble and gets sent to Rabbi Sacks. Nothing matters to her. She's not going to seminary anyway because she thinks none of them'll accept her and we can't pay for it. But I don't want to be like that, so I try to stay in class but I just get mad about it. And I can't talk to my friends, well, most of my friends, because no one understands anything about mental disorders. So I feel like I'm living this lie, all the time."

I paused, pressing my hands against my mouth, physically stopping myself from saying more. The confusion of emotions ravaging my mind was creating a pulsing headache that was making it difficult to think straight.

"I can't believe I just told you all of that." I stood suddenly, grabbing my knapsack and opening her door. "Please forget all of it, it's not important."

Mrs. Zilber put both hands on my shoulder and gently guided me back to the chair. "Rikki," she said gently. "Take it easy. You're doing fine. Just give me a minute to process everything you've said."

The minute felt interminably long. I distracted myself by fingering the scars of my fingertips, still tender from the flames of matches a few days earlier. When she spoke, I had a hard time meeting her eyes.

"I won't pretend to know how difficult this must be for you. To act as though everything's fine, when it clearly isn't, must be taking a tremendous toll on you. When you were talking, all I kept thinking was, *This girl needs a mother.* And I do think that's the truth."

She took my hand in hers and held it lightly.

"Rikki, I'm not your mother. I'm your teacher, and it might seem like you're just another one of my students, but please believe me when I say that I really do care about you. I hope you'll trust me not to judge you because of your mother's issues, and I hope you'll let me support you, however often you need it."

Tears were falling from my eyes, but I made no move to stop them.

"I'm not *your* mother, but I am *a* mother. So if you can, let me take care of you just a little bit."

For the second time that morning, I completely broke down. But this time, when she put her arms around me, I didn't pull away.

During lunch, I couldn't find Daniella and she wasn't answering her texts, so I went looking for Tali instead. When she saw me, she gave me a long hug. I was so worn-out from crying in Mrs. Zilber's office that I barely reacted.

"Do you know where Daniella is?"

"In Rabbi Sacks's office. Where else?" Her blonde hair was pulled into a messy bun on top of her head, accentuating the blue streaks that were even more prominent in her light-colored tresses.

"Did you get in trouble?" I asked, gesturing to the top of her head.

"Not really. Rabbi Sacks wanted us to promise not to do it again. So I did. But your darling sister said she wasn't sure she wouldn't. She said she was still hoping to try green and pink."

I winced. "She really said that?"

Tali nodded, trying to stifle a smile. Slinging an arm across my shoulder, she walked with me toward the cafeteria. "Hey, she told me about what's going on at home. You doing okay?"

I glanced around to see if anyone was listening nearby. "Yeah, I'm fine. Are things okay between you two? She was really upset the other night."

"She was upset? Girl, I was upset! You should've heard her going off on me about going through her phone. You would've thought I stole her credit card information or something. I still think she overreacted."

"She probably did," I said carefully, knowing Daniella wouldn't like this conversation. "But she really didn't tell anyone. It wasn't just you. She's the most private person I know."

Tali shrugged. "I hear you, but honestly Rikki, I thought she was my best friend. But she lied so many times about this. It kind of feels hard to trust her right now, you know?"

I did know. What Tali didn't know was that the lying wasn't over. Daniella was no more capable of being honest now than she was a week ago. Sure, the lies would lessen in intensity, and she'd throw in a bit of truth every so often to keep Tali satisfied. But her armor of lies was still necessary, and no one, not even her best friend, could penetrate it.

"I know. But don't punish her for this, okay?"

Tali narrowed her eyes. "Punish her?"

I swallowed hard. "Yeah. Don't make her feel extra guilty

about it. Though she'll never admit it, she needs you in order to get through this. Even if she can't talk to you about it, having you as her best friend is so important to her. I promise. So just try and forgive her, and if you think she's lying about something, ask me. I'll be honest with you."

It was not a promise I was willing to keep, but one I was willing to make for the sake of this friendship. Tali looked suspicious. "Are you sure you're okay?"

I took a deep breath and nodded. "I'm fine, Tali. I'm fine."

18

When I woke up at 1:34 the next morning, grasping at the sheets and crying out in fear, there was something almost robotic about the way Daniella helped me to the bathroom and into the shower. Bent over under the hot spray, willing my blood flow to resume its normal pace, I realized that we'd both come to expect the nightmares; they'd become as much a part of our routine as straightening our hair and getting dressed in the morning.

It was time to do something about it. Once I had on fresh pajamas, I took out the spiral journal from Mrs. Moskowitz and sat down at my desk. Twenty minutes later, I was still staring at the same blank page, a pen frozen in my hand. I jammed the pen into the paper, creating a long, black gash. My breathing stuttered out of control, and I found myself gasping for air again.

It was so real. I could have sworn she was right there.

Grasping the pen firmly in my hand, I wrote the words that had been bouncing around in my head since I'd heard them in Mrs. Moskowitz's office.

The more you refuse to face the memories head-on, the more they will literally haunt you in your dreams.

What if she was wrong? What if facing them opened up a whole new level of agony that ate me alive? I wasn't as strong as anyone believed. Being talented and popular wasn't a sign of strength. It was just a reality.

My right hand was shaking. My heart was shaking. My whole world was shaking. I slowly brought the pen to the paper again. If I didn't face it, it would kill me. I had nothing more to lose.

She tried to stab me.

The words were small and jagged, so innocent compared to the meaning behind them.

Immediately, I added on, *She didn't mean to. She didn't know what she was doing. She was going through one of her manic phases. She thought I was the devil or something.*

My heart was trying to claw its way up my throat. I watched Daniella sleep for a moment, trying to match my breathing to hers.

I continued on. *She didn't actually stab me. I got away. But in my dreams she does. Over and over. I feel it. The pain and the fear, it's so real, I wake up and I think it's happened. I think she's pinning me down and stabbing me. So I wake up and I go crazy.*

I dropped the pen and pressed both hands against my chest. The pain in my heart was so real I could feel myself bleeding. Except I wasn't.

I know it's in my head, I wrote. *I know it's not real, but I think one day I'm going to wake up and I won't be able to tell the difference between the nightmare and reality. And then it's all over.*

I flipped the journal closed, slid it into my backpack, and set it down next to my desk. Walking back to my bed, I glanced at myself in the mirror and paused. Tears leaked out the corners of my eyes, creating glistening trails that crept down my cheek and jaw. I hadn't known I was crying.

Not bothering to wipe my eyes, I quietly slid into bed and cried myself to sleep.

---

*W*alking into Mrs. Zilber's class that morning required superhuman effort. I keenly regretted my openness from the day before and wished desperately that I could take it all back. For all I knew, she'd snitch on me to Rabbi Sacks and I'd find myself punished for my anti-God sentiments and my plummeting grades.

I considered cutting her class, but didn't want to cause unnecessary drama. Before the period started, my good friends Batya and Vivi cornered me.

"We never see you anymore." Vivi pouted and tilted her head to the side, looking adorably sad.

"It's true. Dance has taken over your life, but we want you back." Batya smiled to let me know she wasn't too serious.

My friends were in ensemble, neither of them being particularly talented in either singing or dancing. The three of us had been friends since sixth grade, when we'd been paired up for a science project that had dyed our hands bright green for two weeks.

"Can you come to my house tonight? Just to hang out. It's been forever," Vivi pleaded.

She was right. Although we had every class together, it felt as though I hadn't seen them for weeks. They were faithful friends. Despite the fact that they'd rarely been to my house and I was evasive about my family to the max, they liked me for who I was.

I, in turn, loved their positivity, their ability to turn even the most boring situation into an opportunity for fun, and their simplicity. There was no drama when I was with Batya and Vivi. They lacked any trace of cattiness, snobbery, or high-strung teenage sensationalism that so many other girls in my grade seemed to have.

"I have practice until six thirty, but I'll come by for a bit after, okay?"

Their cheerfulness hurt. I was a horrible friend to them and sometimes it felt like I used them, just to feel like I had a *chevrah*. I could've easily fit into a number of groups in my grade, but to slide by for years without questions was a blessing.

We talked until the bell rang. I had no idea what we were talking about, but by this stage in life I was a pro at acting present when my mind was a time zone away.

When Mrs. Zilber walked into the room, I was jolted back to the present. My eyes skittered across her face, searching for signs of…pity? Rejection? Dislike?

Why did I even care?

She acted as though nothing was different. She flitted about the room with her usual enthusiasm while reviewing yesterday's lesson and teaching a new *passuk*, apparently oblivious to my acute discomfort.

After I'd finished bawling my eyes out in her office the day before, she made me take down her home and cell phone numbers, saying, "You can call or text me any time, day or night. Don't worry about bothering me, because if I can't answer or get back to you, I won't."

I didn't intend on calling her; I had Daniella.

"Will you check in with me to let me know how things are going?"

That had been the question that made me realize she was serious. Because she could've left it at that one conversation, and left me to decide if I wanted to seek out her help in the future. But she'd insisted on a follow-up conversation to make sure I was surviving.

I had no idea when this follow-up conversation might happen and the uncertainty was making me incredibly anxious.

"Rikki, can you step outside with me for a minute?" I snapped to awareness and saw Mrs. Zilber standing in front of my desk.

Oh. Apparently it was right now.

This was not going to happen. Not when my nerves were wound tighter than a mousetrap and my journal was burning a hole through my knapsack. As soon as we left the classroom, before giving her a chance to say anything, I blurted out, "Can I please go talk to Mrs. Moskowitz? I need to see her, it's really important."

She hesitated, for just a moment, before nodding. "Is Mrs. Moskowitz aware of what's going on?"

"She's trying to help me with the nightmares." I toyed anxiously with a string on my knapsack.

"Rikki." She looked uncertain. I wasn't used to her seeming unsure of herself and I felt inexplicably guilty. "I need you to be honest with me. If it's going to cause you more stress for me to be checking in on you…"

And suddenly I was flooded with panic all over again. "I don't want to take up your time. I'm really fine, so, it's all good."

She narrowed her eyes. "That wasn't my question. I don't need you to try and convince me that things are fine; it's a little late for that. I just want to make sure I'm not making things harder for you by offering my support."

Sensing my confusion, she added, "I want to be here for you. But it needs to be about you, not about me. So is it okay with you if I care?"

There went the tears again. Summoning nonexistent willpower, I kept them behind my eyes and said evenly, "I think so."

She smiled. "Good. I'm glad. Now go ahead to Mrs. Moskowitz. I'll catch you later."

As she stepped back into the classroom, she paused to turn toward me. "Even if you aren't davening, I'm davening for you. He cares about you too, even if it doesn't feel like it."

19

I used the walk from Mrs. Zilber's classroom to Mrs. Moskowitz's office to get myself under control.

I texted Daniella, *everything is making me cry today*. Within thirty seconds she texted back, *(((((((you))))))) sending virtual hugs to wherever u are. love u*, which only made me want to cry more.

I knocked on Mrs. Moskowitz's door, realizing that without an appointment, she might not have time to see me, and knowing that if I didn't do this now, I would chicken out later. She wasn't in her office. She came up behind me, scaring me so bad that I dropped my knapsack and nearly swung at her.

She stepped back, her hands going up instinctively. "I'm sorry, Rikki, I didn't mean to scare you." She'd just arrived, her jacket still buttoned and her briefcase slung over one shoulder. She slid the case down to the floor and pulled out a key to unlock the door. "Did you want to come in?"

I was a mess. Too embarrassed to pick my knapsack off the

ground, I used my foot to slide it into her office and then sank down on the couch. I pulled out the journal and stared at it in my hands, flipping it over and over while she pulled off her jacket and started brewing a cup of coffee from a Keurig in the corner. "Do you want some?" She held a Styrofoam cup out to me and I accepted it gratefully.

When she finally settled down in her chair with her own steaming cup of coffee, she smiled at me and waited for me to say something.

"I wrote something down last night." I held the journal out toward her.

She took it slowly. "You can read if to me if you'd like."

I shook my head. There was no way those words were coming out of my mouth.

She took a long time reading. I stared at her while she read, focusing in on her long, wavy brown sheitel, her knee-length leather boots, her button-down shirt with a vest on top. She wore three bracelets on her left wrist and a long dangling necklace that matched her earrings. Her nails were manicured, which made me look down at my own nails, which were short and ragged.

When she spoke, I didn't want to look at her. "I'm really impressed, Rikki."

"What?" I looked at her suspiciously.

"That couldn't have been easy to write down. It takes a lot of courage, but you did it."

I swallowed hard. "What am I supposed to do about it? I can't keep going through that every night."

"I agree. You can't. Rikki, we need to talk about what happened. I'm going to have to ask you some questions about it."

"What do you need to ask?"

"First of all, when did this happen?"

"Six days before she went into the hospital." Before she could ask anything else, I went on the defensive. "Why, are you going to report this? It's not like she was trying to abuse me. She's sick." This was what I'd been afraid of. My father wouldn't forgive me if he knew I'd shared this information with someone at school, although that was just a guess, since my father didn't even know this had happened.

"I don't know." Mrs. Moskowitz spoke slowly, measuring her words. "Only if I need to. If your mother was hospitalized for this type of behavior, it doesn't seem like it needs to be reported. But first I think we should talk about it."

My emotions were out of control. "I'm not talking to you about this if you're going to report it." My voice contained an unfamiliar note of aggression and I was ashamed. "I just don't want this getting out."

"Out where? Who do you not want to know about this?"

I raked my fingers through my hair, struggling to keep my agitation beneath the surface. "No one. I didn't even want to tell you about this. I just can't deal with the nightmares. Can you just tell me how to fix that? Is there a medicine I can take or something?" My voice was rising, my hands were trembling. I stuffed them under my legs.

The concern on her face was unambiguous. "Rikki, you need to relax. Just sit back, and let your body relax. Try taking deep breaths that go all the way down into your stomach. Let the air fill you up completely and hold it for a beat before letting it out. Good, like that."

I clung to her voice in the way that I listened to Daniella when she talked me out of my dream-induced hysteria. Mrs. Moskowitz's voice was smooth and strong and I felt my body responding to the deep breaths.

"You're safe, right here, right now. Nothing is going to happen to you, and whatever you're feeling, you can handle it." She was watching me closely, continuing her monologue as she slid her chair slightly closer to me.

She reached out and took the half-full coffee cup from my hands. "This may not be the best time to be drinking coffee. You don't need to be any more jittery than you already are." From the back of her chair, she took her jacket and handed it to me. "Put this on for a minute. You're shaking."

Grateful for the warmth and the distraction, I pushed my arms through the sleeves and slid my hands into the pockets. I was breathing steadily now; the frantic fear that had recently coursed through my veins was quiet.

"Take your time." Tears stung in my eyes at the gentleness in her voice. "I won't push you to say anything you don't want to. Rikki, think about this. Did you believe you'd be able to write down your nightmares?"

I shook my head and she continued. "Well then, the same way you believe you can't talk about it now, challenge yourself. Writing didn't kill you, and talking won't kill you either."

"You don't know that."

"Prove me wrong."

She smiled slightly, and I wanted to be angry at her, but it didn't make sense.

"No one knows about this."

She waited.

"Well, maybe my sister knows. I don't really know. She acts like she does, but then again, she acts like she knows everything." That elicited another smile. "I was home alone with her. It was Sunday. I was supposed to be at my friend, but someone was supposed to stay home with her all of the time so I didn't go. I was in my room, and—"

The pressure in my chest made me stop midsentence. Immediately, Mrs. Moskowitz began guiding me through deep breathing as I bent forward, my arms wrapped around myself.

"I can't do this," I choked out. "I told you, I can't."

"You are, Rikki. Take it easy on yourself. You don't have to get it all out right now. You're making progress and that's what's important."

I dropped my head into my hands, feeling miserable. "And then what? What happens after I talk about it — does it stop? Will I stop dreaming about it? What if it doesn't go away?"

She was silent until I picked up my head to look at her. Then she spoke. "Talking about it won't change the fact that it happened. Whatever you went through, that will always be a part of you, but it doesn't have to control you." I slumped back in my seat, exhausted by my raging emotions. "Rikki, what does it mean to you to 'be okay'?"

I bit my lower lip. "No more nightmares. And not being scared of everything all the time."

She nodded. "Good. You can get there. As long as you realize that you're not going to be able to erase the past. This is about taking control over your future and working through the old stuff so that it doesn't keep creating this shadow over your whole life. Does that make sense?"

I nodded, because it did. In fact, it made more sense than anything had in a long time.

I drummed my fingers on the cover of my journal. "I'll try to write more. I just…talking is too hard."

"That's fine. You're doing great." After a minute, she stood and I did the same.

"Thanks a lot…for helping me." I felt awkward and exposed and wanted to create distance. I moved toward the door and out into the hallway.

"Um, Rikki? You're still wearing my jacket."

20

The afternoon felt more like medieval torture than high school dance practice. The move, a double somersault, wasn't particularly difficult, but we were practicing on the unforgiving floors of the auditorium. Each roll was a collision of tender spine and hard flooring, and everyone was in pain.

Ayelet limped over to me at the end, her hands pressed against her lower back. "If I have to do another somersault, I think my spine might start bleeding." She wasn't exaggerating. As one of the skinnier girls in the dance, I knew the move had to be particularly brutal for her.

"Don't worry," I said, gingerly running my fingers up my own spine, feeling the raised bruises. "You have the move down. You can just walk it for the next few days."

"Hey, can I get a ride home?" she asked suddenly. I wondered briefly how she knew I had a car that particular day and then realized that Zehava — my usual ride — had just left. Daniella let me have the car so I could go to Vivi's straight from practice.

"No problem."

Since Ayelet had struck up that first conversation with me, we'd had little time to speak, but our friendship had grown. I was in awe of her dance moves, which, despite her quiet nature, had made her a semi-superstar among the other dancers.

Because I had virtually no free time, I'd written her a letter during class one day, as an alternative to watching the clock tick. I left the note in her locker in between classes and she'd done the same a few periods later. In that fashion, Ayelet and I became friends.

"How are classes going?" I asked as we pulled out of the parking lot. Out of the corner of my eye, I saw her make a face. I'd learned that she had a learning disability and attention deficit disorder, which made classes torturous for her. She was pulled out of thirty percent of her classes for one-on-one tutoring; that was how she stayed in a mainstream school.

"They want me to try a new medication for the ADD."

"I thought meds didn't work for you in the past." Ayelet was very open about her struggles, totally unapologetic about the fact that her brained worked differently than the average person's.

"No, they worked. It's just that I lost my appetite while on them and my parents freaked out when I started losing weight. But now there's more meds out there that don't have that side effect." She rolled down her window and stuck her arm out. "At least I hope not. I hate playing around with new meds, always changing the doses and having to see the psychiatrist. It's irritating."

"I'm sure it is." My stomach tightened at the mention of psychiatrists. The easy thing about being friends with Ayelet was that I never had to talk about myself. There was in implicit imbalance in the relationship that worked in my favor. "Do *you* want to try the new meds?"

She shrugged. "It would be nice to be able to focus. And it

would be nice to not feel like such an idiot all the time, especially when I know that I'm not. It would be cool to find out how smart I really am." I wondered, not for the first time, where her self-esteem came from. She turned to me suddenly. "So how are you always writing letters to me in class? Don't you have to take notes?" The question was innocent enough but it put me on edge.

"I write quickly. So I can take notes and write letters at the same time." It was a lie, and while I felt bad for that, I had no other choice.

"I wish I was more like you."

My stomach twisted. "Why?" The word came out harsher than I'd intended and Ayelet glanced at me sideways.

"You're just chilled. You treat everyone well even though you're popular, so everyone likes you even more." She grinned at me. "I know that sounds cheesy, but I really mean it. I'm glad I have you."

I felt chilled inside. Ayelet shouldn't be looking up to me. She had no idea what I was all about. If she knew — if anyone knew — my reputation would be blown to bits.

After dropping Ayelet off, I drove nearly all the way home before I remembered I was supposed to be going to Vivi's. I was hungry, tired, and wanted nothing more than to have a quiet dinner with Daniella and Uri, but I knew I owed my friends this much.

Mrs. Sommers let me in the front door. "Rikki! It's so nice to see you, it's been so long!" She smiled warmly. "Have you had dinner yet?"

"No, but I'm okay. I'll eat when I get home."

"Aren't you coming from dance practice? You probably haven't eaten in hours. I haven't even put dinner away yet; let me make you a plate." Five minutes later I was sitting at the table in front of a dish piled high with chicken cutlets, rice, and Israeli salad. I'd eaten dozens of dinners here and usually loved Mrs. Sommers's cooking, but the sight of her puttering around the kitchen made me lose my appetite.

"This is really good, but I'm going to finish it later." I slid out of my seat and went down the hall to Vivi's room. I heard laughter inside and steeled myself before opening the door.

"You came!" Batya bounced off the bed and grinned at me.

"I told you I would." I smiled back, wishing my face wouldn't feel so frozen.

"Did my mother try to feed you?"

We settled down, and I felt myself relax as I was engulfed in the familiarity of our friendship.

"Do you remember how you were so sure you wouldn't get picked for dance head?" Batya nudged me with her elbow. "You were like 'I have nothing to lose, I guess I'll sign up, but I doubt I'll get it.'" I had to laugh at her imitation.

"Is Daniella upset that she's not in dance?" Vivi wanted to know.

"Not really. She got involved with scenery. At first it started out as a joke, her and Tali just wanting an excuse to get out of class, but then she started giving them good ideas so now she's officially their consultant."

"I saw it. It's really good." Vivi sat up on the floor where she'd been lying. Batya was sitting in her desk chair and I was sprawled out on her bed. I saw a long look pass between them.

"What?"

"Nothing," Vivi said innocently.

"No, seriously. What's up?" I looked pointedly at Vivi, knowing she was more likely to start talking if there was something that needed to be said.

Batya surprised me by talking first. "We…wanted to talk to you about something."

No. I was done talking about things for the day. "I really should go now. I have homework to do and I told Daniella I wouldn't be out late."

They did that silent-communication-look thing again and I felt my nerves prickle.

"Just stay for another minute," Batya said. "This is important."

I waited for her to continue and when she didn't, I stood, frustrated. That seemed to be all the prompting they needed.

"We're worried about you." The way Batya said it left no doubt in my mind that she was serious.

"Look, I've been busy with dance. It's crazier than I thought it would be, so I don't have a lot of time—"

"It's not about that." They kept looking at each other, little glances that made me want to bolt. "You don't seem happy anymore. Every time we see you, you look stressed-out and sad."

"I'm not. I mean, yeah, dance is stressful, but I'm not…sad." I nearly choked on the word. "Look, you guys are really sweet, but I'm fine. I'm really sorry I haven't been hanging out with you as much. I miss you guys a lot, but after concert, things'll be different." I grabbed my sweatshirt and started pulling it on.

"Is something wrong with your mother?" Batya's words made me freeze.

"What? No. Why?"

I recovered quickly and finished putting on my sweatshirt. Things were getting out of control and I needed to get out.

"You're not being honest with us." Vivi finally spoke. Her normally cheerful face was serious. "We know something's wrong."

"What are you talking about?"

"I don't know. Why don't you tell us?" I glared at Batya. This wasn't a game and I wasn't going to start crucifying myself with information. But I wasn't sticking around to wait for them to talk. I was halfway to the door when Batya shot the first arrow.

"We know she's in the hospital. My little sister's friends with Chevy Hassan. I guess she found out from Tali. Isn't she friends with Daniella?"

Daniella. When she'd find out that Tali had told her sister about our mother, she'd never get over that betrayal.

"I'm not doing this."

"Rikki, we're your friends. You can talk to us about this. It's obvious that something's wrong." Vivi's voice was tentative, yet I felt a surge of anger.

"Don't do this to me." My hand was on the doorknob, twisting it furiously back and forth. "This isn't what I need from you. Can we just act like everything is fine?" My voice was jumping all over the place and so was my heart.

"That's what we've doing for the past five years, isn't it?" Batya's composure stunned me. This wasn't how we operated. Out of the three of us, I was the strong one. I was the one who stayed calm in the face of stress, the one who kept them grounded. Yet with a few sentences, they had flipped the script and now I was the one feeling weak and scared.

"Well, maybe there's a reason it's been this way." I twisted the knob one final time and yanked the door open.

"Rikki, wait—"

"No. I'm not doing this." I walked out.

I walked down the hallway, past Mrs. Sommers, who asked me if I wanted to finish eating, and straight out the door toward the car. Fury set my nerves on fire and I wanted to scream at the top of my lungs at the injustice of it all.

Without even thinking, I slammed my left fist into the side of the car door. Spasms of pain rocked my body. I stumbled back, cradling my injured hand with my good one. I unlocked the car and climbed in, keeping my left hand close to my body. My right hand shook as I tried to put the key in the ignition. When I finally succeeded and the car lights came on, I saw that I'd split open two knuckles.

I started driving, not knowing — not caring — where I was headed. This was it. If Vivi and Batya had gotten this information from a tenth grader, our secret was over; it would be out within a week. As much as we talked about not speaking *lashon hara*, it sure had a way of getting around.

I drove past our house. I didn't want to face Daniella. She didn't know yet that Tali had betrayed her but when she'd find out, things would get ugly. And it was my fault. I was the one who convinced her to be open with her best friend, to trust Tali not to judge her. Daniella would blame Tali, but she would blame me too.

My hand burned with a ferocity that further kindled my anger. My cell phone rang and I nearly smashed into the car in front of me. My heart drumming in my chest, I pulled over and put the car in park. *Ayelet Klein* flashed on the screen. I laughed, a mirthless sound with more than a touch of hysteria. I bet she'd want to be more like me now. I rejected the call and continued driving. I'd hit the highway, and speeding up, I started feeling energy course through my fingertips and collide with the blur of the cars around me.

I rolled down all four windows and hit the Power button on the radio, filling the car with wind and music. And when the roaring of the air got so loud I couldn't hear myself think, I screamed and screamed and screamed.

21

I screamed myself hoarse. I started gagging because my throat was so raw and dry; I had no energy left to even make a small sound. I took the next exit, pulled into a 7-Eleven parking lot, and buried my face in my arms, crying until my eyes ran dry and my emotions exhausted themselves. I saw it was nearly nine o'clock and I'd missed five calls from my father and three texts from Daniella. I deleted them all without reading them. Then I texted her, *I'll b home late. Don't wait up.* When she texted me back, I deleted that one too.

I had three dollars in my knapsack so I bought a decaf coffee, wincing as it hit my throat. I took a moment to look at my surroundings. I was in a neighborhood that had an undeniably more exciting nightlife than our quiet Jewish community did. Around the front door of the store was a group of teenagers, pants hanging six inches too low, cigarettes dangling from their lips, out-talking each other as they attempted to look tough. They'd whistled at me when I went inside, and again when I came back out, but I was emotionless and walked right past them. On any other day, I would've been scared. Tonight, nothing mattered.

I wondered what would happen if I walked over and asked one of them for a cigarette. Before the thought could develop further, I got into the car, reached into my knapsack for a slip of paper, and dialed an unfamiliar number on my phone. Mrs. Zilber answered on the fourth ring.

"Hello?"

"Hi, It's Rikki."

For a horrible moment I wondered if she might say, "Who?" and I considered hanging up the phone, but she was too quick for that.

"Hi, Rikki, I'm so happy you called. How are you doing?"

"Not too good," I said dully. "Am I calling at a good time? Because if it's not—"

"Perfect timing," Mrs. Zilber said smoothly. "I just tucked my nine-year-old into bed and as long as you don't mind me cleaning the kitchen as we speak, then we're good."

I clutched my cell phone tighter and looked down at the dried blood on my knuckles. I had to tell someone what was going on. I was grateful for how dead I felt inside because it made talking easier.

"Some girls found out about my mother. Well, Daniella told her friend Tali, and then Tali told her sister, and now a lot of people are talking about it, and my best friends found out and they tried to stage an intervention because apparently I look sad, but I walked out on the them and I can't go home because I can't tell Daniella this and I have no idea what to do."

"Where are you?"

"I don't know."

"Are you serious?"

"Sort of. I pulled off the highway." I twisted around in my

seat to see if there were any visible street signs. "I'm on Eldorado Avenue."

Now she sounded alarmed. "Near a 7-Eleven?"

"Yeah."

"Rikki, the first thing you need to do is get back on the highway and start coming back toward town." I wondered how she knew Eldorado was in a bad neighborhood, but I obediently started the car and exited the parking lot, looking for signs toward the highway. I put my phone on speaker and left it in my lap.

"Why don't you want to go home?"

"I can't deal with that now. I'm not going to school either. Everyone's going to be talking."

"Rikki, do you remember where I live?" Mrs. Zilber had made a *shalosh seudos* for my class at the beginning of the year. She lived in a newer part of town, where they had nice houses and two-car garages. I'd heard her husband was a doctor.

"Yeah."

"Why don't you stop by for a minute? We can talk about what's going on and then you can decide what you're going to do."

I glanced at myself in the rearview mirror. I looked awful, with bloodshot, swollen eyes, my makeup smudged, and my hair wild and windblown. When I told her that, she laughed and said, "And I'm wearing a *tichel*, so we're even. Do you want me to stay on the phone until you get here?"

I needed time to collect my thoughts. "No, it's okay. I'll call you when I'm there."

Mrs. Zilber was wearing a *tichel*, a zip-up sweatshirt, and socks, which made me feel somewhat better. She hugged me when I came inside, and I accepted it woodenly.

"Did you have dinner yet?" she asked, and I wondered, briefly, why everyone was trying to feed me.

"Can I just have a coffee?" Her house was big and clean, but as we walked into the kitchen, I could see the signs of a family. She was in the middle of washing a big pan of dishes and her refrigerator was covered with children's artwork.

"Absolutely not. I'm not giving you coffee at this time of night. How about hot chocolate?"

"Okay."

She set the drink down at the table along with some chocolate chip cookies, then sat across from me and watched me take a drink. I was suddenly cold and nauseous. I wrapped my hands tightly around the mug and leaned forward so the rising steam could hit my face.

"What happened to your hand?"

I looked down at my swollen fingers and back up at her, wondering what she'd think about me if she knew the truth.

"I got mad and hit something." I waited for her to react, to look at me with fear or pity, but she was unflappable.

"Can I fix that up for you?"

I shrugged and followed her to the bathroom, where she gently rinsed my hand with soap and water, and applied Neosporin and Band-Aids. I felt my emotions flooding back at her motherly touch. By the time she started putting away the first-aid supplies, I was fighting back tears. "Does it hurt?" she asked. I shook my head, with my lips pressed together, afraid I'd cry if I started speaking.

Back in the kitchen, I was eternally grateful when Mrs. Zilber said she was going to finish washing the dishes while I finished my drink. My voice was slowly recovering, thanks to the hot liquid that soothed both my throat and my nerves.

When she finished with the dishes, we went to sit on the living room couches. I spoke slowly at first, my words hesitant and halting, but she was patient, and I told her everything from Daniella's fight with Tali up to when I walked out of Vivi's house and punched my car.

"What do you think will happen when you tell Daniella?" Mrs. Zilber wanted to know.

My answer was immediate. "Once I tell her, she'll be done with Tali. She'll never trust her again."

"And is that such a bad thing?"

"Yes, it is," I said emphatically. "Because everyone is friends with Daniella, but Daniella is friends with no one." She knit her eyebrows together, looking perplexed, so I explained further. "If she knew I was talking to you right now, she'd be really upset. She hates for anyone to know about our mother. She's always lying to people about where she is. She never wanted to tell Tali anything — Tali found out by accident. This'll just prove to Daniella that she can't trust anyone, and that's the last thing she needs."

Mrs. Zilber nodded. "Do you have any family in town? Does your mother have relatives who know that she has bipolar?" I hated — and loved — the way the word rolled off her tongue, as it if was a perfectly normal thing to be discussing.

"You know Shaindy Kliener in ninth grade? She's our first cousin — her mother is my father's sister. But they don't know anything. Last time we saw my aunt, Daniella told her my mother was in the hospital for a hip replacement." Mrs. Zilber raised an eyebrow. "I know, she makes up the craziest stuff. I don't know why anyone believes her."

"Does Daniella know where you are right now?"

The question made my heart twitch. "No one knows," I said slowly, pulling my cell phone out of my pocket. I winced when I saw that I had eighteen missed calls and nine text messages. "I guess they're a little worried." Flipping through them, I saw most were from my father and Daniella, but there were also texts from Kayla, Zehava, Vivi, Batya, and Ayelet.

When Mrs. Zilber saw that, she got serious. "You need to call your father and tell him where you are."

I shook my head. "I don't want to talk to him now."

She held my gaze steadily. "Rikki, as a mother, I'm going to insist on this. Everyone is obviously worried about you and you need to let them know you're okay."

"I texted Daniella. I told her I'd be back late."

"Not good enough. Can I call your father?"

Irritated, I tossed the phone onto the couch next to her. I stood up and started pacing while she called, stopping in my tracks when I heard my father's frantic voice over the phone. "Rikki? Where are you, are you okay?"

Mrs. Zilber was cool. "Mr. Coleman? This is Rachel Zilber, Rikki's Chumash teacher. I just wanted to let you know that Rikki's with me and I'll make sure she gets home safely." My father's voice rose and fell, but I couldn't make out what he was saying. Mrs. Zilber glanced at me a few times, and motioned for me to sit down, but I remained standing, edgy and nervous about going home. "I understand," she said finally. "I'm really sorry you were so worried. I didn't realize you didn't know where she was. I'll talk to her." Just as it seemed like she was about to hang up, she said, "Mr. Coleman? Please don't be too hard on her about this. She's had a rough night."

I cringed and sank down into the couch with my head in my hands. "Why did you say that?"

Mrs. Zilber looked surprised. "Rikki, he called the police. He thought you were kidnapped or in a car accident or something. You can't just disappear for hours like that and expect people not to worry."

"I know, but why did you tell him I had a rough night? He

doesn't need to know that. It's better if he's just mad at me. I don't need him feeling sorry for me."

"Trust me," she said dryly. "I think he'll be plenty mad."

I sat there, lost in thought, picturing the conversation I'd no doubt have with my father. I wanted him mad because that's how I was feeling. I wanted him to scream and yell so I could do the same. I didn't want sympathy or probing questions or anything less than a full-blown fight. I had no idea what I wanted to fight about, but I was hurting inside, and wanted him to feel the same way.

"Do you think you'll tell Daniella tonight?" Mrs. Zilber's voice brought me back to the present.

"I have to. I can't let her go to school tomorrow not knowing what happened."

She nodded. "And will you be okay in school tomorrow?"

"I don't think so. But that's nothing new."

She made me promise to call her as soon as I got home. She brought me my coat from the kitchen, and when I was sitting in my car and stuck my cell phone in my pocket, I saw that she'd packed up my uneaten cookies and snuck them inside. Smiling, despite everything, I buckled my seat belt and started driving home.

22

Daniella was sitting on the front porch when I drove up, the porch lights glistening off her blue-brown hair. "That's the last time I'm letting *you* take the car after school."

She stood, and I could feel the anger radiating from her. I'd counted on my father being mad, but not her. "Do you have any idea what we went through tonight?" She took a step closer to me and I had to force myself not to take a step back. "Uri cried himself to sleep. He was scared you'd been killed. Abba was a mess too." She glared at me, her face unforgiving. "You can't just do that, Rikki."

"I didn't mean to make anyone worry." She was searching for a fight, and although I'd been planning on doing the same thing with my father, I realized now that all I wanted to do was curl up alone and sleep forever.

"Well, it's a little late for that," she sneered. "Congrats, Rikki. You had everyone crying about you tonight."

Guilt flared in me, replaced by cold indifference. "I'm sorry. It's not like I had the best night either."

"That's not the point," she exploded, flinging her hands up in exasperation. "Every night is a bad night around here. And that's why you can't go and disappear. Because this," she gestured wildly toward our house, "this craziness is not something I can handle without you." Her voice caught in her throat and she stepped back, wrapping her arms around herself. "Even with you I can barely handle it. But if you're gone…it's all over."

Now it was my turn to step closer, concern for my sister replacing all other emotion in me. "Daniella, it's all over anyway. I have to tell you something." I swallowed hard, already regretting the words I'd have to say next.

She spoke first. "Vivi and Batya told me." She was in control of herself again, the impassivity creeping back up on her face. She was going to pretend it didn't hurt.

I nodded, scanning her face, desperately searching for some clue as to how we were supposed to react. "Do you know how they found out?"

When she shook her head, I wanted to run. From the truth, from my life, from the pain that Daniella would not own. *Please make this be the right decision.* My silent prayer surprised me, but there was no time to think.

"Tali told—"

"No." She put her hand up, stopping me in my tracks. "No, no, Rikki, tell me you're lying." It was like watching a horrific accident in slow motion. Realization crossed her face and collided with denial and I saw her fight a heroic battle to maintain control over her emotions. Her eyes shimmered with tears but she kept them there, refusing to let even one fall. "I'm going out."

I burst into tears.

That stopped her. "What's wrong with you?"

I was crying so hard that my words came out all hiccuppy and sad. "I need you. Don't leave me tonight." I stumbled over to the front steps and sat down, burying my face in my knees. Deep sobs ripped out from somewhere broken inside of me.

Daniella couldn't leave me then. She cared about me too much and took her role as my protector too seriously to do that. She held me until I'd once again exhausted myself and leaned limply against her. When I spoke, my voice shook uncontrollably, as if I'd just awoken from a long nightmare. "I'm sorry I told you to trust Tali. This is my fault and now everyone knows."

I felt her stiffen at Tali's name. "Don't say that. It's not your fault. It's completely hers." Her voice was dull and emotionless. It occurred to me that if I hadn't been so needy, if I'd let Daniella take her space when she wanted to, she might've been able to grieve over the loss of her friendship. I'd forced her to sacrifice that.

I couldn't remember a time when I'd hated myself quite as much as I did at that moment. "I'm not going to school tomorrow. I'm not going to be able to deal with that. Everyone will be talking about us." I was rambling but I was scared and lost.

Daniella's arms tightened around me. "We're going to school. We're going to face everyone and we won't apologize for lying, because this is our life, and they have no right to make us tell them anything." She pressed her face into my shoulder and I felt her sadness seeping into me. How much pain could she tolerate before she broke?

Before I could respond, the front door opened. My father stood there, illuminated for a moment, taking in the sight of us — my tear-streaked face, Daniella's protective hold. He then slowly lowered himself down on the step, wrapped both of us in his strong arms, and started to cry.

23

"Are you okay?"

Kayla's face swam in front of my eyes and I forced myself to focus. I was sitting at the kitchen table, nodding off over a cup of coffee, waiting for Daniella to be ready for school. My skull was aching and my throat and eyes felt sandpaper-dry, but I was ready to face the music.

"I didn't sleep at all last night," I said, rubbing my eyes blearily. "If I make it through school today in one piece, it'll be a miracle."

Daniella walked into the kitchen, looking worse than I felt. She'd slept in her own room last night for the first time in months. My bed had felt huge and lonely without her, and I'd spent hours writing furiously in my journal, terrified to fall sleep. I had to physically hold myself back from running down the hall to her room, reminding myself that she needed her space.

"Hi, Kayla." Her voice was hoarse. She reached for my mug. "Can I have some?" She drank half of my coffee, and as she drank, I saw her hands were shaking. "Kayla, listen." Her voice was serious. "Some girls found out about our mother. Can you tell us if you hear people talking about it?"

Kayla turned to look at me, bewildered by Daniella's question. Daniella never addressed Kayla seriously about our mother. I shrugged, too worn-out to say anything.

"Okay, sure," Kayla said slowly.

Daniella pulled two yogurts out of the fridge. "Is this good for lunch?"

I shrugged again, then followed them outside to the car, lost in thought. The drive to school seemed both interminably long and frighteningly short. Long before I was ready, we were pulling into the parking lot and were swallowed up by a sea of girls making their way to first period. Before we parted ways, Daniella squeezed my hand tightly. "Text me if you need me. I'll come." I nodded, and swallowed hard past the lump in my throat.

"Rikki!" Zehava came out of nowhere and pounced on me. I forced myself not to fall to the floor and curl up in a ball.

"Hey, what's up?"

"Did you hear? We're getting everyone off first and second period." She handed me a stack of green slips of paper. "Can you give these to the girls in your class? They're announcing it on the intercom soon but it'll go faster this way." She grinned, and I forced myself to smile back.

"Great, I'll be there soon." As soon as I turned away, I made a face, rolling my eyes in annoyance.

"Wow, someone's having a good morning," Ayelet teased, walking up to me.

"Hey." I smiled sheepishly, appreciating the distraction. "Sorry I never got back to you last night. It was a really…busy night."

She raised an eyebrow. "I can tell. You look horrible."

"I do?"

"No, not really. I'm kidding."

I waved the stack of papers at her. "We're getting off for the first two periods. You ready to dance?"

Now she made a face. "Not really. My new meds make me sleepy. I'm not even really awake right now, I'm totally sleepwalking."

I laughed. "You are too cute. Don't worry, everyone is going to be all hyper because we got off. You'll wake up soon."

Eyes half-closed, she started dancing the first steps of the dance in slow motion, moving down the hall with each step. When she was about ten feet away, she opened her eyes wide, flashed me a smile, and disappeared into her classroom.

A smile still playing across my lips, I walked to my classroom and paused outside the door. To walk inside would be to walk into a lions' den. I felt my smile fade as I thought of Vivi and Batya sitting in the classroom, heads bent together, talking about my "problem." I took a deep breath and stepped inside.

Nothing was different. A few girls called out my name and waved. When I sat down at my desk, the same girls crowded around, including my best friends. I struggled to relax and participate in the conversation without looking too guilty. Vivi caught my eye and smiled tentatively. I forced a small smile back. I distracted myself by handing out the green slips to the dancers in my class and by the time I was done, Mrs. Zilber had arrived.

"Girls, today we'll be davening first and learning second. Go ahead and begin. Rikki, can I talk to you for a minute?"

Wow. Forget about subtlety. I followed her outside.

"I just wanted to know how you're doing."

I played with the ends of my hair, unsure how to respond. "I don't think I'm okay really, but I sort of am." She waited. "Like, I was a mess last night. We all were. And I couldn't sleep at all, so it feels like I'm running on adrenaline now. I guess I'll crash at some point, but right now, I don't really feel anything."

Dancing in the Dark

"I'm not sure that's a good thing, but if it's helping you make it through the day…" Her voice trailed off and she glanced down at the papers in my hand. "Do you have enough energy to dance?"

I nodded. "It's about the only thing I have energy for."

She turned to the door as my three classmates appeared with their books in hand, green slips held high. "Go ahead," Mrs. Zilber told them. "Rikki will be there soon."

Tehila Kramer shot me a questioning look as they walked off but I just smiled calmly.

Mrs. Zilber laughed. "You really do know how to keep it together on the outside." She got serious again. "Listen, Rikki, if you need a break today, go lie down in the nurse's office or something. Don't push yourself too hard."

She let me go and I made my way to the auditorium for practice. Chani Jaeger had brought in cupcakes for everyone and the combination of sugar and early morning practice made everyone giddy.

I was licking icing off my fingers when my phone vibrated. I had a new text from Daniella. *Daven for me.* Really? That was out of character.

What's going on? I texted back, but she didn't reply. I threw myself into the dance, allowing myself to get caught up in the high-flying excitement all around me. The motion and music silenced the thoughts in my head and for ninety minutes, I was blissfully unaware of everything that was wrong.

"That was awesome." Zehava grinned at me and gave me a high five. "I'm going to daven in the library before third period. You want to come?"

"Sure," I said slowly. I didn't really, but it was a better alternative to Ivrit, where I was bound to get lost in my own head as soon as my teacher started speaking.

Sitting in a chair in the cool darkness of the library, I gingerly held a siddur in my hands, feeling acutely dishonest. I flipped it open to a random page and stared at the words, trying to remember a time when they'd felt relevant. Then I remembered this wasn't about me.

"Hashem." I glanced around. Zehava was engrossed in her davening, her siddur pressed close to her face. "Don't worry, I'm not coming to ask for anything for myself. I know I don't deserve that. And I'm really sorry I haven't been davening…but right now…I just can't. But like I said, I'm not going to ask for anything for me. This is for Daniella, and I know she davens all the time so she's got to have a connection with You that's worth something." I felt a little dizzy. "Can You help her? She needs You right now because she has no one else she can trust."

I saw Zehava finishing *Shemoneh Esrei* and realized I needed to wrap it up. "So listen, maybe You could just do this for her. And I don't know…maybe if You want to help me out too…I really do need it. And I don't mean to sound ungrateful or anything, I mean, I'm really glad I have people I can talk to, but…maybe You could make my mother okay. Or make my father…start being a father again. I don't know. You probably don't want to hear this from me. Anyway, just please help Daniella."

I closed the siddur and sat motionless. Why, if I was so sure that my prayers were worthless, did I so intensely feel Hashem's presence when I spoke to Him?

24

Vivi and Batya were kind enough to wait until lunchtime to corner me. Before dance, and also before life had become unbearably complicated, I'd always eaten lunch with them in the gym, along with a random assortment of classmates. Lately, I'd either eaten with the dance heads or been occupied with practice. Today, lunch was free.

"Are you coming?" Batya asked pointedly as we stood at our lockers putting our books away. I was arranging and rearranging them with the futile hope that my friends would forget I was there and go to lunch without me.

"I...have to go do something," I said lamely.

Vivi rolled her eyes. "Are you mad at us? Because if you are, you should just say it."

They were both looking at me now, waiting for me to react. "No, I'm not mad," I said slowly. "I have to go talk to...Mrs. Moskowitz." Once I said it, I realized I wanted it to be true. I needed her help.

"Daniella called me last night," Batya said. "She was all panicked because she didn't know where you were." Her gaze shifted sideways. "I kind of feel like it's our fault. Like, maybe you're right, that we should've just left things like they were." She finally looked at me. "So if you want, we won't talk about it again."

The stress and exhaustion were returning. I needed to get away before I said something I'd regret. "Okay. Thanks." I started backing away, needing to put distance between me and the people who knew things they shouldn't.

"Wait," Vivi said, holding one hand out. "Just to make this clear, we'll only be avoiding it because you want us to. Not because it bothers us or makes us uncomfortable."

Batya nodded. "That's right. We could care less about your mother's issues. We like you. Nothing'll change that. If you want to pretend it's still a big secret, then fine, we'll play along. But at least now you know we'll be here for you if you ever want to talk about it."

My eyes flooded with tears. Swallowing hard, I nodded. I didn't even deserve their loyalty. It hurt because I knew they were telling the truth. And it hurt even more because their words made it painfully clear that I was the one judging myself.

I hightailed it to Mrs. Moskowitz's office. She had another girl in her office when I knocked, so she told me to wait outside while she finished up. I texted Daniella while I sat on the floor of the hallway, but all she wrote back was *fine*. I frowned because I'd asked her how things had gone with Tali and I had a strong feeling the answer to that was not so pleasant.

Seriously?

more later.

Mrs. Moskowitz came out and ushered me into her office.

"Your father called me this morning," she said before I had a chance to speak. Immediately, I was on high alert.

"About last night?"

She nodded. "He's extremely concerned about you." She motioned for me to sit as she settled into her chair. "Do you want to tell me about it?"

I was so tired of talking, of breathing, of fighting, of living. "I can't talk anymore." I pulled my journal out of my knapsack and handed it to her. "Can you just read this? I wrote it last night."

She read for a long time, her eyes moving slowly back and forth across the pages. She paused every so often to look up at me, which made me squirm. When she finally finished, she closed the book and looked at me for a long time.

"Rikki." Her voice was so grave that my whole muscular system seemed to seize at the sound of it. "Does your father know about all this?"

I knew what the right answer was. I needed to tell her that he knew, that we weren't keeping any secrets, that she could breathe because the weight of what I'd just revealed wasn't her burden to bear. But my head wouldn't turn and my throat wouldn't open. My brain screamed at me to lie, but I was frozen.

"I'm really sorry this happened to you." She was looking at me steadily, and I was looking back because all I could think was that this was the first time someone who knew everything was looking at me.

"She's sick."

I couldn't say more. I hadn't even wanted to say it, hadn't wanted to justify her actions for the millionth time. How much could we excuse? She'd hurt us, all of us in our own way. With her words and her hands, fueled by the rage and sorrow of a chemical imbalance in her brain, she destroyed our family from within. And my father, blinded by his love for her and his undying faithfulness, had allowed it to happen.

"I know," Mrs. Moskowitz said, setting the journal carefully on her desk. "She's very sick. But she's getting help now. And I think you deserve to get the help you need too."

I started trembling, the reality of exposure shaking my equilibrium. "I think she ruined us."

"No." She was shaking her head vehemently. "Rikki, no. You are so far from ruined. You and Daniella are in tremendous pain, but you're fighting it. The bond you two share is incredible, and it's probably because of what you've experienced that you're so in tune with each other's needs. You've nurtured each other in a way your mother couldn't."

"But there's something wrong with us." She didn't know. She couldn't possibly know how deep the pain ran. We weren't just hurt; we were raised with daily doses of damage.

"There's nothing wrong with you." I started shaking my head. "Rikki, listen. Have you ever heard of post-traumatic stress disorder?"

At the word "disorder" I stopped moving. "What's that?"

"It's what some people develop after they've been through a traumatic event. It might be a one-time event or a series of things over a period of time." I was listening intently. "A lot people are able to return to normal after they've been through a traumatic experience. But for some, the trauma can be too big for them to deal with, and they start having a lot of stress symptoms."

"Like what?"

"It's different for each person. But the common ones are nightmares, reexperiencing the traumatic events, flashbacks during the day, trouble sleeping, being easily startled."

Something was shifting inside of me. It was a spark of awareness and a glimmer of hope. What I was going through had a name?

"I have that." I felt lightheaded with relief. "I'm not crazy."

She smiled gently. "No, not crazy at all. Just in a lot of pain."

"I think Daniella has it too." Puzzle pieces were clicking into place in my mind. The nightmares, her flashbacks, the memories that ran like movie reels through my mind, the way loud noises shook me to my core and left me jittery long after they'd stopped. "Can we get better?" I knew, more than most girls my age, that mind problems weren't easy to fix.

But she was nodding. "Absolutely. You have a long road ahead of you, but I think you can get to a much healthier place than you're at now. You've already come far in the short time I've known you." I wanted to find Daniella, to tell her that something finally made sense. But I needed to stay and find out more. Before I could ask anything, Mrs. Moskowitz continued. "Your mother hurt you deeply, and she's been doing it for a long time. You need to realize that your recovery won't involve changing her."

"What do you mean?"

"She has a mental illness that can't be cured. She hurt you because of her mental illness." She was holding my gaze steadily. "There's a good chance she'll continue to hurt you in the future."

"How can she do that? She won't even see us."

"And isn't that hurting you?"

I flinched. And that answered her question.

"The whole time I was reading your journal, especially the part about how she treated the two of you when you were young, I kept thinking about why things have gotten so bad right now. For the past eleven years you managed to fly under the radar at school, even throughout all of her hospitalizations. Only recently have things reached a new level and you're realizing this can't keep up much longer."

"We're old enough to know it's not right. We didn't know when we were younger. We thought it was just how mothers acted."

She nodded thoughtfully. "So why does it hurt more now, knowing that you were mistreated, and that you didn't deserve it?"

I was silent, twisting her question around in my head. When I finally answered, the words came slowly as the truth teased itself out from the tangled mass of confusion. "There's no one to be mad at. We can't be mad at her, because she's just crazy. We try to get mad at my father, but he just disappears. So Daniella gets mad at everyone, and I just get mad at Hashem."

"And what are you so mad about?"

I looked at her in disbelief, then grabbed my journal and flung it onto the floor. "This. My whole life, okay? I'm mad at my mother for treating me the way she did, and for hurting Daniella. And I'm mad at my father because he was the only one who could've saved us, but instead he just tried to save her."

My voice was growing harsher but I couldn't help it. "And I'm mad that my whole life, no one figured it out. Everyone just looked at us and assumed we were okay. All my relatives, everyone at school, all my friends' parents — they just saw what they wanted to see. If they'd looked a little closer, someone could've done something and made it all stop." The anger was surging forth from a source that had been dormant for too long.

"I'm mad at my little brother because he loves my mother and doesn't care that she's sick. I'm mad at my friends because they have parents who care and don't try to play with their minds or hurt them. I'm mad at Hashem for letting this all happen in the first place." I couldn't even see Mrs. Moskowitz's face through the haze of rage that swept over me.

"I'm mad at Daniella too, for being so good at acting like she doesn't care, and for not being a good mother, even though I know she's not really my mother." I forced myself to draw in a breath before my chest totally caved in. "And me. I'm mad at myself because I let this all happen. I should've fought back, or told someone, or been better at protecting myself."

I snatched my journal off the floor and started ripping out the pages, crumpling them into balls. "I hate myself because of everything that happened. And that just makes me hate everyone else." I dropped the papers and buried my face in my hands as the tears started to flow. "I'm so tired of being angry all the time. It never ends. All night I'm scared and all day I'm angry."

I lifted my head to look at Mrs. Moskowitz and saw she had tears in her eyes. "I need help." Seeing my grief mirrored in her eyes only made my tears flow faster. "I can't feel this way all the time. How can I get better?"

"Like this, Rikki." She wiped her eyes before the tears fell. "By letting it all out."

25

After school, Daniella was waiting for us in the car. She had sunglasses on even though it was barely bright outside. We were silent on the drive home; Kayla knew better than to try talking to us. She left the car and Daniella sat motionless in the driveway.

"What happened today?" I asked first.

She slid down in her seat until her knees were knocking into the dashboard. "I hate everyone in my grade. They're all so shallow and stupid." She ripped the sunglasses off and tossed them aside. "We had seminary interviews today. And Mrs. Landau called me into her office for a long talk about why I'm not 'setting myself up to reach my full potential.'" She made air quotes with her fingers, mocking our assistant principal's words.

"What did you tell her?"

"I told her it was none of her business. I said she didn't know me, or my financial situation, or my mental stability."

"You said that?" I didn't even know why I bothered to be surprised by her anymore.

"Yes. Then she said I had an attitude problem, and I said that's why I wasn't applying to seminary — because no one wants a girl with an attitude problem."

I shook my head. She was miserable but I doubted it had anything to do with seminary.

"What happened with Tali?"

"Tali's not going to seminary. She's going to college."

"I know. I wasn't asking about that."

"Oh." She was silent, and I saw her lips trembling as she tried to keep her emotions in check. "She drove me crazy all morning, asking why I wasn't talking to her. And I didn't say anything at first because I didn't want to start a scene, but then I told her." She paused, pulling in a deep, shuddery breath.

"And?"

"And she said I was overreacting, because it would've gotten out anyway and you can't hide something like that forever." She shook her head in disgust. "She said it was my fault she found out in the first place."

"Danz…I'm sorry. I don't know why she's being like this."

"I do. She's trying to get back at me for lying to her all this time." She looked so sorrowful that I reached out and hugged her. She pulled back, as a sob caught in her throat. "Don't. I'll totally lose it and I've been trying to avoid that all day." She pressed her fingers against her eyes.

I cleared my throat. "Danz, we need to talk. I want to tell you about today but not if you can't handle it."

She slowly lowered her hands and unbuckled her seat belt. "I can't handle anything today, but we might as well talk now. Uri gets back from soccer practice in a half hour so we have some time."

We went into the house, stripping off our coats and knapsacks as we walked. We were moving slowly, as if each step was a battle.

Daniella collapsed onto the living room couch, curling up with her head resting on the armrest. I sank down to the floor in front of the couch, resting my back against it so I was facing away from her. I couldn't watch myself cause her more pain. She reached out and twirled a few strands of my hair.

I forced myself to begin. "I went to Mrs. Moskowitz today, mostly because I had to escape from Vivi and Batya." At the mention of my friends, I was reminded of their loyalty and my cold reception of their acceptance and felt ashamed. "Last night, when I couldn't sleep, I wrote a lot in my journal, about what Ima was like, and what she did to us. And…I showed it to her."

It was deathly still in the room. I wasn't breathing and I couldn't hear Daniella's breath either. I'd just broken the cardinal rule that Daniella had tried her hardest to instill in me for as long as I could remember. I'd spoken the truth and that was tantamount to treason.

After a long pause, Daniella snaked an arm over my shoulder, reaching for my hand. She clasped it tightly and I heard her start to cry. "Good for you."

"What?" I turned around suddenly, unsure if she was being serious or masking her anger with sarcasm. Tears ran sideways down her face and pooled on the fabric of the couch. She reached out and hugged me fiercely.

"I wish I was more like you." She was being completely serious. "Maybe if you talk about it, the nightmares will get better. I wish I could do that."

I told her what Mrs. Moskowitz had said about post-traumatic stress disorder. She sat up, looking at me intently. "You think you have it?"

I nodded. "I know I do. It all made sense. When she was describing the symptoms, it was like she was in my head, talking about everything I was going through." I paused, and then forced myself to continue. "Maybe you have it too."

She shook her head. "No. I wasn't…traumatized." She stumbled over the word, breaking eye contact as she said it.

"Why?" My voice sounded pathetically pleading to my own years. "Why is it so important for you not to act like it doesn't get to you? Why is it okay for me to be traumatized, but not you?"

"You were just a kid when Ima got really sick. You didn't even understand it. That's traumatic all by itself. At least I knew she was sick, so it didn't get to me."

"You're lying to yourself." Anger edged into my voice. She refused to let herself feel pain and that, right there, was the legacy of my mother's abuse living on. "You were a kid too. And you had it so much worse than me. She was horrible to you, Daniella. Don't pretend you don't remember."

"There's no point in remembering. It doesn't change the past."

"This isn't about the past. This is about right here, right now. We're not doing okay, but at least I can admit I have a problem. I don't try to pretend what we went through isn't killing me inside."

Her mask was returning, but right before it smoothed out the creases in her forehead and erased the tears from her eyes, she allowed herself one more moment of vulnerability. "I can't do it, Rikki. You'll get better, because you aren't scared to face everything that's wrong. I know we're falling apart. But the only thing I know how to do is act like I run this world. So until everyone knows I'm a faker and a liar and no one wants to talk to me anymore, I'm going to keep this plastic smile on my face because I can't do anything else."

Before I could respond, before I could even process what she'd said, the window of opportunity had closed and composure slipped over her like a glove. She was back on her feet, asking what I wanted for dinner.

26

As a peace offering, I invited Vivi and Batya over on Shabbos afternoon. That was something I'd done only once in the history of our friendship, during a week when Ima had been hospitalized and I didn't need to worry about her making a scene. My friends took the invitation in stride, hardly mentioning the rarities of the occasion. When Shabbos afternoon rolled around, I paced anxiously in front of the living room window, regretting my decision.

"Now they're going to think I want to talk about everything," I griped to Daniella, who was playing chess with Uri on the floor.

"Just chill out." She didn't look up from the game. "You already told them you didn't want to, so stop worrying. And stop moving, you're making me dizzy."

I stopped in my tracks and watched them play a few moves. "Uri, when did you learn how to play chess?"

He looked up, grinning. "Yoni taught me."

"Who?"

"My mentor."

"Wait, what? You got one? When?"

Daniella looked up and rolled her eyes. "Two weeks ago. You seriously didn't know that?" She glanced affectionately at our little brother. "Uri's been swaggering around like he's six feet tall ever since Yoni came along."

"I have to show you what he got me." Uri popped up from the floor and ran into his room, returning less than ten seconds later with a baseball hat perched jauntily on his head. "Yoni took me to a game. He said he'll take me again if I keep my grades up." He spun the hat on his head so that it was backward and cocked his head, grinning goofily. "Yoni's awesome."

"I can see that," I said, finally sitting down on the couch, my surveillance temporarily abandoned. "Uri, that's really cool. Sorry I didn't realize you got a mentor." He shrugged, still playing with the hat on his head, experimenting with different angles.

A knock on the front door had me jolting out of my seat and him racing for the door.

"Cool hat," I heard Vivi say.

Daniella looked at me and smiled. "You'll be fine," she mouthed.

They couldn't help themselves; they looked around my house as if it were a foreign museum. When they got to my room and saw the mural on my wall, they were rendered speechless. I realized it hadn't existed the last time they were here.

"My mother painted that," I said without thinking.

"Is she an artist?" Batya asked innocently.

Was she an artist? She worked as a freelance illustrator for a children's book publishing company. But only when she remembered to take her medication and wasn't unmanageably manic or cripplingly depressed. In bad times, her artwork took on dangerous tones, definitely not suitable for children's literature. Her themes could be dark, almost demonic, frightening enough that characters she'd drawn often appeared in my nightmares.

But during good times? Armed with her weapon of choice, most often a simple black charcoal pencil, but sometimes vibrant acrylics, glistening oils, or dusky chalk pastels, she was extraordinary. Her imagination seemed to be limitless and she saw the world through a prism of color that somehow she translated through her gifted hands.

"She is," I said slowly. "She's an artist."

At first, the minutes dragged. I tried to stop staring at the clock on my desk that seemed to be moving backward, but found my eyes constantly wandering in that direction. I listened to my friends with an obsessive intensity, trying to determine what they'd say next, based on their current words. I was desperate to know exactly how each conversation would play out, and kept concocting potential distractions to whip out in case things got dicey.

When Uri came in to show us a framed picture of him and his mentor from the game, I was glad for the distraction. I didn't recognize Yoni Shiller, the newest addition to our family, but he looked nice enough in jeans, a button-down flannel shirt, dark blonde hair, and a black velvet *kippah*. In the picture, Uri looked genuinely happy. He was standing on his tiptoes, trying to get his arm around Yoni's much taller shoulders, his head tilted back slightly as he laughed.

I smiled at Uri, grateful he was finally getting some of the attention he deserved. Daniella came in for a while too. She seemed lost with Tali out of the picture; although I knew she had hordes of other friends, she had very little patience for any of them and instead chose to remain aloof and, according to many, downright snobby.

Vivi and Batya were a little surprised, and probably flattered, that Daniella wanted to hang out with us, but I recognized it for what it was; a distraction for her and a show of support for me.

The afternoon passed without a hitch. Thanks to Vivi, the conversation was light and easy, and when *shalosh seudos* rolled around, I didn't mind inviting them to stay. My father was pleasant and friendly, and the meal moved along smoothly.

On Motzaei Shabbos, my friends asked me to come ice-skating and I eagerly accepted. For two hours, we glided along until our noses grew red from the cold and we could no longer feel our fingers. Dozens of girls from school showed up at the rink and I allowed myself to fall into the familiar swing of easy socialization.

On one of my last circuits around the rink, my hands shoved deep into the pockets of my sweatshirt, someone gliding past grabbed me from behind. Before I had time to react, Tali Hassan had me up against the side of the rink, keeping a hand on my arm until I had steadied myself.

"Don't ever do that again." I glared at her, my heart gradually slowing its beat. "You almost gave me a heart attack."

"So I see drama runs in the family," she said drily.

"What's the supposed to mean?"

She gave me an obvious look. "Your sister's being ridiculous. She's acting like I purposely tried to hurt her and it wasn't like that at all. It's not like I broadcasted it to the whole school. I just talked to my sister. Seriously, haven't you ever told Daniella anything that your friends tell you?"

"Not when it was my best friend and it was the one thing I was supposed to keep my mouth shut about." I wasn't going to feel sorry for her. She started to talk but I cut her off. "I told you, okay? I warned you this was big deal. And you knew, Tali. Don't act like I should feel bad for you, because you knew how much she didn't want you to know."

"You can't keep something like this a secret," Tali said, all trace of superiority gone. "Both of you thinking that you can lie to everyone about your mother…it's sick." She ran a hand through her hair, and with her blue streaks catching in the light of the rink, the mannerism was so reminiscent of Daniella that I had to blink hard to get things back into focus.

"No, it's not sick. You have no idea what it's like for us. How do you get to decide who should know and who shouldn't?"

She threw her hands up. "Look, I'm sorry, okay? I should've never said anything. I didn't even mean to tell Chevy. She was looking through my texts and asked me what Daniella was all upset about."

"Don't apologize to me." Her excuse was the last straw. I needed to get away. "You should be apologizing to Daniella."

She rolled her eyes. "Yeah, right. She's not talking to me. You know what she's like."

"Yeah, I do. And maybe you should've thought of that before you opened your mouth."

I skated away from her, trying to shake off the negativity that had wrapped itself around me during our conversation. I thought of Daniella at home, playing games with Uri and cooking her famous pancakes for their own private *melaveh malkah*. She didn't forgive easily, but in this situation, that was completely warranted.

"Are you coming for pizza?" Batya's question snapped me out of my momentary daze.

"Yeah, I'm coming." I pulled my skates off my frozen feet and pulled on my socks and sneakers, letting the swell of conversation around me dispel all thoughts of Tali and Daniella. Vivi was telling a funny story and I laughed, feeling something inside of me ease up slightly.

By the time we made it to the pizza shop, I felt almost relaxed, an entirely foreign feeling. The pizza was hot and cheesy, my friends were funny and caring, and I considered, for a minute, that maybe things weren't as bad as I'd thought. Maybe I was just going through a rough patch, a typical teenage adjustment period, and I didn't have any serious issue related to my childhood trauma. The knot in my stomach eased up and I enjoyed the pizza more than I'd enjoyed any food in the past month.

Weeks later, I would look back on that night in the pizza shop and have the most peculiar rush of emotions. On one hand, it was the last fun time I had before my life took a serious downhill turn; on the other, it represented just how far I'd split off the hurt, aching part of me from the popular, social butterfly that came out in daylight.

In just a few days, both parts would collide.

27

When all the masks came crumbling off, and Daniella and I reached rock bottom, it was so spectacularly horrible that I think all of us were stunned. We should've known things couldn't continue in the way they were. We were on a trajectory toward destruction, and the only question was how long it would take for us to hit a bump in the road that would make everything come tumbling down.

It wasn't any one thing that caused the situation to get so out of hand. It was more a combination of external factors falling down on two girls so worn-out by lies and deception that eventually we couldn't stand on our own two feet.

That Monday started out normally. There was no ominous thunderstorm signaling an impending catastrophe; on the contrary, the sun was strong and bright, making me squint and blink furiously as I walked outside with Daniella and Kayla. In retrospect, maybe Daniella knew we were nearing the end because she was definitely pushing the limits. She wore a hooded sweatshirt with the hood halfway up, her hair cascading out from the collar. Her fingernails were painted blue, the same shade as the streaks in her hair, a definite violation of school rules. With her slim, shaky fingers, she clutched a travel mug of coffee, inhaling the steam as it rose in the cool air.

"Can you drive?"

I took the wheel and pulled out onto the street, my mind blissfully clear. I'd awoken only once the night before, jolted by a dream I didn't remember. A few words from Daniella had lulled me back to sleep and I was more rested than usual. I had an appointment with Mrs. Moskowitz during second period in the afternoon and although I hadn't done any more journaling, there was plenty I wanted to talk to her about. Today I planned on asking her if she'd schedule a time to meet with Daniella. My sister needed help, even if she wouldn't admit it. I was also hoping to catch Mrs. Zilber during lunch to get advice on the Tali situation. I didn't think I'd be able to salvage that friendship but I did need advice on damage control, before the whole school knew that my mother was mentally ill.

For a change, I was able to focus for some of first period. I took half a page of notes, which was one half of a page more than I usually took. When it was time for davening, I chatted with Hashem, once again apologizing for my lack of communication, but requesting His help for Daniella.

Kayla and I were in different classes for second period. "You look good today," she said as we walked out of Chumash. "Did something happen?"

I shook my head. "I just had a pretty good weekend. Skating was awesome." She nodded in agreement, smiling at the memory. "See you in Ivrit."

My concentration seemed to have been used up in Chumash, and I struggled to sit still through second period. I wrote a four-page letter to Ayelet, which only took up a fraction of the class time, and watched the clock tick for the rest of the period. When the bell finally rang, I was out of my seat and in the hallway before it stopped clanging.

Halfway to Ivrit, things started getting weird. Tehila Kramer and Avigayil Fishman greeted me like they always did, but there was something more to it — a shared glance, a spark of pity, a softening around the eyes. Even after I got the same looks from Rachel Landry and Michal Elyon, I convinced myself that I was imagining things. But when Riva Winters came down the hall and gave me a big, tender hug, I couldn't pretend anymore.

"Rikki," she purred. "I'm so sorry about your mother. I'll be davening for her, okay? And if you need anything, or if you just want to talk, I'm here for you."

I disentangled myself from her arms and pulled back, my shock making speech impossible. My friends were all looking at me, waiting for a reaction. I ignored Riva and continued walking forward, not knowing where I was headed anymore. Through the haze of girls I saw Kayla wearing an unsettled expression on her face and I made a beeline for her. She put a hand on my arm and guided me into the library without saying a word. Once inside, she took a deep breath and let it out slowly.

"Don't freak out…but Mrs. Chase made an announcement about you this morning."

"What?"

"I don't know how she knows, and I don't know why she said something, but she was like, 'You girls might not know this, but Rikki Coleman's mother is really sick and has been in the hospital for a while. So keep the family in your *tefillos* and make sure to give Rikki a bit of extra support or a hug and let her know you're there for her.' Rikki, listen, she made it sound like your mother has cancer or something."

That didn't make me feel better. I felt sickened by Riva's hug and wanted nothing more than to leave the school premises immediately. Mrs. Chase's well-intentioned announcement was over the top, and all the positive feelings I'd cultivated over the weekend were gone.

"What am I supposed to do?" I asked desperately. I sat down at a library table and dropped my forehead into my hands. "I hate Riva."

"What?"

"Nothing. I have to tell Daniella. She's going to go crazy."

"Oh, yeah…about that…"

I jerked upright. "What?"

"I heard she's in Rabbi Sacks's office already."

I groaned and shoved back from the table. "I'm going to her."

Kayla glanced out the window into the emptying hallway. "Just wait a few minutes, then you won't run into anyone you don't want to see." She reached out and hugged me tightly, then left.

I stood in the shadow of the door and watched the last few girls disappear into their classrooms, before taking a deep breath and starting toward the office.

I tried shutting my brain off, but it was whirring wildly, attempting to process a dozen thoughts at once. The fact that a random teacher, who only taught me once a week, felt it necessary to share the news with her class stunned me. Why? Were things not complicated enough? Was it necessary to add this burden of exposure and unwanted hugs?

I was grateful that anger made my eyes dry. I wasn't going to cry about this because I'd shed enough tears for a lifetime and didn't have any more to spare. I had no idea what to expect when I found Daniella, but I imagined it wouldn't be pretty; as much as my sister was hard to read, I knew she'd nearly reached her limit.

I had the misfortune of passing Ms. Palmer in the hallway. She tried talking to me about a practice schedule but I blew her off with a made-up excuse and continued walking even after she gave me a strange look. Once in the office, I considered breezing past the secretary and marching straight into Rabbi Sacks's office, but my inner voice of reason told me it wasn't necessary to make a scene.

"Is my sister in there?" I asked her.

She nodded. "Does Rabbi Sacks want to see you too?"

And there was my opening. Without actually lying about it, I indicated that yes, he did want to see me, and no, I did not need her to escort me down the hall to his office. I knocked on his door and pretended that my stomach hadn't just tied itself in knots while I waited for it to open.

The scene was oddly reminiscent of one I'd witnessed several weeks earlier, when Daniella's eye was blackened and I'd clawed my own neck. Mrs. Landau, Mrs. Moskowitz, and Mrs. Zilber sat in various chairs while Daniella stood against the far wall, one foot propped up so that she was leaning back against it, her arms crossed over her chest. Mrs. Romanoff, the twelfth-grade guidance counselor, had opened the door.

Both Mrs. Moskowitz and Mrs. Zilber said something to me, but I didn't hear them. I went straight to Daniella and whispered, "I need to talk to you. Now."

She looked at me with deadened eyes, void of emotion, yet different than her usual simulated calmness. Something was very wrong. Finally turning to the adults in the room, I asked, "What happened?"

"Rikki, sit," Mrs. Zilber said, tapping the chair next to her. "That's what we're trying to figure out."

I didn't sit, but I did focus on her. "I don't get it. Is she in trouble?"

Mrs. Zilber glanced at Daniella awkwardly. "In a sense, yes.

Daniella's been in trouble a lot lately, and to be honest, so have you, with your grades and classroom attendance." That couldn't be what this was about. Daniella wouldn't have had a murderous expression on her face if this was about her GPA.

"Okay, so what's going to happen to us?" I didn't care in the slightest, but I needed to get us out of there so Daniella could help me figure out how we'd show our faces now that everyone knew our mother was in the hospital.

"Well, there's more to it. I know you've been talking to Mrs. Moskowitz, and also to me, and Daniella has been talking a bit to Mrs. Romanoff. It seems that as a team, we've missed a lot of opportunities to help you girls."

My brain had slowed down because it sensed trouble. Daniella was talking to Mrs. Romanoff? That was news to me. And why were our teachers talking as a team about us? It wasn't supposed to be like that. Mrs. Moskowitz was supposed to be keeping everything I told her private. "I don't get it."

"Do you remember how I told you there were certain things I couldn't keep confidential?" Mrs. Moskowitz asked.

"You said you'd tell me if you needed to tell someone. You never said anything."

"I know. I haven't said anything, yet," she said quickly. "But it's reached a point where it's impossible to keep things quiet any longer."

"Why?" I heard my voice rise slightly, and I forced it back down. "Why does it matter now? There's nothing to tell anyone."

The teachers exchanged glances with each other, silently communicating, and I felt heat spreading through my body.

"Can you just tell her already?" Daniella's voice was acidic. She had addressed the question toward the adults, but she was looking straight at me. When none of them responded, she shot them a vicious glare and then spoke directly to me. "They're calling Abba and telling him everything you wrote in your journal." She waited a beat to let it sink in, and then she added, "And he needs to take me to a psychiatrist because they think I'm crazy."

"Daniella." Mrs. Romanoff's voice was exasperated. "We've been through this. No one thinks you're crazy. You just need help."

"For what?" My whole body seemed to have splintered off in several directions. My mind was having a hard time communicating to my lungs that they were supposed to be bringing in air, and I was feeling lightheaded. Then my brain caught up to my mouth and I whirled on Mrs. Moskowitz. "You can't do that. You can't tell my father." Backtracking, I turned to Daniella. "Why do you need a psychiatrist?" Questions were flooding my brain, along with protests and the distinct urge to scream at someone, but I pressed my lips together and waited for someone to say something.

"Rikki, we've talked about this," Mrs. Moskowitz said soothingly. "You and Daniella both need help, but the first thing that needs to happen is your father becoming aware of what the issues are." Daniella's composure was slipping. I could see the anger etched into her face, the rage nearly visible beneath her skin. I glanced at her hands, and sure enough her fingers were shaking. Mrs. Moskowitz continued, keeping an eye on my sister as she spoke. "Daniella has been so busy taking care of you and your brother that she isn't taking care of herself." Seeing the confusion on my face, she explained. "Sometimes it's hard to notice this with people we see all the time, but Daniella has lost a lot of weight in the past few months."

I stared at my sister, and everything took on a new light. Her trembling fingers weren't just slim, they were skeletal. Her cheekbones weren't prominent, they were protruding. I knew that her sweatshirt hid a shrinking frame and yet I'd somehow missed it, so wrapped up in my own problems. I felt the distinct burn of shame swell in my chest at the realization that I'd neglected my own sister.

"I'll make sure she eats," I said weakly. "I'll take better care of her. It's not a big deal, we've just been stressed-out." No one responded. They all watched, with sorrowful eyes, as I tried digging myself out of the situation.

"Forget it, Rikki. It doesn't matter." Daniella's response was unexpected.

I turned to her. "It does matter. I only wrote in that stupid journal because I was trying to get better and I thought she was going to help me." I glared at Mrs. Moskowitz briefly before I continued. "Mrs. Chase told her class this morning that everyone needs to be nice to me because my mother's in the hospital."

"What?" Mrs. Moskowitz and Mrs. Zilber spoke at the same time. Daniella's eyes widened slightly.

I turned to my two teachers. "One of you probably told her. There's no such thing as confidentiality. I should never have believed that."

They were both shaking their heads, but Daniella spoke first. "It wasn't them. And it's not just Mrs. Chase who knows. Half my grade is talking about it."

My vision was blurring. "You can't tell our father." I needed to get it all out before I completely blacked out. "Please don't talk to him, he can't handle this right now. You need to let him take care of my mother. Me and Daniella, we'll take care of ourselves. Just give us another chance." I wondered if I was having a panic attack because all of the sudden the air in the room seemed to have disappeared and my lungs were screaming.

I turned to Mrs. Moskowitz. "I'll keep talking to you. I'll fix the nightmares. I'm fine, okay?"

"It's not that simple, Rikki." When Mrs. Romanoff spoke to me, I wanted to scream at her. She didn't even know me. She had no right to even be there.

"Why?" I kept feeling like I was missing something. Daniella's long silences were getting to me and it seemed as though everyone's voices were being distorted by the chaos in my brain.

"Rikki, sit." Mrs. Zilber took my arm and gently pulled me down into the chair next to her.

I turned to her and asked desperately, "Why are we talking about calling my father? I'm doing fine. I'm talking to Mrs. Moskowitz and to you. I'm getting better. The nightmares have stopped."

"Will you stop saying that?" Daniella exploded. She shoved off the wall with her foot and came over to where I sat, crouching on the floor in front of me. "Stop saying you're fine. I'm so sick of you pretending you're doing better than me because you can talk about what happened in the past."

I stared at her in disbelief. "What?"

"What about now, Rikki? What about what you do right now?" She grasped my wrists, tightening her grip when I tried to pull back. "Do you talk about *this*?" She turned my palms face up. "Did you tell them about this?"

I pulled out of her grasp so hard that I nearly knocked my chair over. "Don't do this," I whispered. Fear coursed through me, shattering any hope of making it out of the office with any shred of our facade still intact. I didn't know why Daniella was doing this, but I knew where she was going.

I was vaguely aware of our teachers moving in toward us, but I couldn't tear my gaze away from her. She was still crouched on the floor, frozen in time while she looked at — no, through — me.

"Daniella." Her name caught in my throat. "Danz, if you tell them, I can't—"

She laughed. "That's what you call being 'fine'?" She turned to look at Mrs. Moskowitz. "Rikki is not fine. I don't know why you couldn't figure that out yourself, but she's going to end up hurting herself really badly."

"What do you mean?" Mrs. Moskowitz was watching me.

"Daniella, stop!" I was torn between begging her not to tell them what I already knew she was going to say, and the desire to escape from it all.

Before I even had time to decide, she made her move. Staring me straight in the eye, Daniella said clearly, "She's playing with fire."

28

There was an awkward silence. My world turned into a slow-motion haze as I watched the adults try to process what Daniella had said.

"Wait," Mrs. Romanoff said finally. "Do you mean that literally?"

Daniella didn't respond, and slow realization started creeping into their faces. Before anyone said anything else, my lungs caved in and I was doubled over, gasping for breath, as terror and grief seared through me. Instantly, Daniella, of all people, was at my side.

"Breathe, Rikki. Just breathe in slowly." She put one hand gently on my back as she spoke.

I shoved her away. "Don't touch me." Mrs. Moskowitz replaced her and coached me until my breathing was semi-steady.

The room was heavy with silence. I forced myself to speak. "It's not true. I did it one time. I just lit a match because I was bored. It's not anything."

Daniella was furious. "Rikki, give it up." Her voice rose in exasperation. "It doesn't matter anymore, don't you get it? There's no point in keeping secrets anymore."

I saw my opportunity for revenge. "So you told them about your flashbacks? And sneaking out at night all the time? And the medications?"

"What?" Four people asked that question at the same time.

It was the perfect opportunity to get out of the spotlight. "She takes my mother's old medications. She just messes around with them and takes whatever she feels like. It's all prescription stuff and she's never even seen a psychiatrist."

Daniella didn't flinch. "So what? At least I'm not going to accidentally light myself on fire one day." She turned to take in the horrified looks of the teachers. "Chill. I'm not overdosing or anything. I'm just trying to keep things normal, okay? I have a lot to deal with."

Mrs. Moskowitz tried to get things under control. "Okay, girls. Both of you, settle down. This isn't the time for you to be turning on each other. We understand there's a lot going on, and that's why you need help."

Mrs. Zilber stood. "I'm going to see if your father is here yet. I think there's a lot that needs to be discussed."

"He's here?" The color drained from Daniella's face. "You already called him?" She looked at Mrs. Romanoff, her face registering the shock of betrayal. "You're all liars." She was backing away from Mrs. Romanoff, who had put a hand out toward her. "You all lied to both of us. You got us to trust you and now you're going to ruin all that by telling him everything?"

Mrs. Romanoff stared back at her. "Daniella, your behavior is increasingly high-risk. If we let this go, one of you will end up getting badly hurt. You've done the best you can acting as a parent for Rikki, but it's not enough. I know your father is preoccupied, but you're his daughters, and from talking to him on the phone, I know you're a top priority for him."

"You don't know anything." Daniella's face had turned to stone. "Don't act like you know anything about either of us." She turned to me. "Don't say anything to him."

Mrs. Zilber called her on that. "Why would you get mad at Rikki for hiding things from us, and then tell her to hide things from your father?"

Daniella's eyes were blazing and I thought I saw a glimmer of fear. "Because you don't have a wife in the hospital. You're paid to be a *mechaneches* for her and Mrs. Moskowitz is paid to be a guidance counselor. So that's why she should talk to you. But my father? My father can't handle anything. My father can barely handle himself."

"Your father," Mrs. Landau said, glancing at her BlackBerry, "is here."

29

That was the last thing that anyone said before Daniella totally lost it. I saw her look at the office door with a combination of fear, anger, and the unadulterated need to escape. I was intimately familiar with that need, but I knew our little showdown had just exacerbated that feeling beyond what she could handle.

I wouldn't find out until later what had led up to that meeting. Daniella, after realizing the news of our mother's predicament was spreading like wildfire, had attempted to leave the school premises. On her way out of the building she was stopped by Rabbi Sacks, who lectured her for wearing a nonschool sweatshirt and having blue nails. After Daniella delivered a few choice words, Rabbi Sacks said he was suspending her.

Once in the office, threats to call my father started to abound. Daniella had asked to speak to Mrs. Romanoff alone, and asked her if she'd make sure Uri and I were taken care of if anything ever happened to her. That made Mrs. Romanoff call in Mrs. Landau and Mrs. Moskowitz, who, in turn, called Mrs. Zilber because she knew of our relationship. The four of them had grilled Daniella until I came along.

Now here we were, with my father somewhere outside the office door, and the look on Daniella's face telling me she felt she had nothing to lose. On any other day, she would've stayed to face him; she would've argued and yelled and lived up to her reputation of having an "attitude problem." But today, she had nothing left to give. I saw her glance at the windows behind Rabbi Sacks's desk, but they were for show, and had no opening.

That didn't stop her. Daniella grabbed a paperweight from his desk and slammed it straight into the center pane; rivers of glass came cascading down on her. Before any of us could react, my sister was climbing through the broken window, ignoring the shards that cut into her arms.

And then everyone reacted at once. Mrs. Romanoff and Mrs. Moskowitz were out the door, sprinting after Daniella. She was headed across the parking lot, toward our car. I edged toward the window, unwilling to face my father on my own.

Mrs. Zilber grabbed my arm, preventing me from escaping. "Get him out of the office," she hissed at Mrs. Landau.

I watched Daniella from the window. She'd reached our car, but was fumbling in her knapsack for the keys. Mrs. Romanoff reached her first and pulled the bag from her hands. Daniella started struggling, trying to get away from them, but they put their arms around her and kept her there. I could see she was putting up a fight. I could only imagine what she had to be feeling for her to lose control in that way. I turned away, unable to watch anymore.

Still holding on to me, Mrs. Zilber led me outside and we crossed the parking lot. As we got closer, I could hear Daniella crying. I'd never seen her cry like that in my life. If Mrs. Moskowitz and Mrs.

Romanoff hadn't been holding her, she would've splintered apart, wracked by grief and crippling emotional pain.

I was crying as well, but I felt disconnected from my body. Mrs. Zilber pulled me close and wrapped her arms around me. "It's okay," she whispered. "It's going to be okay now."

"It's true." My voice was muffled by her shirt and by the tears that now seemed to be choking me. "I play with matches. I light things on fire. I do it when I'm stressed. I don't know why." I was tripping over my own words, trying to spit them out before I lost the nerve. "And I still get nightmares. They're still really bad. I lied about them being gone."

She hugged me tighter. "Shhh…I know, Rikki. I know."

Daniella was inconsolable. She kept pleading with them to let her go and Mrs. Moskowitz kept saying she wasn't safe and needed to calm down before they would take their hands off. Daniella was bleeding from where the glass had cut her arms but she didn't even notice.

I thought of all the nights where she'd woken up to me in a panic, how she'd managed to cut through my terror even though I felt completely unreachable. Mrs. Zilber followed me closely as I approached Daniella. I moved cautiously in front of her, knowing how overpowering these moments could be. The last thing she needed was extra guilt about punching me in the face.

"Danz…" I checked to see if she'd look at me. She was wild-eyed and I had no doubt that she couldn't handle the magnitude of her emotions. She made brief eye contact but I knew she didn't want to see me. I represented the hurt and pain, but at the same time I was the only one who understood its depth. "Danz, listen. We'll be okay. They're…going to help us."

She was moving restlessly still, straining against Mrs. Romanoff and Mrs. Moskowitz.

"I'm sorry I lied." I spoke quickly, wanting to get the words out before she could decide to tune me out. "I won't do that anymore. I'll tell them the whole truth and I'll get help so you won't have to worry about me anymore. You need to focus more on you, so that you can be happy." She was listening. She didn't want to, but she couldn't escape. "I'm sorry I told them that stuff about you, but I'm scared because you have no one to look out for you. We need help and we can get it."

Daniella was quieter now, no longer struggling. Tears still streamed down her face and her body was racked with sobs. When I wrapped my arms around her, she melted against me. I held her tightly and soaked up her grief, wanting to take it from her, to stop her from breaking apart.

It could've been five minutes, and it could've been an hour that we stood there, Daniella held steady against the side of our car by our two teachers, while I held her and waited for the pain to relinquish its hold.

Mrs. Moskowitz brushed Daniella's hair back from her face. "Daniella, I'm going to take you to the hospital to get your arms checked out. I think you might need stitches. Rikki, I want you to come too."

"Why? I'm fine."

She glanced sideways at Daniella. "I think you should stick with Daniella for now."

Mrs. Landau appeared next to us, taking in the scene. "Is she okay?" she asked quietly to no one in particular. Turning to me, she asked, "Can you talk to your father? He's really worried."

I looked to Daniella for the answer but got nothing. Her expression was vacant; only her exhaustion was visible. "For five minutes," I said. "Then I'm going to the hospital with her."

Mrs. Zilber walked back with me into the school. The secretary stared at me as I walked past, and I looked down, self-conscious, noticing I had streaks of blood across my shirt. My father was waiting in Rabbi Sacks's office, leaning forward in his chair, chin resting on his fingertips. He jumped up when he saw me. I moved back, knocking into Mrs. Zilber in my haste to make sure he didn't try to hug me.

"Rikki, are you okay? Is Daniella all right? What happened?" He looked concerned and confused and I wanted to hate him, but instead I felt sorry for him.

"We are not okay. And we haven't been okay for a while." I spoke quietly, calmed by Mrs. Zilber's hand on my back. "You don't even know what's going on with us because you're never home. You only care about Ima."

"What? Rikki, that's not true." The worst part was that he believed it.

"You always say that," I said tiredly. "But nothing ever changes. You're just not there for us." I jerked a thumb back toward Mrs. Zilber. "She knows more about what's going on. So does my guidance counselor. They've been trying to help me. You never even see me."

"Rikki, I'm sorry—"

"Don't apologize." I started to turn away. "Just change things. Just make it better." I was halfway out the door when I remembered something. "And you have to pick Uri up from school today. I'm going with Daniella to the hospital."

30

We rode to the hospital in Mrs. Moskowitz's car. I sat in the backseat with Daniella, not letting go of her hand until we turned into the driveway of the emergency department. When she stepped out of the car, her legs buckled and she crumbled to the ground, pressing one hand against her eyes. "It's getting black at the edge," she mumbled.

The hospital staff brought out a wheelchair and took Daniella inside, quizzing me on her date of birth, medical conditions, and allergies as we walked. They slapped a hospital bracelet on her and told us to wait. Mrs. Moskowitz went to the front desk and spoke to them quietly. A few minutes later, a nurse came over and asked for my arm, holding out a hospital bracelet with my name printed in blue block letters.

I looked at Mrs. Moskowitz and she bit her lip. "I'm sorry, Rikki. I want you to get evaluated by a doctor too."

"Why?"

"I need to know you're safe. The fire setting is serious, and I know you'd never do anything to hurt yourself on purpose, but I need to be sure." She gave me a half smile. "Just consider it something I need to do as a liability if I want to keep my job." When I didn't move, she added, "And this way, they'll let you stay with Daniella."

I stuck out my arm.

Daniella wasn't speaking. Mrs. Moskowitz bought an orange juice from the vending machine and forced her to drink it. When the nurse came to get her vital signs, she stood shakily from the wheelchair and followed her to the back.

When the nurse called me in, I considered refusing, but then remembered that I needed to stick with Daniella. So I slowly followed her to a partitioned area filled with a small exam table and medical equipment. The nurse's name was Annabelle and she talked very slowly. I kept answering her questions before she was finished asking them, but when she asked why I was there, I fell silent. Mrs. Moskowitz answered for me, explaining about my fire setting and aggressive nightmares, and overall making me sound like I was in danger of causing some serious harm. I resented it, but kept quiet.

Annabelle slid my sleeve up my arm and placed the blood pressure cuff on me. She took note of the stain on my shirt. "Where're you bleeding from, honey?"

"It's not mine," I said quickly. She made me roll up my other sleeve as well and she checked my arms, front and back, to make sure I wasn't lying. I heard a nurse talking to Daniella in one exam room over.

"Are you having thoughts of wanting to hurt yourself?"
"Maybe. I guess."
"Do you have a plan for how you would do it?"
"My mom has a lot of prescription pills at home."
"Do you think you'd actually take them?"

"I won't take them if I don't go home. So I'm not going home."

I was overcome by nausea. Annabelle had two fingers of her hand pressed against my wrist, taking my pulse.

"Whoa, honey. Are you okay? You just spiked."

"My sister," I said, gesturing toward the other room. "They can't let her go home. Something will happen if she does."

Annabelle stepped into the hallway. When she returned, she said, "Don't worry about her, doll. They'll take real good care of her." She began writing down my vitals on a piece of paper while I fidgeted on the table. "You look just like her, you know that?" I nodded. "Honey, tell me something. Why is your sister so dead set on not going home?"

I shook my head. "It's nothing like that. My father isn't abusing us. It's the opposite…he's never there." She was watching me skeptically. "Look, it's a long story. She hates him, but not because he did anything to her. My mother did. She was awful to both of us, but now she's in the hospital, and it's like my father took her side."

"You sure about that?" Annabelle was finished with her paperwork and was watching me carefully. I could see she was trained in this, an expert at picking up telltale signs of abuse. I wished I'd met her ten years before.

"Yeah, I'm sure. We're already past that part."

I met Mrs. Moskowitz back in the waiting room. She was finishing up a phone call and I waited restlessly until she hung up. "What am I supposed to do about Daniella?" I asked anxiously. "She can't go home tonight. She'll lose it again if she has to face my father."

"I know." Mrs. Moskowitz looked down at her phone. "I'm working on that." She slid her phone into her pocket and turned to me with a serious expression. "Rikki, they probably won't keep you here tonight. I meant what I said about having them assess you as a formality. And I don't know yet if they'll keep Daniella.

In any case, I don't think you should stay at home tonight. Things seem kind of tense with your father and I would hate for the situation to escalate."

My stomach was doing that clenching thing again. "What about Uri? He won't want to stay home with my father."

She was nodding. "I know. I talked to your father a little while ago. Uri's at a friend and your father gave me permission to decide about you two tonight. Mrs. Zilber has a room for you. It'll just be a one-night thing until we can figure out something more permanent."

I struggled to process what she was saying, but gave up halfway through. I slouched down in my chair, flipping the hood of my jacket over my head. "It doesn't matter."

I met with a psychiatric resident, who wrote me up a recommendation for individual therapy to address the fire setting. He spent fifteen minutes scaring me with stories of teens who'd been charged with arson after they'd accidentally set fires while playing with matches. When he was finished, I pulled off my hospital bracelet and tossed it into the nearest trash can.

The ER doctor decided to keep Daniella for observation overnight, partially because of her ambiguous statements regarding her personal safety and the fact that her blood pressure dropped every time she stood, causing her to black out. "It's probably just a combination of over-exhaustion, stress, and dehydration, but it's best to play it safe. If she's stable tonight, I'll discharge her tomorrow morning."

I went to say good-bye to Daniella, who was curled up in a hospital bed, the blankets wrapped tightly around her. An IV snaked out from under the covers and traveled up toward a bag of fluid. Her eyes were half-closed, and at first I thought she was sleeping, but then she spoke. "Where are you going?"

I filled her in on my conversation with Mrs. Moskowitz. "You'll be out tomorrow and then we'll figure out what we're going to do." Glancing over my shoulder to see if anyone was listening, I bent down toward her. "Promise me you won't do anything stupid."

A ghost of a smile played across her lips. "Who, me?"

"No, I mean it," I said urgently. "Promise me you won't hurt yourself and you won't try to run."

"I promise," she whispered. She reached out with a shaky hand, moving carefully not to disrupt the wires and tubes, and grasped my arm. "And promise me something."

I leaned closer, waiting.

"Promise you won't let today change anything. Everything I said and did…I don't want it to change things. Like, don't judge me…" Her voice trailed off.

Navigating carefully, I hugged her as tight as I dared. "I love you. Nothing about today matters except that we can be honest now. With each other, and with Mrs. Moskowitz, Mrs. Romanoff, and Mrs. Zilber. I think they'll help us." I pulled back and looked her straight in the eye. "If I was judging you, it would be in a good way, because today you finally did the right thing for both of us."

She raised an eyebrow ironically. "Now that's a nice way of looking at it." Smiling, I kissed her forehead, and left the room.

It was after nine o'clock at night when we left the hospital. We hadn't been able to leave for hours because they'd needed a signature from my father in order to keep Daniella overnight. Daniella had nearly panicked when she heard my father was coming, but after being assured repeatedly by Mrs. Moskowitz and the nursing staff that she didn't have to talk to him or even see him, she had calmed down. When he arrived, I watched the nurses watch him with suspicion. They were jumping to conclusions as to why Daniella refused to see him and it bothered me.

"He's not a child abuser," I said irritably to Mrs. Moskowitz.

"No, but he's married to one."

I had refused to speak to her for a half hour after that, not so much upset at the bluntness of her words, but confused as to why they sounded so true. She'd taken the opportunity of my stubborn silence to educate me on the dynamics of abusive families.

I recoiled at the word, so eventually she started replacing "abusive" with "dysfunctional," which was a lot more tolerable. When I finally decided to speak, I said, "I don't care if he was an abuser or if he allowed abuse to happen, I just don't want anything to do with him right now."

That's when she started telling me about the concept of a respite home. "It's someone who's like a foster parent, but just has kids come live with them short-term while things get worked out in their own homes. We have a few *frum* families in town who have respite homes for situations like that."

"You want us to go live with some random family?" Now that I was separated from Daniella, I felt her absence like a missing lung, not quite able to breathe without her. I was lost, not knowing what to say and what to feel.

"The other option is for you to stay with relatives for a while. Don't you have a cousin in ninth grade?"

"No. No way," I said quickly, wincing at the thought. "We lied so much to my aunt, she'll never take us. And I can't deal with my cousins."

"I was thinking that you and Daniella might do well in a home without any kids. There's this woman I know, she's widowed and all her kids are grown — I think she'd be ideal. I know other kids who've stayed there and it's the perfect place to be if you need peace and quiet. I think that's exactly what you and Daniella need right now."

"I don't know." It was definitely surreal, to be sitting in my guidance counselor's car, on the way back from the emergency room, talking about moving into a quasi-foster home. "My father will let?"

She shrugged. "It sure sounded like it tonight." She sighed. "Rikki, your father isn't a bad person or a bad parent. I don't want you to think we're trying to say he is. He's doing the best he can while being married to a woman with a severe mental illness. But it's just not enough for you and Daniella." She turned on to Mrs. Zilber's street. "I think if you and Daniella try to deal with everything that's been building up while you're still living in the place where it all happened…"

"It won't work," I finished for her. "We hate it at home. That's why Daniella was leaving every night. And I only stayed for Uri."

We pulled into Mrs. Zilber's driveway and Mrs. Moskowitz killed the engine. "Rikki, thank you for trusting me today. I know you were upset that we were talking with each other to try and figure out how to help you, and I hope that won't change our relationship in the future, because I'm looking forward to seeing the progress you make over the next few weeks."

"Thanks for your help today," I said awkwardly. "Sorry I got mad at you. I know you really didn't break confidentiality. I just got freaked out."

She smiled. "Yes, there was definitely some 'freaking out' going on today, but this was pretty much as bad as it gets. The only way to go from here is up." She opened her car door and stepped out. "Come on, let's go get you into bed."

31

Mrs. Moskowitz passed me off to Mrs. Zilber, who greeted us at the front door.

"How are you holding up?" she asked as I stepped inside.

I shrugged my coat off and was hit with a wave of exhaustion. "I think if I could have a shower and a bed, I'll be okay."

They both laughed, even though I was being totally serious. Mrs. Moskowitz put a gentle hand on my shoulder. "I'll be in touch with you tomorrow, Rikki. I hope you sleep well."

My eyes widened in panic. "Wait…I can't stay here." Mrs. Zilber looked at me quizzically. "I can't sleep without Daniella. I'll get crazy nightmares, I'll wake up the whole house. I can't stay."

Mrs. Zilber waved Mrs. Moskowitz on. "I'll deal with this." She steered me softly toward the kitchen. "Let me show you were you'll be sleeping." When I started to protest, she continued speaking. "Yes, you'll be sleeping here, and if you wake up from a nightmare, we'll deal with it."

In the guest bedroom in the basement, there was a shopping bag in the center of the bed. "Your father dropped off some clothes for you. If he forgot anything, just let me know and I'll get you what you need." I looked inside the bag and felt oddly pleased to see that he'd accidentally packed Daniella's pajamas instead of mine.

I sat gingerly at the edge of the bed, fingering the fabric of the thick comforter. "I'm serious. I can't sleep without her." Fatigue was tugging at my eyelids, but fear of causing a scene in the middle of the night prevented me from giving in to it.

"What's the worst thing that can happen?" Mrs. Zilber asked reasonably. "We'll all wake up? That's fine. We'll go back to sleep." She watched me struggle to keep my eyes open. "Get some sleep, Rikki. You can shower in the morning." She headed toward the door and paused to look back at me. "Call me on my cell if you need anything. Just try to relax, okay?"

It was easy for her to say. I didn't bother telling her that my cell phone was still in my locker at school so I couldn't have called her if I'd wanted to. She'd done enough for one day and I'd deal with this night on my own. I would've skipped a shower if I my skin hadn't been crawling with the grimy feel of a hospital emergency room. I nodded off at least twice while standing under the hot spray, and when I finally dragged myself into bed, I fell asleep without even having time to worry.

When I opened my eyes again, I was looking into the face of a small girl. She looked about four years old and was peering at me with undisguised interest. When she saw that I was awake, she smiled bashfully. "My mommy said you should come upstairs for breakfast."

I smiled back at her, my mind still hazy with sleep. I'd made it through the night. For one split second, I wondered if I'd woken up screaming and just didn't remember it, but I decided that was unlikely. I forced myself to sit up in bed. "Do you know what time it is?"

She disappeared for a minute and then returned. "The clock says seven-four-two." She grinned proudly, as if she'd just figured out some complicated mathematical equation. Then she edged toward the door. "Are you up for sure? My mommy said to make sure I woke you up for real and that you didn't fall back asleep."

She was so cute, I felt a sudden pang of absence as Uri's face flashed in my mind.

"I'm up for real," I assured her. Thinking about Uri had wiped away the sleepiness, and the steady thrum of stress was now coursing through my veins. "I'll be there in five minutes."

My father hadn't packed my hair straightener or my makeup, so all I could do was wash my face, put on my uniform, and pull my hair into a ponytail. I refused to look in the mirror before I went upstairs, for once not caring about how I looked to anyone else.

"Good morning," Mrs. Zilber greeted me, looking wide awake as she poured a bowl of Cheerios for her younger daughter.

I tried to smile at her, I really did, but it fell flat. "Hi."

She offered me cereal, toast, oatmeal, pancakes, eggs, and French toast. I passed on all of them and asked for coffee, but she said I couldn't have coffee unless I ate something first. Sitting at the table, I crossed my arms and rested my head on them, not sure I could deal with such a monumental decision that early in the morning. Her daughter, finished with her cereal, walked over tentatively and leaned against the side of my chair, smiling sweetly up at me. "I'm three," she said proudly.

I smiled at her. "You're cute." I turned to Mrs. Zilber. "Your daughters look so much alike. Do people ask you if they're twins?"

"All the time." She set a cereal bowl and spoon in front of me, and then brought over three cereal boxes. "Choose one. People probably ask you and Daniella that pretty often, don't they?"

At the mention of Daniella's name, I fought the urge to sweep the bowl and cereal straight off the table. "Sometimes. Can I see her? Do you know if she's okay?"

"Eat, Rikki. You need to keep yourself healthy." She stared me down until I picked up a box of Crispix and poured about eight pieces of cereal into the bowl. Sighing, she reached over and took the box, filling my bowl halfway. I pouted, but eventually poured some milk and started eating. When I was halfway through, Mrs. Zilber brought me a mug of coffee as a peace offering.

"Thanks."

"Daniella's fine," she said, returning to my previous question. "She's being discharged at eight. Mrs. Moskowitz will pick her up and take her to school."

I nearly choked on my coffee. "She's going to school? After yesterday?"

Mrs. Zilber handed me a napkin. "Not to class. We have a meeting scheduled today, for you, Daniella, and your father. We have to figure out how to move forward and decide what the best setup for you girls is."

"Mrs. Moskowitz said maybe we could stay with someone else until things calm down."

Mrs. Zilber nodded. "I heard. But your father needs to be on board. Plus, we need to figure out exactly what we want to happen over the next few weeks while you girls are out of the house. We don't want to waste an opportunity to get you girls help."

I stared into my coffee mug, wishing it held some answers because I had none. "How does everything change so fast?" I asked quietly. "I just want the world to slow down for a minute, so I can catch my breath."

Her smile was sympathetic, but she didn't say anything. Because Mrs. Zilber, just like me, had no answers.

32

When we pulled up to the school, my heart started pounding. Mrs. Zilber glanced at me sideways and asked if I needed help. "Is Daniella here?" I gasped through clenched teeth. She looked around the parking lot and shook her head.

A knock at my window had me nearly strangled in my seat belt, and I wasn't much calmer when I saw Kayla standing there. I panicked. "What am I supposed to do?"

"Do you want to talk to her?"

"I don't know…yes. No. Maybe."

Kayla was looking at me in confusion. Unable to stand it any longer, I cracked the car door open. "Are you okay? I've been going crazy trying to figure out where you were. Your father said Daniella was in the hospital but he wouldn't say where you were. What's going on?" She looked past me at Mrs. Zilber and gave her a small nod. "Rikki, I don't get it. Is it your mother?"

I needed several hours to fill Kayla in on everything. There was no way I could package the events of the last twenty-four hours into a concise answer that would satisfy her. "Sort of. We're going through stuff, and everything is just crazy now."

She looked unsatisfied. "I don't understand."

"I don't either. I want to talk to you about it." When I said that, I realized how much it was true. Suddenly, I wondered if Kayla knew more than she let on about the events in our home. We'd been neighbors for eight years and a lot of heartache had happened during that time. I knew she was familiar with my mother's dramatic mood swings, but I didn't know what she knew about her way of treating Daniella and me. "Can you call me later? Right after school. It's really important."

"Of course." She reached out and squeezed my hand, then turned to walk away. She paused mid-step and turned back. "Daniella…is she in a regular hospital? Or…"

"Daniella's not in any hospital," Daniella said smoothly, walking up next to Kayla. Mrs. Moskowitz followed closely behind. She looked thin and tired, but not nearly as fragile as she'd seemed when I'd seen her last.

I couldn't help myself. I started grinning and climbed out of the car to hug her. She hugged me tightly and then reached out and hugged Kayla too. Kayla stiffened in surprise, but didn't say anything.

"That's for leaving you stranded at school yesterday and not giving you a ride this morning," she explained. "Sorry about that." Kayla softened and Daniella continued. "And I was in the ER, not the psych ward, so don't get any funny ideas."

Kayla shook her head. "I've got no ideas at all. What happened?"

Daniella pulled up her sleeve and held out her arm, which was wrapped in white gauze. "Twelve stitches happened. I broke some glass."

Mrs. Zilber interrupted. "Kayla, I think we both need to get to class."

"Can she bring me my cell phone?" I asked, feeling disconnected without it.

Mrs. Zilber hesitated and then nodded. "She'll bring it to you in the office." She looked at Daniella and then back at me. "Good luck."

I saw my father's car pull into the school parking lot and I felt the anxiety stirring. As soon as Mrs. Zilber and Kayla were out of earshot, I turned to Mrs. Moskowitz. "I don't know what to say at this meeting. What's going to happen?"

Daniella turned too and when she saw my father's car, her composure slipped and I saw a glimpse of the hopelessness from the previous day. "I don't know if this is a good idea." She bit her lip and turned to Mrs. Moskowitz. "Maybe I shouldn't be there. I always get mad at him and say things I shouldn't."

Mrs. Moskowitz motioned for us to follow her toward the school building. "You'll both be fine. Just let me take the lead in this meeting and it'll all make sense. Daniella, I'm trusting you to be respectful. I don't think that's too much to ask for."

We entered the school building. The first bell had already rung but there were a few girls still straggling through the hallways. I kept my eyes on the floor, not wanting to see any of my friends. "I don't want to do this," I whispered to Daniella. She, too, hadn't had access to a hair iron or makeup that morning. Her tangled hair was pulled back into a messy bun and her eyes were bloodshot and swollen. Aside from the bandage on her arm, she had a piece of gauze taped over her hand where the IV had been inserted.

"Me neither." She was looking around warily, sneaking glances over her shoulder, as if she were being hunted. "You think she'll tell him everything she knows?"

Mrs. Moskowitz was unlocking the door of the conference room. I knew that at any minute, my father would walk through the front doors of the building and I felt entirely unprepared. "Does confidentiality count for anything now?" I asked her.

She looked surprised. "Of course it does. That's why I'm hoping you'll speak for yourself today. That way I won't have any issue with breaking it." At the look on my face, she added, "Or you could just tell me right now that you give me permission to share the things you've told me with your father."

Between a rock and a hard place. That phrase had never seemed so real to me as it did now. Either she'd pressure me to say aloud the things I'd only written, or she'd have the freedom to divulge my secrets.

The main doors to the school opened and my father walked inside along with Rabbi Sacks. My father was looking at my principal as he spoke, and didn't see us right away. Daniella was quietly freaking out, fingering the bandage on her arm nervously and moving backward. Mrs. Moskowitz shoved the door open and ushered us inside.

"Look, I want to explain something to you before this meeting gets started." She shrugged out of her coat and draped it over the back of an empty chair. Her leather, fur-lined jacket reminded me of the coat my mother had once tried to shoplift from a department store. I shook my head to clear out that image and focused on her. "I think you girls need to be out of your house for a while, at least until your father figures out how he's going to care for your mother in the hospital *and* his three children at home."

"That's impossible," Daniella said. "There isn't time to do both."

"Maybe. But I don't know that he's even tried. I do know that your father is completely unaware of how much you've both been affected by your mother's illness over the years. I'm not sure if he chose to be ignorant or if he truly never knew, but that has to stop. He needs to know what your mother did and he needs to know what it's resulted in."

My heart was racing and I stared hard at her, trying to match her breathing. "Why does it matter so much if he knows?"

"Because how else will he be able to help you? If I were to ask your father right now, 'What do you think Daniella and Rikki need?' what would he say?"

"That I need an attitude adjustment," Daniella said cynically.

"He would say I don't need anything," I added slowly.

"And is that the truth?" Her question was gentle, but her point was clear. We both shook our heads. "How can I even suggest that you stay somewhere else for a while if that's what he thinks? He doesn't have any idea why you ran from him yesterday." She looked pointedly at Daniella. "Without knowing anything else, it would make sense for him to assume that it's all part of your attitude problem."

"How do we—" I stopped speaking when the door opened and my father stepped inside.

33

An unnatural and intensely awkward silence filled the room. Daniella was looking down at her fingernails and I was staring at her, afraid to look anywhere else.

"Mr. Coleman, thank you for coming. Please, have a seat." Mrs. Moskowitz's voice was so smooth and calming; she was in full-on social worker mode and I'd never been more grateful for it.

My father sat carefully and folded his hands on the table in front of him. "Hello, Daniella… Rikki…" He sounded so tentative that I felt sorry for him. I gave him a small nod.

"Mr. Coleman, we've spoken a few times, so you already know that I'm the school social worker and I've been meeting with Rikki pretty regularly. Rikki, have you ever told your father why you started meeting with me?" When I shook my head, she said, "Why don't you start by telling him how that happened."

Traitor. I just barely stopped myself from glaring at her. She certainly didn't waste time getting straight to business. Suddenly, a disturbing thought popped into my head.

Looking directly at my father, I jumped right in. "Have you ever woken up in the middle of the night because I was screaming?"

"What?"

"Screaming. The middle of the night. I get nightmares all the time. I wake up screaming my head off."

He stared at me blankly. "What?"

"How could you never have heard me?" I demanded in frustration. "I used to wake up hoarse all the time because I screamed so much. Are you trying to say you never once woke up because of that?"

He looked at me like I was crazy. "Rikki, no. I never woke up from you screaming. I wouldn't ignore that if I heard it." He caught the skepticism on my face. "Rikki, I'm being honest. If I'd ever heard you screaming in the middle of the night, I would've been there in a heartbeat. You know I've always been a deep sleeper. Uri got that from me."

There was no arguing with that. "Well, that's why I went to Mrs. Moskowitz. One time I hit Daniella in the face when I was still half-asleep and we got sent to the principal because they thought you were beating us. So that's when I started seeing her."

I could see him trying to fit all of the pieces together, both realization and confusion crossing his face. "What are you having nightmares about?"

I'd been talking about this to Mrs. Moskowitz and Mrs. Zilber for the past several weeks now, reliving the secrets of my childhood and talking about things I'd long kept hidden. But to speak about it to my father, with Daniella sitting quietly by my side, seemed impossible. As if she could read my mind, Daniella leaned in toward me, turning her head to whisper in my ear. "You can tell him. We have to tell him now. It's okay."

Relief surged through me, and I cast her a grateful look before I started to speak.

Twenty minutes later, I was still speaking. My voice was hoarse and I was speaking in a monotone, but I was getting the words out and, more importantly, my father was listening. I could see from his face that he hadn't known. He hadn't known that my mother had targeted Daniella from a young age and had tortured her emotionally with lengthy silent treatments and a steady stream of degrading comments. He hadn't known that Daniella had been desperate to break through my mother's silence, and had been willing to try anything, no matter how dangerous.

He hadn't been there when Daniella had talked back, refused to eat, broken dishes, screamed, ran into busy streets, and acquired all sorts of accidental "injuries" in an attempt to make my mother notice her. He hadn't been around to see my mother beat Daniella for her behavior, and then go right back to ignoring her. He didn't know that Daniella had preferred the beatings to the silent treatment. And he hadn't known that I'd had to watch it all happen.

I explained how my mother had used me to further hurt Daniella, lavishing me with praise and gifts and constantly wishing out loud that I was her only daughter. Only when she'd descend deep into her depression would her rage spill over to me. During those times, my status as the favorite child disintegrated. With her fists and with her words, my mother made it clear that both of us were a burden. We retreated from her and bonded over our bruises and aching hearts. As I got older and saw how much Daniella suffered, I tried to stop playing my mother's games, but I was young and confused and didn't know how to stop it.

To complicate things further, Daniella insisted that I never tell. Not my father, not my teachers, not our neighbors. No matter how much my mother hurt her, Daniella never broke. When my mother turned her anger toward me, Daniella directed it back to herself. When Uri was four, he spilled milk on the living room carpet. My mother hit him so hard that his head snapped back and hit the leg of the coffee table. It was the first time she'd laid a hand on him. Daniella picked up the cordless phone, walked over to my mother until she was mere inches away, and said clearly, "If you ever hurt him again, I will call the police and tell them everything." Five minutes later, ten-year-old Daniella was curled up on the floor in pain, but my mother never hit Uri again.

As we got older, the physical abuse lessened. Once we were closer in size, my mother backed off and relied on her mouth to keep us in line. By the time we were in middle school, she'd mostly stabilized on medication, and the endless pit of rage that seemed to boil within her was, for the most part, quiet. Her relationship with Daniella was volatile. In many ways it seemed like Daniella was intent on pushing her buttons just to see if she could make her crack.

My mother gave Daniella the silent treatment for months at a time, only speaking to her at family gatherings or when my father was around. She tried to win me over, but my loyalties were with my sister, my protector. My mother turned all of her attention to Uri, mothering him in a way she'd been incapable of when we were young. In some ways, she'd redeemed herself in our eyes by treating Uri as her favorite.

My father had created his own oblivion. He was obsessed with his work, and, to be fair, he had to be. My mother worked when she felt like it, and, while offers to do freelance artwork came easily, she lacked the focus to complete them and follow up on payments. To compensate, my father worked seventy-five-hour workweeks at his real estate office, coming home after we were already in bed. We viewed him as a safety net, even though he was completely oblivious that his very presence protected us from the worst of my mother.

In recent years, my mother had achieved respectable periods of stability, and during those times she was fun and sweet. We grew up in the shadow of her bipolar, but both Daniella and I knew that something much darker than that lurked beneath her skin. All we ever wanted was her love and approval, but that had been too much to ask for. Daniella received an endless flow of pain and punishment, while I served as the pawn to make it hurt more.

On the days when my mother woke us up at six in the morning to tell us that we were taking a day off from school to go to the beach, we were out of bed in thirty seconds flat, whispering to each other, "She seems like she's in a good mood. Maybe we'll have fun today." We'd then spend the rest of the day searching her eyes for signs of approval, for some indication she was doing this because she loved us and wanted us to have fun, and not just because she was starting a manic streak.

As I spoke, I worked my way forward. I kept my eyes focused on a spot on the table where someone had lightly carved their initials with a sharp object. I traced my finger repeatedly along the lines, moving from my childhood, into adolescence, and right up to the present.

"A while ago, she tried to stab me. It was the Sunday right before she was hospitalized. You weren't home."

My father blanched. Throughout my narrative, he had kept his face solemn, yet attentive, making it clear that he was listening and it was okay to continue. This was the first sign of distress.

"She thought I had some sort of spirit in me and she wanted to get it out." I felt the familiar fear that accompanied my nightmares start throbbing in my chest but I ignored it. "She chased me with a kitchen knife and I had to lock myself in the bathroom for over three hours until you came home." My heart stuttered as I remembered how I'd nearly lost my mind with fear and how even after I'd heard my father's car pull into the driveway, I'd remained lying on the floor of the bathroom, paralyzed with terror, until Daniella found me later that night. "That's what I have nightmares about," I finished quietly. "She's chasing me…and she catches me."

Silence spread gently across the room. I picked my head up to look at Mrs. Moskowitz and she gave me a small nod and a tiny smile. I could almost hear her saying, "You did good, Rikki," and that image eased the muscles in my chest off my heart. I breathed deeply, pulling the air into my lungs, allowing them to fill completely, reveling in a brand-new feeling.

This was what honesty felt like.

34

Waiting for my father to respond would normally have been a nerve-inducing experience, but all I felt was a sense of peace. I'd given it everything I had, not holding back even though I was scared, and now the ball was in his court. Would he even believe me? I didn't dare look at Daniella, but I could imagine she was eager to hear his response as well.

He cleared his throat and adjusted the collar of his shirt. I was grateful that he hadn't gotten emotional while I was speaking; I didn't want him to act like a victim. It took him a few tries to start speaking, but finally he coughed and looked me straight in the eye.

"I had no idea. I could never have imagined anything you just told me, and I can't even tell you how sorry I am." He looked past me at Daniella. I could feel her presence next to me, but she was completely still. "Daniella, I would never have thought she was capable of doing that. You shouldn't ever have had to experience even one day of that treatment." His voice was getting stronger and I thought I detected a hint of anger.

He continued, measuring his words with deliberate slowness. "But…"

I held my breath. *Please*, I thought silently. *Don't make excuses. Don't say it was because she was sick. You'll ruin it if you say that.*

"But I should have known."

His admission stunned me. I didn't move, just kept my eyes trained on his face.

"I'm your father. I should've known everything that was going on. I have no excuse for not being there and for allowing it to take place while I was out. It breaks my heart to think that every time I came home, I was signaling the end of another day of abuse." His voice cracked, but he forged on, not letting his emotion take over. "I wish you would've told me. I wish I'd known she was doing those things."

"Would it have made a difference if you'd known?" Daniella asked quietly.

He considered her question. "I'd like to think it would have. At the very least it would've changed how I saw your behavior. It makes a lot more sense to me now why you'd ask me to divorce her."

I saw a muscle in Daniella's cheek twitch at that reference. "So what are you going to do now that you know?" There was defiance in her voice, a challenge for him to make things right.

He sighed, a deep, heavy exhalation that spoke volumes. He turned to Mrs. Moskowitz. "I don't know. Legally, is there something that needs to be done? I don't see what good it would do to report it." He winced, paused, and then added, "But I will if I need to."

Mrs. Moskowitz was prepared. "I'll be reporting it. Based on experience, I don't think anything will happen because your wife is already receiving mental health services and you're the sole caretaker of your children right now and you have no record." My head spun but I tried to hang on to what she was saying.

Thankfully, Mrs. Moskowitz seemed to sense my confusion. "As a social worker, I need to report all incidents of child abuse. What your mother did to you and Daniella would be considered abuse. The department of social services will decide what happens next. They may assign a worker to your case to monitor the situation, or they may just document it and do nothing, since your mother is already in treatment. Either way," she continued, turning toward my father, "your wife's doctors need to know all of this information if they're going to be able to treat her effectively enough to return home."

My father nodded. "I'll tell them everything."

"What'll happen when she gets out?" I asked.

"I don't think that'll be happening any time soon," he answered. "But it's still a good question and I don't exactly know."

"Are you going to stay with her?" Daniella asked pointedly.

"Can I suggest that we hold off on that topic of conversation right now?" Mrs. Moskowitz interrupted. "Let's focus for a minute on the present. Mr. Coleman, the message that I'm getting from Daniella and Rikki is that they don't feel safe at home. There's too much emotional trauma there and too little support for them to be able to focus on healing."

My father looked crushed by her words, but didn't argue.

"This isn't an attack on your parenting," she clarified gently, "but something needs to change. We spoke briefly about this yesterday, so how would you feel if the girls stayed somewhere else for a while?"

"What sort of place would they stay at?"

"I have someone in mind. She's an older woman with several grown children. She's taken care of teenagers in the past and she's very warm and nurturing. Daniella and Rikki need some motherly love and I think they'll get it there."

For as much as Mrs. Moskowitz said she wasn't attacking

my father's parenting, it was patently clear that she thought he couldn't take care of us. He knew it was true and it hurt him.

He swallowed hard. "Will I still get to see them?"

"Of course. You can see them as often as they want. This isn't a punishment to you."

"What about therapy? Will they get help?" He wasn't looking at us. He was looking at Mrs. Moskowitz as if she had all of the answers, and I related to that feeling.

"Absolutely. That's one of the first things we'll work on. Both girls will need a good therapist and eventually, I think you should be doing family therapy with them."

Daniella made a small noise of protest, and then fell quiet.

My father was silent for a long time. When he finally spoke, he looked directly at Daniella. "If I say that it's okay, will you understand that I'm doing this for you, and not because I want to get rid of you? Because I don't want you to ever think that I'm allowing this to happen because I want you out. I would never even be considering this if I wasn't being told it's the right thing to do."

I glanced at Daniella and registered the shock on her face, and I knew, immediately, that he had figured her out. After all this time of chalking everything up to her "attitude problem," my father had somehow accessed the convoluted thought process in my sister's brain and had identified the key to this dilemma. If he'd agreed immediately, Daniella would've never forgiven him for giving us up. If he'd refused to let us go, she would've never forgiven him for denying us the chance to heal. In a lose-lose situation, he'd figured out how to win her over.

A sheepish smile slowly spread across her face and I was pleased to catch a glimpse of the carefree Daniella who I loved with all my heart.

"You should let us go," she said to him. "It'll be good for all of us."

35

My father drove us home so we could pack up our stuff. To say we were all feeling overwhelmed would've been a gross understatement; the tension in the car was so epic that there simply weren't words to talk about it. Everything felt eerily off-kilter. It was eleven o'clock on a Tuesday morning. My father was out of the office and we were out of school, preparing to pack our bags and move out of our home for an undetermined amount of time. Daniella was in her own world, staring fixedly out the window and I was attempting to look nonchalant, but my fingernails were digging into my palms. As hard as I tried to steady my breathing, my heart was beating a staccato beat in my rib cage.

My father brought two large suitcases down from the attic and set them on the floor of my room. "Let me know if you girls need anything," he said, standing awkwardly in the doorway before backing out.

"This is weird," I said, mostly because I didn't know what else to say and I needed to fill the silence with something. Daniella was standing in front of my closet, staring. She seemed to be doing a lot of staring and it was getting to me. "You seem really spaced out. Are you okay?"

Her head snapped around at my question. "Yeah, sorry. I'm just…" She floundered around for the right word, and then gave up with a shrug. She walked over to my bed and sat down gingerly. "I can't stop thinking about Uri. We can't just leave him here."

I sat down on the bed next to her, close enough so I'd feel her arm against mine. "I know. I can't stop thinking about him either. Like, I know we need to do this for us, but it's just so wrong."

"He's not going to understand. He'll think we're leaving him."

"And he can't stand being around Abba. He won't last without us."

We were silent. The hope I'd felt at the prospect of going to a safe place was rapidly shrinking. We had no right to sacrifice our little brother for our own peace and comfort.

"We can't go," I said miserably.

Daniella turned toward me and stared me down. "I can't go. *You* are going."

Instantly, I was on my feet. "Don't you dare."

She didn't respond.

"You're always doing this." My voice rose in frustration and I made no effort to control. "Could you, for once, just stop acting like such a…martyr?"

Her face darkened. "You think that's what this is about? You think I'm trying to be all selfless and sacrifice myself? That's not it, Rikki, okay?"

"Well then, what is it? Seriously, please tell me, because that's exactly what this looks like."

She grabbed my arm and pulled me back down on the bed. There was no gentleness there and I could see that everything about her was raw and hurting; she was not attempting to hide her emotions and this was so new that I could only watch.

"I don't care what happens to me. My life is a mess, because of everything she did to me back then, and because of everything I've done to myself now. I don't have a future. But you do. So maybe leaving would be good for me too, but in the long run, it doesn't matter. You're a different story. You have so much going for you. If you can get out now, you'll get help and you'll get better. And you'll be able to move past everything that happened. It's too late for me, so the least I can do is make sure Uri doesn't suffer."

I pulled out my cell phone and started dialing.

"Who are you calling?"

I ignored her and waited. Mrs. Moskowitz picked up on the third ring. She'd been waiting for us to call and tell her we were packed and ready to go. Before she got the first sentence out, I started talking, fast. "Daniella says she's not going and that she has to stay with our brother and that it's too late for her to be helped anyway and I need you to change her mind because I won't go without her."

Daniella lunged for me, trying to grab the phone from my hand, but I jumped back, out of reach. "Rikki, leave her out of this," she hissed, but I kept talking.

"We didn't even start packing, but can you please come now? I can't deal with this now."

"Rikki, calm down." Mrs. Moskowitz sounded alarmed, which did little to calm my nerves. "Can you put Daniella on the phone?"

I tossed my cell phone to Daniella. "She wants to talk to you."

Daniella hit the End button, severing the connection. "What are you doing?" She glared at me. "You can't not go just because I won't. You know they didn't even want to put us together?"

"What are you talking about?" There was something between us at that moment that was highly unsettling. I was angry at her, but needed her more than ever.

"It's true. Mrs. Moskowitz tried to talk me into it. She said we're too close, that we're too dependent on each other, and that I control you." She watched me carefully as she spoke, gauging my reaction. I thought I detected a hint of malice in her voice but quickly pushed that aside.

"They can't separate us. So what if we're dependent on each other? Why wouldn't we be? And you don't control me."

"That's where you're wrong, Rikki," she said evenly. "I do control you. And that's where I messed up really badly. I thought I was protecting us by not letting you tell anyone. I convinced myself that I was the only one getting really hurt." She held my gaze, the pain in her eyes so deep and sincere that I felt my eyes burn. "That was my biggest mistake. And Mrs. Moskowitz is probably right. You'd be better off away from me because even when I think I'm helping you, I'm just letting you down."

She broke eye contact and stood quickly, walking back over to the closet. Opening the door, she grabbed a handful of clothes and threw them recklessly onto the bed. She then began folding them furiously, shoving them into the suitcase with such force that I stepped back to watch. It took me a minute to realize that she was packing all of my clothing and had left her shirts and skirts hanging in the closet. Irrational rage flooded through me and I marched over to the closet, seized a set of uniform shirts off their hangers, and flung them into the other suitcase.

"Give it up, Rikki."

"No. I need you."

"No you don't," she insisted. "I'll just hurt you more. I'm trying to do the right thing by letting you go, so don't make this harder."

"I'm not the one making this harder." I was fighting back tears now. "Why didn't you bring this up at the meeting earlier? Why did you agree to it then? You said it would be good for all of us."

"I know, but I wasn't thinking about Uri. I couldn't help you,

Rikki. So at least let me try to help Uri." I could see that she was close to tears as well.

A new voice spoke from the doorway. "Daniella, why are you so insistent on helping everyone but yourself?" Mrs. Moskowitz stepped inside the room and closed the door behind her, surveying the scene of scattered clothing. "You deserve to get help and be safe just like Rikki and Uri. If anything, you need it more." She took a step closer to both of us and I felt the tears straining at the back of my eyes. She leaned against my desk and studied Daniella for a moment before asking, "Why are you so afraid to let yourself have what you need?"

It took a long time before Daniella could formulate an answer. When she finally choked out, "I don't deserve to be helped," I lay down on my bed and curled into a ball, letting the tears flow into my clenched fists.

"Rikki," Mrs. Moskowitz said gently. "Why are you crying?"

I forced myself to sit up. The pain of Daniella's words were like a knife in my heart. "Because she is so wrong, but she believes it's true." I pressed my hands against my chest, trying to stop the ache. "Because it's what my mother would've wanted her to believe about herself."

Daniella pressed her lips together tightly, but that didn't stop the tears from leaking out of her eyes.

I continued. "Because it's what my mother believed about herself. And that's why she could never stay stable — because every time she started to get better, she'd do something to mess it up. She'd stop taking her medications because she couldn't stand everything being normal. So it didn't matter if we weren't happy or if she was hurting us. She just had to get things back to crazy." The words felt like acid as they tripped off my tongue. I didn't even know how I knew what I was saying, but it seared through me in the way that only truth could.

"Stop." Daniella pressed her palms against her eyes, trying to stop her tears, but her shoulders were shaking. "Don't compare me to her."

"You're not like her at all," I said fiercely. "So stop acting like her."

"Daniella, you're nothing like your mother." Mrs. Moskowitz knelt on the floor right beside our bed. "Rikki's right. Your mother refused to help herself, even when she was destroying everyone around her. Don't let yourself be fooled by your fear of facing the truth. Do you think that if you don't get help now, you'll be of any use to Uri in two or three years? You'll be too broken to be there for him."

"What about now?" She brushed her tears away, trying to steady her breathing. "I feel like I'm abandoning him and I'm the only mother he has." The word "mother" started the tears flowing again.

"You have to give your father a chance to step up," Mrs. Moskowitz insisted. "If you continue to take care of Uri, your father will never be able to take over as a parent. You're not doing anyone any favors if you stay here right now."

"I hate this," Daniella mumbled.

"I know, but you need to do this for yourself."

Daniella glanced at me. "It's easier to do stuff when I think that I'm doing it for someone else." I nodded, understanding what she meant.

Mrs. Moskowitz nodded too, but she wasn't letting Daniella off so easily. "If that's what it takes to get you out of this house, then you can tell yourself that you're doing it for Uri or for Rikki, because they need you to get better, but at some point, you're going to have to realize that you deserve to be safe and happy. You can't forget that."

Daniella looked so appalled at that idea that I had to smile. I wrapped an arm around her shoulder and squeezed, relieved that she wasn't fighting anymore. She leaned into me and spoke without looking at me. "Are you sure you want me to come with you? Because I don't want to control you anymore; I seriously keep messing that up. So if you want to be on your own, I totally get it."

"Daniella, you're coming with me."

Mrs. Moskowitz smiled. She left the room to speak with my father as we finished packing. The tension was still there, but this time it was laced with sorrow rather than anger. When both of the suitcases were packed full of clothing, accessories, shoes, make-up, and our hair straighteners, we dragged them out to the living room.

"I'm going to take you over to Mrs. Baumgarten's now to get settled," Mrs. Moskowitz explained, "and your father will bring Uri over a bit later so you can say good-bye. Are you girls ready?"

My father took our suitcases outside and heaved them into the trunk of Mrs. Moskowitz's car. Then he turned to Daniella and me and wrapped his arms around both of us, pulling us in tight. "I love you both so much," he whispered fiercely. "I don't know if I can ever make up for everything that's happened, but I want you to know that I'll do whatever it takes to try and make it right. Please, just give me a chance."

To my surprise, Daniella hugged him back, but I was too worn-out to do anything. We piled into the backseat of the car and watched my father standing on the front porch until we turned off the street. Thankfully, Mrs. Moskowitz didn't try to talk to us during the twenty-minute drive to our new home until we were five minutes away. "Do you want to know a little about where you're going?" she asked cheerfully.

"Um, I guess," Daniella answered. The truth was that I didn't care, and from what it sounded like, she didn't either. At least Mrs. Moskowitz's voice drowned out the confusion in my head.

She told us that Mrs. Baumgarten was sixty-four, widowed, and had three grown children, two of whom lived out of state. She was a retired nurse and now volunteered for the local *bikur cholim*. She'd taken in a lot of kids before so this wasn't anything strange to her. She knew very little about why we were coming to stay with her and we shouldn't feel pressured to tell her anything.

Once Mrs. Moskowitz stopped talking, Daniella and I started asking questions, which she answered easily. Yes, Uri could visit us there. No, he could not live with us. No, Mrs. Baumgarten was not being paid to take care of us. Yes, we had to go to school.

"She'll tell you what rules she has at her house." Mrs. Moskowitz pulled into the driveway of a simple, two-story home.

"This is awkward," I said to Daniella, and she laughed. The small sound of joy brought a smile to my face and gave me the courage to open the car door and get out. Mrs. Moskowitz was trying — and failing — to haul our suitcases out of the trunk, so we went to help her. When we finally set both of them on the ground and prepared to pull them toward the house, we saw that the front door had opened and Mrs. Baumgarten was standing on the porch, coming to greet us.

36

Things got a lot worse before they got better. Mrs. Baumgarten — or Mrs. B., as she told us to call her — was wonderful. She was tough and loving and gave us our space, while letting us know she was right there if we needed her. But we had a rocky start; about five minute after we walked in the house, Mrs. Moskowitz insisted on checking our suitcases before she left. We both protested, way more than what would've been rational, and by the time she was done, she had a four-pack of lighters and a bottle of prescription pills dated three years earlier in her pocket. Mrs. B. immediately laid down the rules. We were not to be in possession of any weapons, drugs, or otherwise harmful contraband. We had a curfew of eight o'clock on school days, eleven o'clock on weekends.

"I'll be checking on you periodically to make sure you're both accounted for," she said, looking directly at Daniella.

We could have friends come over, but no boys. We needed to keep kosher and Shabbos in the house; what we did outside was none of her business. We would attend school every day, and do our homework before we did anything else fun. We were responsible for keeping our room and bathroom clean, and were expected to clean up after ourselves.

"Do you have any questions?"

"No ma'am."

When my father brought Uri by that night, he sobbed inconsolably for what felt like forever. He only calmed down after Mrs. B. took him aside and promised him he could visit any time he liked. As soon as he left, Daniella broke down, and nothing Mrs. B. or I could say was enough to ease her guilt.

That first night, I had a nightmare so bad that I woke up choking and screaming. Dazed and disoriented, I bolted out of bed, stumbled around until I found the bathroom, and vomited until nothing was left in me. Daniella held my hair back while my body spasmed and tried to rid me of the terror that seemed to have attached itself to my very core. Mrs. B. brought me a cup of ice chips and encouraged me to suck on them as my stomach stopped revolting. I cried and cried and had no idea why I was crying or what I was feeling. I only knew that something inside me hurt so badly and wouldn't stop.

That's what stood out most from the first week that we lived with Mrs. B. The incessant flow of tears. I cried, Daniella cried, Uri cried, my father cried, even Kayla cried when I told her why we'd left home and what I'd been hiding from her for eight years. Mrs. Moskowitz insisted we return to school on Wednesday, and at least seven times over the course of the day I found myself locked in a bathroom stall, my hands pressed over my mouth, trying to muffle my sobs. From Daniella's red-rimmed eyes, I knew she wasn't doing much better.

"I can't stand this." I gritted my teeth as I wiped away tears from my cheeks. I was in Mrs. Moskowitz's office after lunch on

Thursday and no matter how hard I tried, I couldn't stop crying. "I don't know what's wrong with me. I never cry like this and I can't stop. It's driving me crazy."

"Don't you think you have enough to cry about?" she asked rhetorically. "Stop trying to fight it. It's normal for it to be coming out now, when you're finally safe enough to let yourself feel."

She was all about feeling. She wanted Daniella and me to allow ourselves to experience our emotions and stop bottling them up inside. On a theoretical level, I understood why that was necessary, but on a practical level, the nonstop flood of tears was unbearable. My friends knew something was wrong. I was no longer able to maintain my facade of having it all, and they were utterly confused. Kayla was the only one I'd come clean with. All of my other friends had subscribed to the rapidly circulating rumor that my mother was hospitalized with some terminal illness. Thankfully, they chalked up my excessive emotions to my apparent concern for her well-being. I didn't bother to correct that notion.

Dance, which had once been my escape, had started to feel like a burden. When I was actually dancing, I could shed some of the constant ache that had burrowed under my skin, but when the music was off and we were teaching new steps or critiquing moves, the pressure of human interaction was almost too much to bear.

Ayelet watched me. She knew something was up, but apparently the rumor about my mother hadn't yet circulated to the ninth grade so she had no idea as to why I was suddenly avoiding her. I wasn't sure why I was avoiding her myself, but I appreciated that she gave me the distance and didn't pry. Zehava asked me point-blank if my mother was sick. I said that she was and that I didn't want to talk about it. She gave me a hug and told me she was there for me; while I recognized her sincerity, I couldn't help but remember Riva Winters's unwanted affection, and had to fight the urge to shake her off.

My teachers were terrible. Without fail, they each pulled me aside to offer their support and express their concerns. Most of them couldn't resist mentioning that they'd "noticed" that Daniella had been struggling for some time and wanted to make sure I wasn't going through anything similar. I hated them for doing that, and couldn't stand the way they expected me to pour my heart out to them.

"Thanks, but I don't need anything from you," I told them coldly. To Mrs. Chase I added, "Maybe you should've asked me this before you started talking about me to your class." I walked away before she had a chance to answer. Of course, I walked straight to the bathroom, where I spent fifteen minutes crying my eyes out.

Batya and Vivi were fantastic, but I felt so terrible about how I'd treated them I couldn't get over my awkwardness. They waited expectantly for me at lunch every day and kept up light conversation so I could either participate or just listen. Whenever anyone would broach the topic of my ailing mother, they would swiftly change the topic. When Batya found me standing at my locker at the end of the day, choking back tears as I packed my books into my backpack and tried to psych myself up for yet another dance practice, she leaned close and said, "Listen, we're still going by the 'don't ask, don't tell' thing, but you can change your mind at any time. Seriously, we're here for you." Then she walked away before I had a complete meltdown.

If Mrs. B. thought our crying was excessive, she didn't mention it. On our second night there, she served us macaroni and cheese along with a fresh salad. Daniella picked at her food, arranging her carrots, tomatoes, and green peppers into geometric designs.

"Daniella, stop playing with your food. You need to eat it." Her tone was firm, but gentle.

Daniella bit her lip and tears slowly pooled in the corners of her eyes.

Mrs. B. considered her for a moment, and then asked, "What is it?"

Daniella stared at her fork. "It's just cool that you noticed that I wasn't eating. I used to try that all the time when I was a kid, and my mother never noticed." Then she excused herself and left the room before she started really crying.

"It's true," I told Mrs. B., remembering Daniella's antics at mealtimes. "She would try everything to get her to pay attention. She once even threw an entire plate of food at my mother. I think she was like, eight or something."

Mrs. B.'s eyebrows shot up. "How did your mother react to that?"

"She didn't really. That was the worst part. She made me clean it up, and then for the next week, when she set the table for dinner, she wouldn't set a place for Daniella. She wouldn't give her any food and acted like she wasn't even there." I pushed my plate of food away, sickened at the memory. I looked directly as Mrs. B., as a certain realization dawned on me. "She was terrible to her. And I just went along with it. I never stood up to her." I stood abruptly, my chair rocking precariously on its back two legs.

"Just let her be," Mrs. B. said quietly as I moved in the direction of our room. "Let her cry now."

37

When the tidal wave of unhappiness finally started to ebb, it felt like being reborn. The sun seemed brighter, the sky seemed bluer, and Daniella's eyes were clearer than I could ever remember. It was a Sunday. We'd been at living away from home for six days, though it felt like eternity. Daniella woke me up early and I could see, immediately, that she felt the difference. I chalked it up to the first Shabbos in years during which we'd been completely unafraid.

"Wake up, Rikki. We have a lot to do today." She bounced up and down lightly on the edge of my bed. Although we shared a room, Mrs. B. insisted that we sleep in our own beds. She said she didn't mind if I "screamed the entire house down every night." It was more important for me to learn how to sleep without Daniella by my side. Motzaei Shabbos had been the first night since our arrival that I hadn't woken up from a nightmare.

"What's happening today?" I asked, rubbing my eyes as I sat up. Daniella was fully dressed, her hair pulled back into a loose bun. Somehow, neither of us seemed to have the energy to iron our hair into submission every morning. It seemed rather inconsequential to have our hair looking like a shampoo advertisement when we were fighting for our emotional survival. I thought Daniella looked even prettier with her hair pulled back, plus, it made her growing-out blue streaks blend nicely into her hair.

"We're going to visit Ima."

"We're *what*?" In typical Daniella fashion, she'd managed to jolt me fully awake within ten seconds of conversation. She grinned at me.

"We're going to visit—"

"No, I heard you. But what are you talking about? She doesn't want to see us."

"So? That doesn't mean we can't visit. Let's just go and see what happens." Seeing the doubt in my eyes, she tried harder. "Please, Rikki? I have to do this and I need you with me. Just this one time."

"Why?" I reached over and the pulled the blinds open, squinting as sunlight streamed into the room. It felt as though it pierced my heart and warmed me up inside. Why would Daniella want to ruin a perfectly good day by visiting a psychiatric hospital?

"I don't know." She twirled a piece of her hair nervously. "I just want to try and talk to her. Ask her some questions."

"You're not going to get any answers from her."

"I know that." She looked down at her hands. "Look, I just…I know it's right that we're here. At home, it was like being stuck all the time. I could never get past what she did. But now that we're out? I don't know…last night…it felt like the first time in my life that I could actually breathe."

I knew exactly what she meant.

"Now that we're talking about it," she continued, "now that it's not this big secret anymore, I'm not that scared of her. And I kind of want to see if that's just in my mind, or if it would be the same way in real life, too."

"Scared? I didn't think you were ever scared of her," I said slowly. "You never backed down from her."

Daniella laughed, and there was less bitterness than usual. "Rikki, I was terrified. You have no idea. I was just more scared of being invisible."

She stood up, pulling my covers back with her. "Come on, get dressed. Visiting hours start at eleven and we have to go now because Abba will be there later and I don't want to run into him."

I couldn't help but notice she was dressed up, and I felt a small flutter start up in my stomach at the prospect of seeing our mother for the first time in months. I ate breakfast as if I wasn't nervous at all, trying to trick my body into thinking that today was just like any other day.

"You girls look nice," Mrs. B said, coming into the kitchen. "Are you going somewhere?"

"Yeah," Daniella said nonchalantly. "We have this thing for school."

I kicked her under the table. I wasn't going to let her start lying to Mrs. B. and ruin this arrangement.

"Ouch. Okay, forget that. We're going to visit our mother." Daniella glared at me, but it turned into a grin halfway through. She was nervous and excited.

Mrs. B. poured herself a cup of coffee and sat down at the table with us. "Does she know you're coming?"

Daniella couldn't bring herself to tell the truth about that so I answered for her. "No, we're just going to try and see if she'll let us talk to her. We know she might say no." I stared at Daniella as I said that, but she just looked back innocently.

Mrs. B. looked back and forth between the two of us. "I don't have any problem with that, as long as you don't go there with high expectations." She fixed her gaze on Daniella. "Especially you."

I smiled as Daniella started protesting. That was one thing I liked best about Mrs. B. She kept it real all of the time.

"Call me and let me know what happens."

Daniella kept watching the clock. "I want to daven first and then we'll go. Rikki, will you be ready in twenty minutes?"

"Yeah, I guess I'll daven too."

Mrs. B. and Daniella exchanged glances, which I pretended not to see. They knew I didn't daven, but never pushed it. Although I hadn't made much progress in the area of formal *tefillah*, I'd been sending up personal prayers with increasing frequently. I found that I could talk to Hashem as long as I could first make a disclaimer that I wasn't asking for anything for myself. I kept my *tefillos* related to Daniella and the rest of my family.

I joined Daniella in the living room and pulled down a siddur from the shelf, more for a prop than for practical purposes. I sat in one of the well-worn armchairs, under a row of framed pictures of Mrs. B.'s smiling children and grandchildren. In addition to the photos of her children, she also had pictures of other teenagers who'd stayed at her house over the years. Some of them had been photographed with their husbands and children as well. I wondered if she'd ever have pictures of Daniella and me hanging on her walls at some point in the future.

"Hashem, thanks for giving us Mrs. B. That was pretty cool of You. I guess You knew we needed that." I paused to watch Daniella daven, concentration and emotion evident in her face. "Can you keep an eye on Daniella today? I don't have a good feeling about what we're about to do but I know I can't stop her. Just please don't let my mother hurt her again. Please don't let my mother make her feel invisible anymore."

My gaze was pulled toward the picture window that held the

view of the backyard, scattered with picnic tables and chairs; the scene of a happy family. "Do we even have a future? Is there anything good for us out there? I don't ever want to feel as miserable as we did this past week. I don't even know how we made it through that. And I know I'm supposed to feel like You're always with us, even when things are bad, but I did *not* feel that You were watching out for us last week. Well, I guess You were, because we're okay now, but was that really necessary? All that drama? You couldn't have helped us out in a less painful way?"

I struggled with the guilt and confusion that were warring inside my heart. "I guess I'm being ungrateful but this is just really complicated for me. It's like You're helping me and hurting me all at the same time. I mean, You put us in this situation in the first place, and now You're helping us, so we're supposed to be grateful?"

I was suddenly fearful that my ingratitude would ruin any chance of today going right. "I'm sorry," I added quickly. "Forget what I said, okay? I didn't really mean that. You've been awesome. Like I said, thanks for Mrs. B., and please look out for Daniella." I watched my sister close her eyes and tilt her head back slightly, as if she were communicating directly with Someone above.

"And maybe, please, could you help me have some of this faith that Daniella has? I guess that's how she hasn't broken yet. She's always held on to You. I want that, but I don't know how to get it. So help me?"

38

Daniella drummed her fingers against the steering wheel for the entire eighteen-minute drive to St. Lucas Hospital. It was beyond annoying, but I didn't have the heart to ask her to stop. I tried starting a conversation a few times, but she was so distracted, she kept asking me to repeat myself and eventually I gave up. When the big stone building came into view, an arching sign announcing its presence to the world, my heart was beating somewhere in my throat.

Daniella pulled down the visor and studied herself in the mirror. "I wish I'd ironed my hair."

"You look fine. Are you sure you want to do this? Because we could turn around now and go back. I wouldn't care."

She opened the car door and got out, stretching her limbs gracefully. "No, let's do this."

I was self-conscious as we walked down four long corridors toward the adult psychiatric unit. We passed cafeteria workers, nurses, doctors, medical technicians, patients and their families.

Some of them glanced at us as we walked by, but most were oblivious to our presence. None of them seemed as out of place as we felt.

At the door to the unit, Daniella hesitated, looked around like she wanted to bolt, and then in once swift motion, reached out and rang the bell. There was a moment of silence and I could've sworn I heard Daniella's heart beating. Then the intercom crackled to life and a disembodied voice said "Unit 2C, who are you here to see?"

I couldn't have said anything even if I wanted to. Daniella leaned forward slightly, closer to the microphone and spoke clearly. "Aviva Coleman."

"Okay, someone will be with you in a minute." The intercom went silent.

Daniella looked at me with a dazed expression. "That was it?"

I shrugged. A few minutes later, the door clicked open and a young African American nurse stepped outside. She wore black scrub pants, a teal scrub shirt and matching teal crocs. Her hair was long and sleek and was pulled into a ponytail that was draped over one shoulder. Her nametag read *Brianna* and she looked surprised to see us standing there. "Who are you here for?" she asked again.

Daniella repeated my mother's name. Brianna cocked her head to the side. "Does she know you're coming to visit?"

I could see in Daniella's eyes that she wanted to lie, if that's what it took to see our mother, but she overcame that urge. "No. She doesn't know."

Brianna looked us up and down. "I'm going to check with her and see if she's up for visitors now." She hesitated. "Are you her daughters?"

We nodded.

"Are you twins?"

We shook our heads.

"I'll be right back."

We listened as the door clicked closed behind her.

Daniella was standing too straight, her shoulders pulled back stiffly. I wanted to put an arm around her and tell her it would all be okay, but I could barely stay upright and present myself. If Brianna returned and told us to come onto the unit, would I even be able to follow her?

When the door opened again and she stepped outside, allowing the door to close behind her, I already knew the answer. "Ladies," she said gently, "your mom isn't up for having visitors today. I'm sorry."

Daniella flinched. My lungs constricted. Daniella recovered faster than I did. "I bet she'll be up for a visit when my father comes later, won't she?" Before Brianna could answer, she went on. "I bet she's never once told him that she wasn't up for his visit. She's ridiculous."

Brianna was watching her carefully. "What's your name?"

Daniella scowled at her.

"Look, I know it must be hard having your mom in the hospital, and I'm sure you both miss her a lot. But sometimes people need space when they're trying to get back on solid ground after dealing with mental illness."

"We've given her space," Daniella muttered. "She hasn't seen us once since she got here."

"I'm sorry," Brianna said again, and I knew she meant it. "Do you want me to pass along a message to your mom? Or maybe you can write her a note."

"I'm not writing her anything," Daniella said defiantly. "But I'll send her a message. Tell her we hope she rots in here."

Brianna raised an eyebrow.

"Don't tell her that," I said quickly.

Dancing in the Dark | 229

Daniella glared at me. "What do *you* want to tell her?"

I shrugged helplessly. "I don't know. Tell her that she's losing us. We're not going to wait around forever for her to decide that she wants to see us again."

Brianna nodded, and waited to see if there was more.

Daniella was rapidly cycling through emotions. I could see anger, then grief, then frustration, then loss cycle across her face. Crossing her arms over her chest, she said, "Tell her I'm done."

There was nothing for me to say. I looked down at the floor, not wanting to see pity in Brianna's eyes, but when she spoke, I felt anything but pity. "You ladies may not know this, but your mom is a very special woman."

"Special?" Daniella laughed, the sharp edge of anger unmistakable. "You think she's special? You don't know anything. She's ruined our lives. She tried to kill my sister with a knife. She beat me so badly she broke two of my ribs. Even now, we can't eat, we can't sleep, we're failing school, we're living without any parents. That's how special she is. She's a selfish child abuser. That's all."

Brianna nodded. "I believe you that she was abusive. It's not easy having a mentally ill parent. But you need to realize that it's not easy to be mentally ill. Your mom hasn't always been in control of her actions."

"And that makes it okay?" Daniella cried. "I'm so *sick* of people excusing her behavior. I don't care what she has. It makes no difference." She was getting emotional, the tears that I hadn't seen since Friday pooling in her eyes again. My heart ached for her. "Let's go."

I started to follow, but stopped when Brianna said, "Wait. Just hang on a second, I want to get something for you." She slid her electronic card on the entry pad and pulled the door open. She paused momentarily to ask, "Will you wait here?" and once I nodded, she disappeared inside. Daniella walked about ten feet away and leaned against a windowsill, her arms wrapped tightly around herself. I distracted myself by reading the signs warning visitors that all patients on the unit were an "elopement risk" and that doors should only be opened when no patients were around.

Brianna came back out holding a stack of pamphlets and a flyer. Sitting at a table in the lobby, she spread them out in front of her and motioned for us to sit down. Daniella came reluctantly. "If you don't understand how mental illnesses work, you'll always be taking your mom's actions personally. That's just going to cause you a lot more grief than necessary." She slid the pamphlets toward us. "Read through these. You can do it right now so you can ask me any questions. It'll be good for you to understand."

"Why?" Daniella asked through gritted teeth. I echoed her question in my mind.

"I don't get it. So what if we understand? How does it change things?" I added.

"Because then you can stop being mad at your mom and start being mad at the disease," Brianna said simply. She gave us a moment to digest her words before continuing. "When I said your mom was special, I meant that. When you take the disease out of the equation, you mom is talented and kind and creative. You have so much anger toward her so it's hard for you to see that."

We were silent. The rage was leaving Daniella's face, leaving in its wake raw, agonizing sadness. I felt it too, but knew it didn't even compare to what she was experiencing. Brianna seemed to sense it as well, and reached out to cover Daniella's shaking hand with her own. "Sweetie, the only thing harder than having a relative with a mental illness is *having* a mental illness."

A single tear trickled down Daniella's cheek. I felt it like a knife in my heart. "You have to let her go," I said quietly. "At least for now. She's not going to be able to give you what you want. I don't think she can help it."

"She has this power over me," Daniella choked the words out. "I always tell myself I won't care what she does…but I do."

"It's no power," Brianna said. "She's your mom. That's just the way kids are about their moms. We love them even when they don't treat us right." After a moment of silence, she smoothed the flyer onto the table. "There are lots of teenagers like you whose parents are dealing with a serious mental illness. We have a support group on Tuesday nights for the teens to get together and talk about what it's like and give each other support. I think you might benefit from it a lot." A beeper buzzed at her waist and she glanced down to look at it. Rising, she leaned toward us one last time. "I have to go, but seriously, consider coming to the group. You'll see, you're not alone."

"Can you tell her one thing?" I asked.

"Sure, what is it, sweetie?"

"Tell her we're not coming again. She made her choice and now we're making ours."

39

When we walked away from the unit, Daniella ducked into the nearest bathroom and I knew she was crying. As I waited for her, my phone vibrated in my pocket and I saw I had a text from Mrs. Zilber. *Mrs. B. told me where you were going. Are you doing okay?*

I texted back, *I don't know. She refused to see us, Daniella's crying in the bathroom now.*

Twenty minutes later, Daniella was still crying in the bathroom. She'd asked me not to follow her in there, and had said she needed some space, but this was making me nervous.

I took a deep breath and pushed open the door. She stood at the sink, staring at herself in the mirror. Daniella's eyes were red and raw and her face was flushed. She caught my eye in the reflection. "I'm sorry. I'm just trying to pull it together and every time I think I'm okay I start crying again." She turned to look at me, and her face crumpled. "I thought this part was over."

I pulled her close to me, letting her cry against my shoulder, grateful that I was feeling strong enough to support her. "Don't apologize. It's okay to feel this way. Just let yourself cry."

She laughed through her tears. "Thanks, Mrs. Moskowitz."

Smiling, I pulled back so I could look at her. "Let's just go. Who cares if you're still crying? We're in a mental hospital, so I think anything goes."

"Go where? It just feels like everything is useless."

I shook my head. "That's not true. She just makes you feel that way. You need to get away from her. Let's go back to Mrs. B.'s. We can chill there."

She splashed cold water on her face and dried it with some paper towels. Blowing her nose one last time, she straightened her shoulders and exited the bathroom. She didn't cry as we walked back down the corridors to the lobby. "I hope I never end up here," she said quietly as a girl our age wearing jeans and a sweatshirt walked by, escorted by a nurse.

"You won't. Don't even think about that."

"You don't know that. Seriously, either of us could just totally crack at some point. We have it in our genes to go crazy."

I gritted my teeth. "Can we please not talk about this now?" Daniella had triggered something in me. It occurred to me that she probably shared my fears of inherited mental illness, and I wondered why I hadn't talked about this with her before. "Later, okay? I just really need to get out of here."

When we hit the main lobby, I stopped dead in my tracks. Daniella, one step behind, banged into me. "Ouch. What's up?"

I just stared. Sitting on a couch right inside the entrance of the hospital was Mrs. B. She smiled when she saw us.

Daniella was speechless for a minute, but recovered quickly. "Is she here for us? Did you ask her to come?"

"No, I had no idea she'd be here."

Daniella's expression was unreadable. Before I could say

anything more, Mrs. B. had waved us over.

We approached her hesitantly. "Are we in trouble or something?"

Mrs. B. smiled. "No, you're not in trouble. I just heard from Mrs. Zilber that things didn't go too well with your mother so I wanted to be here for both of you. I'll never take her place, but at least you have someone."

Daniella's eyes welled up with tears, while I felt a distinct warmth radiate from my core. "I finally just stopped crying two minutes ago and now I'm at it again," Daniella said wearily, wiping her eyes.

"So what?" Mrs. B. said. "I'd be crying right now if I was in your shoes." She patted the couch next to her. "Come sit." Daniella sat warily, and Mrs. B. gently placed an arm around her shoulder. Daniella leaned forward, burying her face in her hands and Mrs. B. held her tighter.

I went to sit next to them. "We had such a good weekend," I said, frustrated. "And now this. I shouldn't have let her come."

"I guess you wanted to see her too?"

Mrs. B.'s question made a lump well up in my throat. "Yeah, I guess I did."

In the end, Daniella left with Mrs. B. I was glad that Daniella trusted her, because my sister needed to be able to talk to someone. We'd both started individual therapy at a nearby clinic. I connected immediately with Yocheved, my social worker, who had fifteen years of experience with teenagers and PTSD. Daniella was having a more difficult time, as she really disliked the middle-aged lady she was supposed to open up to. Despite her relationship with Mrs. B. and the fact that she was definitely more talkative about the past, I knew there was a lot she was holding inside.

On my way home, I called Mrs. Moskowitz and asked if she had time to talk. We met at a nearby Starbucks and I filled her in on that morning.

"Brianna sounds nice," she said. "Were you able to ask her questions about the reading material she gave you?"

I shook my head. "She got paged to go back onto the unit. But I read them. And…"

Mrs. Moskowitz waited patiently while I tried to force the words out. It took some time before I finally said, "It had some statistics in there." I sucked in air, willing my lungs to expand, before plunging forward. "Daniella and I have a fifteen to thirty percent chance of having bipolar."

Once I said it out loud, it seemed less terrifying than when it had been in my head. The probability still loomed over me, but it had somehow diminished in size once it had been verbalized.

"That must be really scary."

"It is. If I get bipolar, I think I'd just kill myself. There's no way I'm going to take the risk of hurting people the way she did." I looked directly at Mrs. Moskowitz, daring her to tell me I was crazy for even talking that way.

She just nodded in understanding. "There are a few things you need to understand, Rikki. First of all, not everyone with bipolar is like your mother. Plenty of people don't beat their kids and play mind games with them. Lots of people with bipolar are kind and sensitive and caring. They can hold down jobs and raise large families and be contributing members of society." I was listening intently.

"Your mother did a lot of damage to herself by not managing her illness properly." She was watching me carefully, gauging how I would take her words.

"And my father did more damage by letting her get away with that. And Daniella was the victim of all of that."

"And you," she said gently.

I flinched.

"You won't be doing yourself any favors if you make it seem

like Daniella is the only one who was affected." She paused to let that sink in. "Can I ask you something?"

I wrapped my hands around my latte, clinging to its heat. "Yeah."

"Why fire? Why did that become something you turned to?" I shifted uneasily in my chair and she immediately backtracked. "You don't need to talk about this if it makes you uncomfortable."

"No, it's fine," I said slowly. "I guess I don't really know. I've asked myself that a hundred times." Images of flames flickered across my mind, and I felt a glimmer of the calm that I'd come to associate with the blaze. "I remember the first time I did it. I was upset because we'd gone to my cousin's bar mitzvah, and my mother had been ignoring Daniella for over a month, but when we were in shul, everyone kept complimenting Daniella on her outfit and my mother just started complimenting her too. She acted like a perfect mother in front of all my aunts and cousins." My face felt hot as I remembered the scene that had occurred when we'd gotten home after shul.

We'd walked home together, Daniella simmering with barely concealed rage. When our front door closed behind us, she lost it. "You faker," she screamed at my mother. "*Oh, Daniella, you look so gorgeous. Doesn't she look great? She looks so thin.*" She mocked my mother fearlessly.

My mother looked bewildered by her attack. She never seemed to fully understand her interactions with my sister. "Daniella, you do look good. I meant it."

Daniella shot her a look of pure hatred. "You're crazy." The words were flat and cold, and with that, she walked out, not returning until after Shabbos.

During *shalosh seudos*, my mother had railed against Daniella while my father listened patiently, Uri played with his food, and I wanted to stab my mother with my fork. After twenty minutes of hearing my mother call Daniella selfish and rude, I'd had enough. As soon as Havdallah was over, I pocketed the book of matches and retreated to my room. With my back against the locked door, I lit the matches, one by one, and let them burn until my fingertips were singed. The sharp smell of phosphorus and smoke and the dull ache in my fingers completely overpowered my feelings of helplessness. I was immediately hooked.

Playing with matches had escalated to lighting other things on fire, just to watch them burn. Candles, paper, tissues, toothpicks — as long as it would light, I'd burn it. I kept the fire contained, either in the sink or in a metal trash can, but the more stressed I was, the more careless I became. Small black holes in my clothing attested to times that the sparks had gotten the best of me. I sustained a large burn across the palm of my hand when a large piece of tissue had floated out of the trash can and had landed on my carpet.

I was ashamed of the fire setting, especially after my mother began imagining that the flames of the Shabbos candles could speak to her. I figured I was starting my own journey into mental illness but was too embarrassed to ask even Daniella about it. Presumably, she'd known all along, yet had chosen to keep quiet for fear of ruining the one thing that could calm me down even in the worst of times, similar to the way I'd kept my mouth shut about her pill popping. Admittedly, both of our decisions had been poor.

"I think I might end up like her," I said miserably, looking down at my scarred fingertips. Repeated burns had left them calloused, and although I wouldn't have admitted it to Mrs. Moskowitz, simply rubbing my fingertips together provided a sense of relief.

"Why do you think that?"

"I know what you think. I know what everyone thinks."

"You do? What are we all thinking?"

"That I play with fire because of her," I said impatiently. "So I'm crazy in the same way she is."

Mrs. Moskowitz raised an eyebrow. "You just said you started setting fires before she started being obsessed with it. How does that fit your theory?"

"I don't know." I sighed, running my hands through my hair. "It doesn't make sense. But it doesn't mean I don't still think it."

She set her coffee cup down on the table and took both of my hands in hers. "Rikki, look at me."

Reluctantly, I did.

"Do you think you have bipolar?"

I hemmed and hawed and started and stopped my answer a few times, but eventually, I blurted out, "No."

"Good," she said, looking me straight in the eye. "Because you don't. So stop torturing yourself."

"Then why do I like setting fires?"

She shrugged. "It's an addictive, unhealthy coping skill. What's so fascinating to you about fire?"

I hesitated before answering her, still concerned she'd find my answers indicative of mental instability. "It's something I can control. Well, usually. I can choose what to burn and how long to let it burn."

She was nodding. "Doesn't it make sense that if you're living in a chaotic environment with an unpredictable mother, that you'd want something you could have control over?"

"Yes."

"Well then, that makes you normal."

40

We had the entire morning off for dance practice. The production was only three weeks away and we were working on perfecting our dances, down to the smallest details. For the jail dance, we'd created an intricate move involving one girl literally flying across the stage. The dance was split into eight "prisoners" and four "wardens." We'd adopted a cheerleading move where three of our prisoners launched one prisoner over a wall of four wardens, to be caught by the other four prisoners.

We knew our teachers would never approve the move if they heard about it before they'd seen it, so we'd practiced in secret, actually posting lookouts while Ayelet Klein flew across the room into the arms of our waiting dancers. It'd been risky, and even with the use of double-layered crash pads borrowed from the gym, she'd sustained quite a few bruises and scrapes, but she'd insisted she was up for the challenge.

That morning, a panel of teachers would be viewing our full dance for the first time and giving us the approval we needed to get on stage during concert. Ms. Palmer had sufficiently terrified Zehava and me with a horror story about how the teachers had once insisted she change approximately one-third of her dance moves two weeks before concert since they were too "modern." I was fairly certain our dance was kosher, but I didn't know if they'd let us keep the flying move, and even though the rest of our dance was good, everyone knew that with that move, it would make history.

We'd executed the move perfectly eighteen times in a row and were feeling pretty confident. Mrs. Landau, Ms. Palmer, and four other teachers sat in a row of chairs at the front of the gym and waited for us to perform.

"What if she crashes?" Zehava whispered to me frantically as the girls took their places. "They'll cut our whole dance out."

She wasn't exaggerating. One of Atara and Laya's dancers had fallen on her head while practicing a flip and had been carted off by Hatzalah in an ambulance. She was fine, but rumor had it that Rabbi Sacks had threatened to the pull the dance.

"Zehava, she'll be fine. She can do it perfectly and we all know exactly what we're doing. She won't crash."

"Yeah, but if she does, she'll totally kill herself."

"I can hear you, you know," Ayelet said wryly. "And I'm fine. As long as you all catch me, I won't get hurt." She turned back to us once last time before striking her starting pose. "Oh, and if I do crash? Just pretend it was part of the move. They won't know the difference."

I started laughing, but Zehava looked ready to pull her hair out. Before she could say anything else, Ms. Palmer turned on the music and we scrambled into our positions.

I wouldn't have admitted it to the girls in my carousel dance, but the jail dance was my favorite. The music throbbed and swelled and made me feel alive. The moves were razor-sharp and unique, channeling what we assumed an imprisoned person might feel. The thing

Dancing in the Dark | 241

I liked best about the jail dance was that we didn't need to smile. In every dance I'd ever been in, we were required to plaster on shining smiles throughout the whole performance. In this dance, it was unnecessary to pretend that we were happy; we were prisoners.

In the seconds leading up to Ayelet's shining moment, time seemed to slow down. I saw the concentration on everyone's faces as three girls swung her up and over. Her body was perfectly arched, toes pointed, arms extended. Then she was coming toward us, exactly as we'd practice, and we caught her in our arms, waiting until she was secure, before setting her back on the ground and striking our final pose. We executed it perfectly.

The music stopped and there was dead silence. I held my pose, allowing my mind to return to the present. I hated the moments after the music stopped and electricity sizzled out of my fingertips. I focused in on Mrs. Landau, who was staring at us, wide-eyed. None of the other teachers moved, except for Ms. Palmer, who gave us a tiny thumbs-up.

Just as the silence started to get awkward, I heard clapping start from across the room. In the middle of a circle of girls who had been watching us, Daniella was cheering. As the others girls broke into applause, she stuck two fingers into her mouth and wolf-whistled. The room exploded into an excited frenzy as girls who hadn't seen our move before closed in on Ayelet, congratulating her on her bravery and talent.

Mrs. Landau waved us over and Zehava and I stood nervously in front of her. The noise in the background faded away as I waited to hear her opinion.

"That was by far the most dangerous move I have ever seen in a Bais Yaakov dance."

I swallowed hard, knowing what that meant.

"We can do it perfectly. We haven't messed up even once," Zehava said.

"I know, but all it takes is one mistake, and Ayelet could snap her spine."

I shook my head. "That's really unlikely. Even if we don't catch her perfectly, there's four of us there but only three girls actually catch her. Zehava is the spotter so if we'd mess up, she'd make sure Ayelet wouldn't get hurt."

One of the other teachers I didn't recognize leaned over. "I agree with Mrs. Landau. That was definitely the most dangerous thing we've seen." Before we could say anything, she continued. "But that was also, by far, the coolest move anyone will ever see at a Bais Yaakov concert."

Zehava and I grinned at each other as the other two teachers started nodding. Mrs. Landau looked unconvinced, but she couldn't help agreeing with them. She called Ayelet over from her circle of admirers. "Are you okay with this move? You know how risky it is."

Ayelet shrugged. "Yeah, I know it's risky, but I'm okay with it. I know Zehava and Rikki have my back. Literally."

She was so cool, I wanted to hug her. Except I hadn't talked to her in a while, so it would've been weird.

Mrs. Landau was the lone holdout. She held up a finger so she could think in peace, without Zehava making various arguments as to why we should get to leave the move in. Finally, she said, "Here's the deal. From now until concert, you need to have crash mats at every single practice. If she falls even one time, the move is out. If she doesn't, you can go ahead with it."

"Yes!" Zehava jumped about three feet in the air and grabbed me in a huge hug, pausing momentarily to include Ayelet in it as well.

Mrs. Landau was shaking her head, saying, "I have a bad feeling about this…" but she was smiling.

41

At the end of practice, Ayelet pulled me aside. "Rikki, can I talk to you?"

I hesitated, suddenly nervous. I wasn't sure why I was avoiding her, but I suspected it had something to do with the fact that I felt like the world's biggest faker, and having Ayelet look up to me and tell me she wanted to be more like me just drove it home. Still, she looked a little desperate, so I decided to adopt some of Daniella's selflessness and get over myself.

"Sure, let's go outside."

We walked across the parking lot, toward two iron benches that faced the back of a quiet shopping center. Ayelet jumped right in. "Look, I know you're going through a lot right now, something about your mother, I'm not really sure what, no one seems to know, so maybe I should just be giving you your space, but…" She trailed off, looking lost. Summoning up more courage, she soldiered on. "And I keep wanting to tell you that you can talk to me about stuff if you want, but then I feel really stupid because I know I'm younger and you probably wouldn't want to talk to me."

I had no idea where she was going with this.

She took a deep breath. "And maybe this is selfish of me, but I just really need to talk to you." She looked at me bashfully, and I realized that was it. She didn't want anything from me other than support and a listening ear. Ayelet didn't care about my mother. To her, I was an older friend, who was too blind to see that my support meant something. I suddenly felt deeply, seriously ashamed.

"Ayelet, I'm so sorry I've been wrapped up in my own life. Things are really crazy, you probably wouldn't even believe me if I told you. Still, you can always talk to me."

She looked doubtful, and I didn't blame her. "Are you sure? Because I don't want to be a burden or anything."

"I'm sure. What's up?"

Now that Ayelet had my full attention, she looked like a deer in headlights. She laughed self-consciously. "This is harder than I thought it would be… You know how I went on those new meds?"

I nodded.

"They're really working. They don't make me lose my appetite or make my heartbeat go crazy. They just work. And I'm doing better in school too. They said if I keep this up, I'll be in all mainstream classes next year."

I had noticed that she seemed a lot calmer at practice. I'd even seen her sitting down for longer than two minutes at a time.

"So…isn't that a good thing?"

She sighed. "I know, right? I should be really happy about that."

"But you're not."

She shook her head, her blonde hair falling partially across her face. She was avoiding my gaze, tipping me off to her anxiety. Finally, she spit it out. "I'm on medication, Rikki."

I waited. With a start, I realized what her problem was.

"And that bothers you?"

She looked at me with her eyebrows raised. "It wouldn't bother you? To be on psychiatric medication? I know I've talked about it before like it's no big deal, but it is. It was easy to talk about being on meds when I was younger, but now that I'm actually on them again, I hate it. It's so embarrassing."

I was stunned into silence. How ironic.

"Ayelet, can I be honest with you?"

"Yes."

"It's really not a big deal."

"That's easy for you to say." She slumped back against the bench in frustration.

"No, it's actually not."

She looked at me warily. "What do you mean?"

"Exactly that." I glanced around, making sure that no one was around. "I have post-traumatic stress disorder. I don't know if you know—" She nodded. "I'm seeing a psychiatrist about it on Wednesday for the first time. If he prescribes me something that'll stop the nightmares or make me less anxious all the time, I'll go on meds too."

"Seriously?"

"Seriously. I wouldn't joke about this. Look, I get it. No one our age wants to be on meds because there's so much shame attached to it. And then you start thinking about *shidduchim* and all that…"

She was nodding, listening hard.

"But who cares? You're doing awesome now. Who cares if you need to take a pill every morning to make your brain work right?"

She started to protest, but suddenly, I needed to finish my thought. "Just imagine if you refused to take it because you were too embarrassed to be on medication. You'd be making yourself miserable, you'd be making your parents miserable, and you'd be making your future husband and kids miserable too, all because you were too proud to help yourself."

She considered that. "But you always hear people saying that ADHD is all hype, and it's not a real disease, and people who need meds are just weak and don't have enough self-control."

I started laughing. "Ayelet, none of those people have seen you try to sit through a class unmedicated."

She tried to keep herself from smiling, but couldn't do it. "I know. I know I have it. Thanks for putting that in perspective."

We were silent for a few minutes, both lost in thought. I marveled at the irony of Ayelet seeking advice from the one person who was likely to be as pro-medication as possible. I also marveled at the fact that she hadn't flinched when I'd revealed that I had post-traumatic stress disorder.

She hadn't flinched, but apparently she hadn't forgotten it either.

"Rikki, why do you have PTSD?"

My jaws clenched and anxiety twitched in my stomach. "It's a long story. And I think I'll probably tell you sometime, but not right now, okay?"

She nodded in understanding, then reached out and hugged me, quick and fierce.

"What was that for?" I asked, smiling.

She was blushing, but looked positively happy. "I'm just really glad I have you to talk to again. You're like the big sister I always wanted."

As we walked back toward the school, it occurred to me that even if my life was currently in shambles, at least to one person I was exactly who she needed. And that realization was almost enough to make me feel whole again.

42

Yoni Shiller, Uri's mentor, brought him by after school on Tuesday to visit us. I was surprised to see that my little brother looked a lot calmer and more confident than the last time I'd seen him.

"What have you two been up to?" Daniella asked. She was sitting on the couch next to Mrs. B., learning how to crochet. I thought it was hilarious that Daniella, who had little patience for anything, was learning how to crochet, but Mrs. B. said she had natural talent. I think Daniella liked it because it kept her hands from shaking. I still wasn't sure if that was a sign of anxiety or malnutrition or a side effect from the random pills she'd been experimenting with, but I knew it bothered her.

"We went roller-skating and bowling." Uri couldn't contain his glee when he was around Yoni. He basked in the coolness of his mentor and seemed less needy when he was around. "And we're going to the aquarium this weekend."

Yoni nodded, smiling affectionately at Uri. "Yeah, Uri's full of ideas, always keeping me on my toes. I don't think I'll ever get bored with him." He reached over to give Uri a high five, and Uri positively beamed.

"You know what Abba told me?" Uri paused in the middle of the card game he was playing with Yoni and focused his gaze toward Daniella and me. "He said the next time he goes to visit Ima, he's taking me with him."

Daniella dropped the ball of yarn she was holding. It slowly rolled off the couch and made its way toward me. I tossed it back to her as we exchanged meaningful glances. I knew, without communicating, that she was wondering just how much Yoni knew about the situation.

"Abba said that?" Daniella's voice was perfectly calm. "Uri, that's awesome. She'll be really happy to see you." I wondered how she managed to say that with perfect sincerity, but one look at Uri's hopeful face revealed the answer. She loved him fiercely and I knew that despite her pain at my mother's rejection, she was genuinely glad that Uri would get to see his mother.

"Yeah, Uri's psyched about that," Yoni said nonchalantly. "He really misses your mother, but I'm proud of the way he's been sticking it out at home with your father. We've been hanging out together some nights."

I looked at Yoni with newfound respect. "Really?"

"Sure. Me and Uri make a wicked team. We crushed your father in Monopoly the other night." Both he and Uri laughed at the memory.

Daniella raised her eyebrows at me and smiled.

Uri and Yoni stayed for dinner, and Mrs. B. was delighted with the company. Yoni was hilarious and had all of us laughing at his jokes. I couldn't take my eyes off Uri, thrilled at how happy he seemed. After they left, Daniella and I remained at the table with Mrs. B., not wanting the meal to end.

"Do you think it's true about Abba taking him to visit Ima?" I asked.

Daniella poked at the food on her plate. "It better be. It'll break Uri's heart if it's not."

"Daniella, please eat your food instead of playing with it."

Daniella started to scowl at Mrs. B., then thought better of it.

Mrs. B. started washing the dishes, and I went to help as Daniella dutifully began eating her food. She was eating more, now that Mrs. B. was preparing three meals a day and running the household. At mealtimes, Daniella often seemed lost, like she wasn't quite sure what to do with herself.

"Good job, sweetie," Mrs. B. said gently as Daniella placed her empty plate in the sink. Daniella gave her a halfhearted smile.

"Girls, don't forget about your appointment first thing tomorrow morning."

We were scheduled to see the psychiatrist at eight o'clock and eight thirty. My therapist wanted me evaluated for post-traumatic stress disorder and anxiety, as well as the fire setting. As for Daniella, I wasn't exactly sure what they wanted her to be evaluated for. My sister was complex, the type that defied labels.

Although her relationship with Tali had completely disintegrated, her popularity at school continued to be epic. She was a livewire, injecting energy and exhilaration into the most mundane situations. I'd seen her transform crowds into hotbeds of energy with her infectious smile, her quick wit, and easy compliments. She fed off the energy of others and reflected it back to them, one hundred times brighter.

But that was the Daniella the rest of the world saw. Those closest to her got to see beneath her beautiful, sparkly mask. Beneath it all, Daniella was deeply wounded. I hoped she'd put her prejudices toward authority aside for long enough to be honest with the psychiatrist. If Daniella didn't get help now, I didn't know when she would.

As if she was reading my mind, Mrs. B. said, "Girls, I hope you both make the most of the appointment tomorrow. Don't hold back anything." She reached out and squeezed Daniella's shoulder. "Especially you, sweetie. I know you'll be tempted."

Once she let go, Daniella turned away to hide her smile.

Later that night, after we were already in bed, Mrs. B. came in to check on us. Daniella was in my bed, where we'd been talking about Uri and the affect Yoni was having on him.

"Daniella, back to your bed," Mrs. B. said, hands on hips, smiling affectionately.

"Yes, Ima," Daniella said automatically, sliding out of my bed. She paused, and corrected her mistake. "I mean, Mrs. B."

As Mrs. B. tucked both of us in, leaning down to kiss us on our foreheads, it occurred to me that maybe Daniella hadn't made a mistake after all.

43

Thankfully, Uri had been telling the truth. Daniella and I were both thoroughly impressed to hear that my father had told my mother that he would not be visiting her again until she agreed to let Uri come as well. After five days of no visits, which meant five full nights of board games for Uri and Abba, she acquiesced and Uri got to see her for the first time in over three months.

After speaking to him on the phone, unable to keep myself from smiling at the excitement in his voice as he described Ima's "cool" hospital socks with grips on the bottom, I asked Daniella if it bothered her.

She shrugged. "It doesn't really matter, does it? She'll never treat me the same way she treats him. Or you."

Her tone was matter-of-fact, and for once, I believed that she meant what she said. Daniella was changing. We both were. Our visit to the psychiatrist had been incredibly enlightening. While it was no surprise that I was diagnosed with PTSD, Daniella had been just as shocked as the rest of us when she exited the office with not only a diagnosis of depression and PTSD, but of ADHD as well.

"It kind of makes sense," she admitted as we sat waiting with Mrs. B. at the pharmacy. Both Daniella and I had been prescribed low doses of an antidepressant, and she was given medication for her ADHD as well. It was a little overwhelming to be inducted into the world of psychiatric labels and medications, but Mrs. B. was making it seem so normal that we just followed her from the doctor's office to the pharmacy like dazed little puppies.

"I don't know why I didn't ever think of this," Daniella said, twisting her fingers together. "I mean, people always joked around and said I was ADHD because I have all this energy, but I never took it seriously. And I could never sit through class, but I thought that was just because I was stressed." She pulled her legs up to sit Indian style in her seat. "I'm failing all of my classes."

This was news to me. "Since when?"

She gave me a ghost of a smile. "Since me and Tali haven't been friends."

"What does that have to do with it?"

"What did you think I was doing every night at her house?"

"I don't know. Dying your hair blue?"

She laughed. "That was one time. The rest of the time, she taught me everything we learned in school that day. I had no problem learning when she taught it to me, because it took her, like, ten minutes, when it took the teacher fifty." She stopped laughing and looked off wistfully into the distance. "Now I'm lost again. She actually offered to keep tutoring me, but I said no. I don't think I could deal with that."

I took a minute to digest everything she had just told me.

"Do you miss her?" I asked quietly.

Daniella didn't answer right away, and when she did, she allowed there to be sadness in her voice. "I do. But even if I start being friends with her again, I know it'll never be the same." She leaned forward, resting her elbows on her knees. "Even though Tali messed up at the end, I never really gave her a chance. So even though we were best friends, we were doomed from the start."

I nodded, recognizing the truth in her words.

She turned toward me. "What's up with you and Kayla? Are you still close?"

I hesitated, not liking the answer. "I think I'm avoiding her. I keep feeling so awkward around my friends, and even though she knows the most, it's like I don't know how to be around her. Like, do I pretend things are the same, or do I acknowledge everything that's happened?"

"You should invite her over," Daniella said casually. I smirked as I turned to look at her, stunned.

"Why? You don't even like Kayla."

"What? Yes I do. I think Kayla's awesome."

I narrowed my eyes at her. "You had both of us fooled."

Daniella took a deep breath. "Okay, maybe I was just the tiniest bit jealous that you had someone you could talk to. She looked at me sheepishly. "I'm sorry."

I scowled at her for a minute, before it slipped off my face, and I grabbed her in a big hug.

"Hey, what was that for?"

I couldn't wipe the grin off my face. "These days, you're just so…human."

Daniella rolled her eyes. "Way to make me feel self-conscious." But she was smiling too.

I pulled out my phone and texted Kayla, despite the fact that she'd be in class. *Come over later? At our new place.*

I noticed Mrs. B. heading toward us, a small white paper bag in one hand, and inspiration struck. "Hey Daniella, this ADHD thing? I know someone you can talk to."

44

I saw Kayla at school before she had a chance to respond to my text.

"I've missed you," she said, as we stood by our lockers, exchanging our books. "I'll totally be there after school. Is Daniella going to be around?"

I thought about telling her what Daniella had admitted, but decided it was unnecessary. I had a feeling Daniella would be acting differently around Kayla from here on out.

"She is, but she'll be nice. She actually gave me the idea to invite you. I hadn't even thought about having friends over there."

We started down the hall toward our next period and I realized how much I'd missed Kayla over the past couple of weeks. For that matter, I missed all of my friends. I wanted to go back to how things were before our private life had been exposed and we'd been cast into a state of turmoil, but I knew there was no going back. We had to recreate from the ashes of our smoked facades. I could pick and choose pieces from my past as I built my new future, and Kayla was definitely one remnant I was bringing along.

I reached out impulsively and hugged her, although that was more Daniella's style than mine. "I've missed you too. I have so much to tell you."

We passed by Mrs. Zilber in the hallway. She flashed me a quick smile as she passed and I smiled back. At first, it had been awkward to see her at school, knowing that she knew so many personal things about me. She'd quickly proven she could maintain a professional distance in the school building, even while she cultivated a nurturing relationship with me outside of it. I'd become somewhat of a regular visitor at Mrs. Zilber's home, and her two young daughters were die-hard "Rikki fans," as she called them. She'd more than made good on her offer to provide some motherly support.

I didn't focus very well in Ivrit. The prospect of taking medication that would subdue the night terrors and give me some relief from the pervasive anxiety was alluring. As I had told Ayelet, I wasn't particularly bothered by the idea of taking psychiatric medications. I wasn't about to share it publicly with my class, but I knew it was unnecessary for me to suffer if I could take something to regulate the chemicals in my brain.

The psychiatrist had provided Daniella and me with a crash course in how traumatic experiences affect the brain. He showed us diagrams of how the release of too much stress hormones caused biological changes in the brain, which, in turn, cause all sorts of symptoms for the victims of traumatic experiences.

Daniella told me after that he'd speculated that her ADHD symptoms were strongly related to the trauma she'd experienced as a child. "He said it doesn't matter where it came from, and as long as I'm dealing with the trauma in therapy, the ADHD meds can only help."

I spent the rest of Ivrit writing a letter to Ayelet. Daniella didn't need help accepting her diagnosis, but she did need some help in overcoming her ego and accepting tutoring. I was still stunned by the fact that Tali had singlehandedly kept Daniella's grades at an average level for three years, which gave me a greater appreciation for the friendship that Daniella had lost.

Maybe you can talk to my sister. She just got diagnosed with ADHD and she's struggling with school a lot. Can I tell her about you?

When class was over, I stuck the note in Ayelet's locker and headed to gym for practice with the carousel dance. By the end of practice, I was in a great mood, my endorphins running high and my heart pumping from the fast-paced flow of the dance.

"Someone took their happy pills today," Zehava joked, noticing my improved mood.

She had no idea why I thought that was so funny.

We finished practicing with five minutes of lunch left to spare. I called Mrs. B. to ask her if it was okay for Kayla to come for dinner. She sounded pleased that I'd be having a friend over. "Sweetie, you can invite anyone anytime you like. You know there's always room for one more at the table."

I passed Mrs. Landau on my way to English class. "How's that flying leap coming along? Actually, forget it, I don't want to know," she said. She paused for a minute and pulled me to the side, waiting until two girls passed by before she asked, "How are things going, Rikki? I know you've been talking with Mrs. Moskowitz and Mrs. Zilber, so you don't need to give me any details, but I don't want you to think that I don't care. I've actually been thinking about you and Daniella a lot."

I didn't know how I felt about her questioning me, but I did appreciate her sincerity. "We're doing a lot better. It was good that things sort of exploded that way, I guess. It was hard, but I think we'll be okay. So…thanks for doing something."

She waved away my gratitude. "You know, Rikki, I really admire you. I think a lot of people do, because of how talented and kind you are, but what they don't know is how you've overcome so much adversity. Other people would've become bitter and hurtful, but you haven't let that happen." I was blushing now. "You should be proud of yourself. I know you'll do great things."

When I'd overcome my embarrassment enough to talk, I asked, "What do you think will happen to Daniella next year? I know she didn't apply to any seminaries, and she didn't apply to college either. It's like she refuses to think about the future."

Mrs. Landau nodded thoughtfully. "I know. I've been speaking to Mrs. Romanoff about that." She hesitated, clearly not sure of how much she should share with me. "Rikki, you know better than anyone that Daniella has a lot to deal with right now. I'm pretty sure her future is not at the top of her list of priorities."

I nodded in agreement.

"Still, we're working on finding some options for her. We'll talk to her about it soon, so try not to worry, okay? We'll make sure that she has plans. Trust me."

And I did. Even though my school was full of people like Mrs. Chase, whose misguided good intentions had caused me pain; and people like Tali, who spread secrets that weren't theirs to share; and Riva Winters, whose whole personality was like nails on a chalkboard, it was also full of people who cared about me and my sister as if we were their own children. People, who, despite having families of their own, had made room in their hearts for two motherless girls.

45

Dinner that night was an epic affair. Joining us were my father and Uri, Kayla, and Mrs. B.'s youngest daughter, son-in-law, and four children. It was noisy and slightly chaotic, but there was no denying it was fun.

After dinner, Kayla and I retreated to my room and I filled her in on life's happenings since we'd spoken last. It was surprisingly easy to tell her about my new diagnosis and medications.

"That's awesome," she said sincerely. "I really hope it helps."

I lay back on my bed, exhausted by my own honesty, and she lay down next to me. It was a position we had assumed so many times before, as I had never been able to look her in the eye when I spoke the truth about my life.

"Rikki, things make so much more sense now."

"What do you mean?"

"I never realized how bad things were at home. I mean, I knew your mother was not emotionally stable, but I promise I didn't know she was hitting either of you or neglecting Daniella that way." She propped herself up on one elbow and looked down at me. "Please believe me that I would've said something if I'd known."

I nodded.

"I always wondered why you kept our friendship so separate. Like, I knew you were more honest with me out of anybody, but that was only on nights and weekends. At school, you always put up this wall between us, like you were scared I'd start talking about your mother in the middle of class or something."

"I did?" I considered that momentarily. "I guess I did. I was scared. I was always scared that my home life and my school life would collide. And then they did and it was horrible, but it was the only way things could change."

"What's going to happen when your mother gets out?"

Cold fear flickered somewhere inside of me, but I forced it down. "I can't even think about that. Daniella will never be able to live at home again. She knows that and everyone else knows it too. But I'm not so sure about me."

"Are you happy here?"

"Yeah. I really am. It's hard sometimes, living with Mrs. B. now, and seeing what mothers are supposed to be like. I'm seriously jealous of her kids." I laughed self-consciously. "But there's no use thinking like that."

There was a knock at the door and Daniella stepped inside. She hesitated when she saw us, but I waved her inside.

We made small talk for a few minutes before Daniella finally bit the bullet. "Kayla, listen, I'm sorry if I ever treated you…in any way…that made you uncomfortable. I know I can come on a little strong sometimes, and I just had a hard time with you knowing so much. But still, that wasn't your fault. So I'm really sorry."

Kayla smiled, and I saw, from the relaxed slope of her shoulders, that for once, she felt comfortable around my sister. "I think

I get it now, so don't worry about it."

Daniella hung out with us for next few hours until Kayla had to leave. After walking her to her car, we made our way to the kitchen to receive our medications for the first time. I knew I would've been trusted to take my medication independently, but with Daniella's track record of psychiatric drug experimentation, Mrs. B. was going to be keeping our medication under lock and key.

We tossed back our pills with some water and Daniella smiled at me devilishly. "I feel better already, don't you?"

I rolled my eyes, laughing, and even Mrs. B. couldn't help herself.

46

I wish I could say the medications kicked in right away, but that wasn't the case. For two weeks, I was plagued with nausea and headaches, side effects of my antidepressant. To make matters worse, my therapy sessions involved digging up painful memories from the past that triggered ferocious nightmares that woke me dripping with sweat, screams ripping from my throat.

Daniella struggled too. While the stimulant medications almost immediately had a positive effect on her ability to focus, her therapy sessions were triggering a lot of flashbacks and intrusive thoughts. It was painful to watch. It was usually triggered by something external — a certain food, smell, song, or phrase. Her face would tighten, her eyes would go blank. I could stand six inches from her face, and she wouldn't be able to focus on me. Afterward, she'd sometimes share what she'd remembered with me; other times, the memories would haunt her for hours or days until she found the courage to share it with Mrs. Romanoff, Mrs. B., or her therapist.

What she remembered blew my mind. In therapy one day, I told Yocheved, "Every time she tells me stuff, I feel like I'm being traumatized all over again. I think I'll have PTSD forever at the rate this is going."

That sentiment must have somehow been filtered back to Daniella, because at some point, she stopped sharing the details with me, and I was selfishly relieved.

At the same time that we were navigating the mine-filled roads of trauma recovery, we received word that our mother was stabilizing. We weren't exactly sure what that meant on a practical level, but my father explained that they doctors had found the right combination of mood stabilizer and antipsychotic meds so she was no longer experiencing hallucinations and delusions, nor debilitating mood swings.

"Does that mean she's getting out?" Daniella asked dully.

"Not yet," my father said carefully. He'd taken us out for lunch on a Sunday afternoon. Since we'd started staying with Mrs. B., we'd seen more of our father than we had when he lived with him. He was making a conscious effort to spend more time with us, and his rejuvenated relationship with Uri had restored a lot of our faith in him. "Don't worry, I'll let you know long before that actually happens."

Daniella looked amused. "Don't worry? Okay." Her characteristic sarcasm didn't grate as much when she used it sparingly.

"She's been asking about both of you."

"Asking what?" we said at the same time.

"Just how you're doing and if you've been managing okay."

Daniella stabbed at her slice of pizza with her fork. "I don't get her. Does she care or does she totally not? She can't have it both ways. I hope you didn't tell her anything about us. She doesn't deserve to know."

"Deserve?" my father repeated. "Daniella, she doesn't deserve a lot of things because of what she did to you."

Daniella was looking down at her plate, dissecting the pizza into geometric shapes. I couldn't stop watching her.

"But then again," my father continued, "there are a lot of things that I don't deserve either. Because of how I let you down."

Now I was watching my father watch Daniella. He cleared his throat, pushed his plate back, and leaned toward us. "Do you girls remember Ima from before she got sick?"

I shook my head because, in my mind, there was no before. It all seemed like one endless loop of sickness. Daniella didn't move.

"I dated for six years before I met her. I started thinking I might never meet a girl who was everything that I wanted. But then my roommate set us up, and there I was, on the first date with her, and for four hours, the only thought in my mind was 'She exists. This girl of my dreams exists.' She almost didn't go out with me again because I seemed spacey." My father laughed self-consciously. "She was everything. She was funny and smart and beautiful and so incredibly alive with energy and excitement."

"So, basically, she was manic when you met her," Daniella said flatly.

"No." My father shook his head swiftly. "She wasn't manic. At least I don't think so. When we were first married, we were so happy that people always commented that we seemed as if we had been married for longer. She was so intuitive and considerate, it was like she thought of everything I might want or need before I even became of aware of it."

My father's eyes were focused somewhere over our heads and I sensed that although he was sitting at the table with us, he wasn't exactly present. Daniella and I exchanged looks, but let him continue.

"And then she started having these moods. It was so hard

watching her struggle, but when she'd come out of it, she was the same person I knew and loved so I accepted it. I didn't think it was something she could help or we could fix." He shook his head, as if silently berating himself for his lack of knowledge. "After she had you, Daniella, she became so depressed that for the first time, I thought she might not come out of it."

Daniella twitched in her seat. This was not something we'd ever heard before.

"She loved you." My father's gaze settled on Daniella's face and she looked down. "She loved you so much and it broke her heart that it wasn't enough to make her happy. She was hospitalized for the first time when you were three weeks old."

Daniella was fighting back tears. I reached out and silently clasped her hand in mine.

"She was hospitalized again right after you were born, Rikki. And that time, they diagnosed the bipolar that had been there all along. She was put on mood stabilizers and she came back to life."

I didn't speak, didn't want to ruin the moment.

"When you girls were younger, you were her life. She spent all day, every day with you. She taught you how to draw and paint, she took you to parks and museums and fairs. She sewed matching clothes for you and for your dolls. If I ever had to work on Sunday, I knew you would all show up with a picnic lunch and we'd get to spend time that way. I know you two were happy when you were younger." He broke off, looking back and forth between the two of us. "Do you remember, at all?"

"Why does it even matter?" Daniella asked, quiet and raw. "Even if we did remember, she went and ruined everything."

"I wish you could've known her before." My father clenched his fists in frustration, pressing them into the tabletop. "You didn't have enough time with her before things got so bad." He took a deep breath before pressing on. "When you think of her now, all you see is her illness. All you remember is the pain and the hurt that she caused you. You have so many bad memories that even if you had good ones, they would seem insignificant. But it's not like that for me." Here, my father's eyes filled with tears. "I look at her, and all I see is that beautiful girl, sitting across from me in a hotel lobby, making me laugh and open up and believe, for the first time, that I have met my soul mate."

I bit down hard on my lip and pressed a fist to my mouth.

"I don't think I'll ever stop seeing her that way. Even though she's in the hospital, even though I now know what she's done, I can't change how much I love her."

"But what about us?" Daniella was squeezing my hand so hard that my fingers were beginning to go numb, but I couldn't move. "Didn't you love us?"

"Of course I did — I do." My father spoke the words so vehemently that a girl at the table next to us turned to look at us. I caught her eye and stared hard, until she awkwardly dropped her gaze. "I love all of you so much. I just…I want you to understand why I didn't leave her, even when I knew she was sick. I need you to understand that I didn't know what she was doing, because I never could've dreamed that up in a million years. The woman who I loved and knew" — he caught himself — "who I thought I knew, she wouldn't have hurt anyone."

He meant it. One look at his face and I knew, without a doubt, that he sincerely thought the world of my mother. Mood swings, postpartum depression, and bipolar disorder were no match for his love for her. But the way he looked at us now, there was also no denying that his heart was big enough for all of us, and that confused me more than I could put into words.

"Why didn't you try to tell me?" His tone was desperate as he leaned toward us, his attention focused mostly on Daniella. "Maybe I'm not supposed to be asking this, and trust me, I still take full responsibility for not knowing, but why didn't you come to me for help?"

Daniella struggled to find the words and looked at me helplessly before she finally shrugged her shoulders in defeat and said, "I didn't know I could get help."

47

"Can I tell you a secret?" Daniella bounced up and down on the edge of my bed, vibrating with energy. She was crocheting a green-and-teal striped scarf and I couldn't comprehend how she was able to keep track of her stitches while she was so active.

"You can, but I'm not keeping it."

"What?" She stopped bouncing and stared down at me, where I lay reading a book.

"Seriously. You can tell me, but I won't necessarily keep it a secret."

If there was anything I'd learned in therapy, it was that the secrets Daniella and I had kept for each other had been toxic, eating away at us from the inside, and although we'd both thought our loyalty to each other was of the utmost importance, we'd been wrong.

Daniella pouted. "You're no fun."

I shrugged, knowing she'd tell me anyway. Sure enough, after less than fifteen seconds of silence, she tried again. "It's really no big deal."

"So just tell me."

"But I only want to tell you. I don't want the whole world knowing."

I tossed my book aside, unable to concentrate with her speaking in riddles. "Is it something dangerous?"

"What? No." I was having a hard time reading her and didn't have the slightest idea as to what her secret might be, but there was definitely a healthy dose of anxiety mixed with excitement radiating from her.

"Just tell me already," I said, elbowing her lightly. "You know you want to."

She pressed her lips together, as if trying to keep the secret contained, and then blurted out, "I found something."

"You did?"

"Yeah. Something that belongs to Ima."

"What did you find?"

She paused for a moment, either for dramatic effect or from nerves, and then said, "Her old journals. From, like, the past twenty years."

I shot upright, sending Daniella's yarn and needle clattering to the floor. "Did you read them?"

"Chill, Rikki." She retrieved her needle and sat staring at me thoughtfully, tapping it against her chin. "Why, do you think I should?"

"Are you kidding? Of course not." In reality, I couldn't have thought of a worse idea. "Where are they now?"

She looked slightly deflated by my unenthusiastic reaction. "They're still at our house. I found them when I was packing up more clothes. I went to see if one of my shirts was in Ima's closet. Seriously, I wasn't looking for them. I just found them."

I had my doubts, but there was no use arguing. "You have no idea what you could do to yourself if you read them."

She looked annoyed. "Don't you think we deserve to read them? She ruined our lives. At least we should get to know what she was thinking while she did it." She pushed up off my bed and crossed the room to go sit on hers. "It would be nice to understand some things."

I crossed over to her bed and sat next to her, suddenly feeling old and wise. "Yeah, it would be nice, but you're not going to find reasonable explanations in her journal. It'll probably make things worse because she's so sick. Danz, she'll probably just be justifying what she did. Do you really want to read about how horrible she thought we were?"

Her shoulders sagged and she didn't answer. I felt obligated to continue. "Look, I know it's hard to let it all go and I'm shocked that you didn't read them already. I didn't know you had that much willpower." I grinned at her to let her know I was joking, which elicited a half smile. "We're moving past her. Even if she gets out, no one's going to make you go home. You know that."

And that was the truth. I knew my return home was still up for discussion, but the unspoken agreement was that Daniella would most probably never live at our house again. There were too many memories for her there.

"I'm not so worried about that," she said, finally sitting up straight again. "I'm going to California next year." And just like that, she had shaken off the cloud and was furiously knitting green and teal stripes.

"You are?" I gently, but firmly, removed her crocheting project from her hands and placed it on the floor. "Can you please focus and tell me everything instead of just throwing out shocking bits of information like you seem to enjoy doing?"

She pulled me over to the desk computer and pulled up a website from her saved favorites. "I'm going here next year." I took a moment to browse the website of a school called Eden. It was located in Northern California, and advertised itself as a "therapeutic seminary." Run by renowned educators and therapists, I had to admit that it looked like the perfect place for her.

"When did this happen?"

"Yesterday. Mrs. Landau put in an application for me a few weeks ago and I just got accepted. My application was really late but I think they accepted me out of pity."

"Who cares? They're lucky to have you."

"Awww, you're sweet." Daniella hugged me lightly. "You should come visit me there. It says family can visit."

I continued clicking through the website. The school had a maximum capacity of eighteen students, ranging from ages seventeen to nineteen. It was dual program, allowing the students to earn college credits while taking many *kodesh* classes that would be offered in an Israeli seminary. Therapy was a strong component as well, including art, dance, and equine therapy. There would be frequent trips, many with outdoor and survival themes, all designed to build character and foster teamwork.

"This is awesome. Did you tell Abba?"

She grimaced. "Not yet. Tuition is ridiculously high. I'm going to write an essay and try to win some scholarship money, but Mrs. Landau said if that doesn't work, they'll help with funding. I really don't want handouts."

"Okay, but if it comes down to that, you're taking them. This is too good to pass up."

"I know." She reached out and grasped my hand. "I'll miss you."

My heart twitched, as if it were already feeling the loss of my sister. "It's the right thing. Don't ever doubt that," I said firmly. "Oh, and by the way? I'm not keeping that secret."

She rolled her eyes at me. "Who are you going to tell? No one cares if I read that stuff."

I pulled out my phone. "Oh, really? Let's see if Mrs. Moskowitz cares. Or Mrs. Zilber. Or Abba."

She grabbed it from me. "Okay, Rikki, relax. You're overreacting. Just forget I said anything and leave it at that."

"I'm sorry, Danz. But I don't trust you on this. If someone doesn't get rid of them, I know you're going to go read them. And if you get hurt by what you read, it'll be partly my fault."

She was shaking her head vehemently. "No. Rikki, you're wrong. I don't need anyone to treat me like a baby. I can decide what I should and should not do."

I stood and stuck out my hand for my phone. "Daniella, I love you more than anyone, okay? And I would never do anything to purposely hurt you or break your trust, but I just can't keep any more secrets and you knew that before you told me this. So I'm going to tell Mrs. B. or you can come and tell her yourself."

Reluctantly, she followed me into the kitchen where Mrs. B. was baking. "What have you two been up to?" she asked, dropping scoops of chocolate chip cookie dough onto baking sheets.

"I just thought you should know," Daniella said casually, "I found my mother's journals at our house and I'll probably read them if they're still there next time I go to get more clothes."

I almost had to laugh at Daniella's lack of introduction.

Mrs. B. smiled pleasantly. "Thanks for the heads-up. I'll make sure they aren't there."

Daniella gave me a fake smile.

Mrs. B. caught it, and laughed as she slid a tray of cookies into the oven. "Did you make her tell me that, Rikki?"

I nodded, appreciating the calm feeling that accompanied a good decision. "Daniella, have you talked to your therapist about this?" Mrs. B. asked.

Daniella shook her head meekly. "I will."

"Good," I said. "Because if you don't, I will."

48

The Shabbos before the concert was peaceful. Kayla slept over, and time passed quickly with her and Daniella to keep me distracted from the big night ahead. Shabbos ended and a flurry of activity ensued. After stopping at Kayla's house to pick up her costumes, Daniella drove us to the theater. The whole building was alive with activity and frenetic energy that only a group of overexcited teenagers could produce.

Our teachers attempted to keep the chaos at a minimal level, but there was too much excitement to contain. Zehava French-braided my hair as we quietly conferred over last-minute dance details.

"I still don't know if Chevy can get the flip right," Zehava griped, as she pulled my hair back so hard that my eyes watered. "Should we switch her with Shira?"

A few feet away, Ayelet laughed at my faces of mock agony. I focused on Zehava and attempted to calm her nerves. "No, Zehava, stop trying to change things. Everything will be fine. We'll do great tonight."

When our hair had all been sufficiently styled, Daniella began doing the makeup for both dances. The carousel dancers wore bright makeup with colorful-bordering-on-garish splashes of eye shadow and blush. The prisoners and wardens were all dark eyes and sculpted cheeks. The carousel dance was toward the beginning of the concert while the jail dance was almost at the very end. Zehava and I would need both a costume change and a dramatic makeover between the two.

Onstage, the concert had begun. The concert heads welcomed the crowds and the choir began singing the theme song. Approximately ten minutes before the carousel dancers would prance onto stage, Zehava and I corralled the group for a quick pep talk. "Remember," she said, leaning in toward the middle of the group, "we're excited. We're happy. We're at a carnival and there are kids and cotton candy and Ferris wheels and clowns and rides so we're smiling and laughing the whole time. Got it?"

And they did get it. They danced their hearts out and the audience loved every minute of it. When I first got on stage and struck my starting position, I'd needed to force the smile on my face. Then the lights went on, and in the second row of the audience, I saw Mrs. Zilber, with her two daughters on either side of her, all beaming at me. After that, my smile was effortless and real.

Backstage, my carousel dancers squealed and hugged each other and basked in the afterglow of a performance well done. Grinning, yet still apprehensive about the upcoming dance, Zehava and I changed into our orange prison suits. Daniella removed our colorful makeup and transformed us into haunted prisoners.

The pep talk for our jail dance differed greatly from the previous one. Although Zehava gave the usual "You guys are all awesome and we're so proud of you and we know you can do great" speech, the unspoken message that everyone heard loud and clear was, "Don't drop Ayelet."

If Ayelet was nervous about her upcoming flying leap across a stage in front of several hundred audience members, she certainly wasn't showing it. She looked calm and composed, the dark makeup on her face contrasting eerily with her pale skin and fair hair.

At just the right moment during the play, we stormed the stage. We were more than a dance; we were a dramatization of the most theatrical part of the entire concert. We represented a struggle for freedom and we'd trained our dancers to embody the role we'd been given.

From the moment we arrived, the audience was in an uproar. They quieted down somewhat as we began our dance, a slow buildup of deceptively simple yet seemingly complex moves. Prisoners against wardens. Freedom against incarceration. Good against evil. The music swelled inside my head and I was lost in the rhythm. We moved in perfect harmony, each of us transitioning from one move to the next, channeling hours upon hours of practice, sweat, and determination.

The end was approaching. I was completely in the moment. We were all aligned. Ayelet was flung skyward, soaring higher and higher, her body a picture of strength and grace. I watched her move with a sureness and confidence that we had come to expect after dozens and dozens of practices. She trusted us one hundred percent and did not doubt for a moment, that when she fell back toward the earth, we would be there to catch her with open arms.

I thought of my own journey out of the darkness and how I'd learned to lean on a new family I'd created for myself. Aside from Mrs. Zilber and her daughters in the front row, I knew the audience was dotted with people who cared about me and had opened their hearts so mine could begin to heal. I knew they were watching me, and I hoped I was making them proud.

I thought of Mrs. B., who'd bought concert tickets for her

daughter and granddaughters because she wanted them to be there while she *shepped nachas*. I thought of her daughter, who'd traveled in from out of town with her two girls, just to see me perform. I thought of Mrs. Moskowitz, who'd hugged me tightly before I went on stage, telling me that I looked beautiful and was "positively shining."

I thought of Daniella, and the future lying ahead of her, bright and open. I thought of Ayelet, unknowingly causing me to love myself more than I'd thought possible. I thought of Uri, growing into a confident and happy young man.

The muscles in my arms contracted. I lifted my eyes up, focusing in on Ayelet's landing, and despite the fact that I was dressed as a prisoner, despite the fact that I was caked in makeup designed to make me look somber and grim, despite the fact that Zehava and I had drilled our dancers specifically not to do this, I couldn't help myself.

I smiled.

About the Author

Shoshana Mael is a social worker who has worked with troubled youth in Baltimore City. She wrote *Dancing in the Dark* with the hope of bringing a new level of emotional intensity to young-adult Jewish literature. In her spare time, Shoshana enjoys photography, rock climbing, and drawing with Sharpies.

Shoshana was raised in Baltimore and now lives in Philadelphia. She can be contacted at shoshanamael@gmail.com.

This is her first novel.